Heartbeats in He

A Tale of Love, Healing, and th[illegible] We Share

Rebecca Wells

First Edition: August 2024

Table of Contents

Chapter
Arrival in Heartsville

The first light of dawn had not yet broken over Heartsville when Dr. Nora Flynn unlocked the doors to her beloved canine clinic. Despite the early hour, her steps were light, her demeanor infused with a serene anticipation of the day to come. Inside, the clinic was still in the gentle embrace of the predawn silence, the quiet only interrupted by the soft clicks of Nora's heels on the polished floor as she moved about, preparing for the day.

She started with the basics, methodically checking the stock of medical supplies—vaccines, bandages, and the like—ensuring everything was neatly arranged and within easy reach. The reception area was next, where she straightened magazines and aligned the rows of pet care brochures, her motions fluid and practiced. With each water bowl she filled and each waiting room chair she adjusted, Nora's mind steadily shifted from the lingering residue of sleep towards a sharp focus on her responsibilities.

As the sky outside tinted with the earliest hints of azure and gold, the quiet was punctuated by the sounds of Heartsville waking up. The distant hum of early morning traffic, the sporadic barking of dogs from nearby homes, and the soft chirping of sparrows created a backdrop to Nora's meticulous preparations.

The clinic, a cozy yet cutting-edge facility, was more than just a medical establishment; it was a community hub, a place where people and pets alike were treated with warmth and respect. Nora had taken great care to make it feel welcoming—the front porch had comfortable seating, and the large windows let in ample natural light, creating a space that felt more like a home than a clinic.

As the clock neared the opening hour, the first clients began to arrive, heralding the start of the rush. Dogs of various breeds and sizes pulled their owners into the clinic, tails wagging with unrestrained enthusiasm. Nora greeted each by name, her voice a soothing melody amidst the growing chaos. She knelt to welcome a sprightly Beagle, receiving a joyful lick on her cheek as a reward.

"Good morning, Buster. How are we today?" she asked, rubbing the dog's ears affectionately as she spoke to his owner, Mrs. Henderson, about his recent bout of allergies.

Her interactions were a delicate dance of professional care and personal charm, each pet receiving her undivided attention, each owner treated with genuine interest and kindness. A Labrador with a limp was examined with gentle hands, a nervous Pomeranian was soothed with soft words, and a pair of Dachshunds were praised for their playful spirit.

Mid-morning brought a brief lull, and Nora took advantage of the moment. She stepped out to the back of the clinic where a small garden offered a quiet sanctuary. Here, surrounded by blooming flowers and the soft rustle of leaves, she allowed herself a few minutes of solitude. This garden was her haven, a place to gather her thoughts and recharge amidst the demands of her day.

The peace was fleeting, however, as the clinic's doors swung open again, ushered in by the sound of paws on tile and the happy chaos of Heartsville's pet community. With a contented sigh, Nora stepped back inside, ready to embrace the challenges and joys of another day at the clinic. Her heart was full, her mind clear—she was exactly where she belonged, at the heart of a community woven together by the love of pets.

- - - - - - - - -

The brief quiet of the clinic was shattered as the clock struck ten, marking the arrival of the morning rush. Dogs of all sizes and breeds, from majestic Great Danes to tiny Chihuahuas, tugged at their leashes, eager to enter the bustling clinic. Nora stood at the center of this controlled chaos, a calm presence as she greeted each new arrival with a cheerful, "Good morning!"

"Dr. Flynn! I'm so glad you're here—Baxter's been limping since yesterday," called out a worried young woman, clutching a sandy-colored Cocker Spaniel.

Nora knelt beside Baxter, her tone soothing. "Let's take a look at that leg, shall we, Baxter?" She gently examined the dog's leg, her skilled fingers probing delicately. "It might just be a sprain, but let's do a quick X-ray to be sure, okay?"

As Baxter was led to the imaging room, a lively Golden Retriever burst through the door, its leash flying behind like a banner. The dog's owner, a tall man with a jogging suit and headphones around his neck, apologized as he caught up.

"Sorry, Dr. Flynn! Marley just couldn't wait to see you," he laughed, a bit breathless from his sprint.

Nora laughed along, scratching Marley behind the ears. "I'm always happy to see Marley too. How has he been doing with the new diet?"

"Much better, thanks to your advice. His energy is back, and he's been like a puppy again," the man replied, his face brightening.

"That's wonderful to hear! Keep up the good work, Marley," Nora said, giving the dog one last pat before turning to the next patient, a shy little Shih Tzu peeking out from behind her owner's legs.

Nora's clinic wasn't just a place for medical care; it was a lively community center where pet owners shared news and sought advice. As she treated a tabby cat with a minor ear infection, Nora overheard two pet owners discussing the latest neighborhood news.

"Did you hear about the new dog park they're planning to open next month?" one owner asked, a sprightly Jack Russell Terrier pulling at his leash.

"Yeah, I heard it's going to have an agility course and everything. Should be great for getting some of that excess energy out," replied another, her calm Dalmatian sitting by her side.

Nora chimed in, "It's going to be a fantastic addition to Heartsville. Great for socializing and exercise. Make sure you all check it out!"

The clinic door opened again, and in came a familiar face, Mrs. Weber, with her two Pugs in tow. "Dr. Flynn, I'm at my wit's end," she sighed, adjusting her glasses. "Cookie and Cream have been up all night barking at the new puppy next door."

Sitting on a stool, Nora brought herself down to eye level with the concerned pet owner. "Let's talk about it. There are a few strategies we can try to help Cookie and Cream adjust to their new neighbor."

As Nora discussed behavioral techniques and environmental adjustments, more clients filled the waiting area. Each person and their pet added to the lively tapestry of the clinic's morning rush. Conversations overlapped, dogs barked and whined in excitement or impatience, and Nora, ever the conductor of this symphony of sounds and souls, moved with purpose and grace.

"Mrs. Weber, try these calming treats and maybe a bit more exercise in the evening. It might help them sleep a bit sounder at night," Nora suggested, handing over a small sample bag of treats.

"Thank you, Dr. Flynn. I'll try anything at this point!" Mrs. Weber replied, her voice laden with gratitude.

With each consultation, Nora not only treated her patients but also wove herself deeper into the fabric of their lives, becoming as much a part of their daily routines as their pets were. As the clinic buzzed around her, she filled out a prescription, calmed a nervous beagle, and planned a follow-up appointment, all with a smile.

The morning progressed, each minute filled with the fulfilling chaos of veterinary care and community interaction. Nora took a moment to glance out the window, the sun now high in the sky, bathing the clinic in warm light. It was shaping up to be another beautiful day in Heartsville, filled with challenges, chatter, and the undeniable joy of caring for the pets and people who made her clinic a cornerstone of the community.

As the morning rush began to wane, the atmosphere inside Dr. Nora Flynn's clinic shifted subtly. The frenetic pace of the earlier hours eased into a steady rhythm of arrivals and departures. It was during these moments that the clinic truly transformed into a community hub, a place where relationships were nurtured just as much as pets were healed.

Nora moved from room to room, her presence a reassuring constant. With each pet owner, she shared not just medical advice but also moments of genuine personal connection. It was this unique blend of professional expertise and personal warmth that had made her clinic a beloved part of Heartsville.

In one corner of the waiting area, Nora noticed two of her regulars, Sarah and Tom, exchanging shy glances over their coffee cups. Sarah's terrier, Max, and Tom's boxer, Bella, were tangled in what seemed like an enthusiastic conversation of their own. Smiling, Nora approached them.

"It looks like Max and Bella are getting along quite well today," she remarked, watching the dogs play.

Sarah looked up, her face brightening. "Yes, they've become quite the pair. We've been meeting up at the park after our visits here."

Tom nodded, adding, "It's been great for Bella. She needs the exercise, and I think we do too."

Nora laughed softly. "It's wonderful to see. It's not just about the pets, you know. It's about building connections—helping each other out. That's what community is all about."

Her words seemed to linger in the air, reinforcing the sense of camaraderie that the clinic fostered. As Sarah and Tom continued their conversation, Nora excused herself to attend to a new patient, a nervous-looking spaniel named Ginger.

"Dr. Flynn, I'm worried about Ginger here. She's been scratching a lot lately, and nothing seems to help," explained Ginger's owner, a middle-aged man named Richard.

Nora knelt beside Ginger, examining her skin carefully while speaking in soothing tones. "Let's take a closer look, Richard.

It might be allergies, but we'll do a test to make sure. How has her diet been?"

As Richard described Ginger's meals and recent behavior, Nora listened attentively, occasionally nodding or asking a question. It wasn't just about diagnosing an ailment; it was about understanding the life of her patient and offering solutions that fit seamlessly into their daily routines.

Throughout the clinic, conversations like this unfolded. Each dialogue was a thread in the fabric of the community, each story shared added depth to the bonds formed within these walls. Nora was more than a veterinarian; she was a confidante, a community anchor who facilitated and strengthened the ties between the people of Heartsville.

Later, as the lunch hour approached, Nora stepped outside to check on the clinic's community bulletin board. It was a colorful mosaic of flyers and notices—everything from lost pets and local events to a bake sale fundraiser for the animal shelter. As she pinned a flyer for the upcoming "Mutt Mixer Monday," she felt a tap on her shoulder.

Turning, she saw Mrs. Ellis, an elderly woman who frequented the clinic with her poodle, Coco. "Dr. Flynn, I just wanted to thank you again. The arthritis supplements you recommended have made such a difference for Coco," she said, her voice trembling slightly with emotion.

Nora smiled warmly, touching Mrs. Ellis's arm gently. "I'm so glad to hear that. Coco is such a sweetheart; she deserves to feel her best."

As they chatted about Coco's improvements and the upcoming community events, it was clear that these interactions were about more than just pet care. They were about comfort, support, and the shared love of animals that brought everyone together.

As noon drew near, Nora returned to the clinic, ready to tackle the afternoon appointments. The morning had been a vivid tapestry of medical care, laughter, and shared stories, a testament to the role her clinic played in the heart of Heartsville. Here, in this space, every person and their pet were part of a larger family—a community brought together by Nora's dedication and the universal love for their animal companions.

- - - - - - - - -

As the clock ticked past noon, the morning rush finally began to subside. The last of the morning appointments wrapped up with a Labrador puppy, whose joyful unawareness of his own size brought a smile to Nora's face and a few laughs from the staff as he clumsily made his way through the clinic.

"Looks like Max is going to be a big boy," Nora commented as she gave the puppy a final pat before handing him back to his owner, Mr. Jenkins.

Mr. Jenkins chuckled, holding Max steady. "That's what you said last time, Dr. Flynn. At this rate, he might need his own room at home!"

"I wouldn't be surprised," Nora replied with a laugh. "Just make sure he's getting enough exercise and not too many treats, alright?"

"Will do, Doctor. And thank you again. We're so lucky to have you in Heartsville," Mr. Jenkins said, sincerity warming his voice as he headed towards the exit.

Once the clinic was quieter, Nora retreated to her office, a small but cozy room filled with books on veterinary medicine, framed certificates, and photos of various pets she had treated over the years. Here, she took a rare moment for herself, sinking into her chair with a sigh of contentment mixed with fatigue.

Her gaze drifted to the window where she could see the small park across the street, dotted with people enjoying the sunny day. The sight brought a moment of introspection about her role not just within the walls of her clinic, but as a part of the broader community of Heartsville.

The door to her office creaked open, and her assistant, Lisa, peeked in. "Dr. Flynn, do you have a minute?"

"Of course, Lisa, come in. What's on your mind?" Nora responded, her tone inviting as she motioned towards the chair across from her desk.

Lisa sat down, her expression a mix of concern and curiosity. "I was just going over our schedule for the next few weeks. We're pretty booked, but I've had a few calls asking about more community events. I know we're busy, but do you think we could maybe fit something in?"

Nora considered this, her mind weighing the clinic's capacity against her desire to meet the community's needs. "What kind of events are they interested in?"

"Well, there's been quite a bit of interest in another pet care workshop. And maybe something fun, like a pet photo day? People love getting professional shots of their pets," Lisa suggested, a spark of enthusiasm in her voice.

"That sounds wonderful," Nora mused aloud. "Let's do it. It's important to balance the workload with community engagement. It keeps us connected and reminds us why we do what we do. Can you start organizing it? Maybe reach out to that new photographer in town?"

"Absolutely, I'll get on it right away. And, Dr. Flynn?" Lisa paused, a smile spreading across her face. "Thanks for making this such a great place to work and for all you do for Heartsville."

Nora smiled back, touched by the compliment. "Thank you, Lisa. It's a team effort, and I couldn't do it without you and everyone else."

As Lisa left, Nora turned back to the window, her thoughts drifting to the people and pets she'd helped that morning. Each thankful smile, each wagging tail, reinforced the impact of her work beyond the medical care she provided. It was about fostering a community, about creating a space where people felt supported and connected.

Nora stood up, stretching slightly before heading back to the front lines of the clinic. There were more appointments to tend to, more pets and people to help. But that brief moment of reflection had recharged her, reminded her of her purpose, and reaffirmed her commitment to the community that had embraced her and her clinic with such warmth and trust.

With renewed energy, she stepped out of her office, ready to continue her day, each step echoing softly in the now peaceful clinic. The heart of Heartsville beat on, and Dr. Nora Flynn was its steadfast rhythm, ever present and ever caring, as the day unfolded around her.

Chapter 2
First Impressions

Jake Carter was a journalist known for his incisive writing and a healthy dose of skepticism that colored his view of the world. Sitting in the cluttered comfort of his office at the local newspaper, he flicked through his emails with a furrowed brow, each message a reminder of the day's deadlines and expectations. His editor, Marlene, a sharp-witted woman who knew how to push Jake's buttons, walked briskly into his office, her heels clicking authoritatively on the linoleum floor.

"Jake, do you have a minute?" Marlene asked, leaning against the doorframe with a manila folder in her hand.

Jake swiveled in his chair, raising an eyebrow. "For you, Marlene, I have five. What's up?"

Marlene tossed the folder onto his desk. It slid across the clutter and stopped against his keyboard. "I've got your next assignment. It's a feature piece on unconventional matchmaking services. And before you say anything, yes, it includes animals."

Jake's expression soured immediately. "Matchmaking? With animals? You're kidding, right?" He flipped open the folder with a flick of his wrist, his eyes scanning the contents quickly.

"No joke. There's a clinic in Heartsville, run by Dr. Nora Flynn. She's doing something unique—using pets to help people connect. They say it's a big hit. Could be a nice human interest piece," Marlene explained, watching him closely.

Jake scoffed, leaning back in his chair. "Sounds like fluff, Marlene. Since when do we cover matchmaking gimmicks?"

Marlene smirked slightly. "Since they involve the whole community and could be a gold mine for readership. People love these kinds of stories, Jake. It's feel-good, it's different, and who knows, you might actually find it interesting."

Reluctantly, Jake flipped through the documents, his curiosity piqued despite his reservations. "Alright, I'll bite. But I'm going in skeptical. If there's nothing to this, I'm writing it that way."

"That's all I'm asking. Go, interview Dr. Flynn, see what the fuss is about. And Jake? Try to have a little fun with it," Marlene advised before leaving his office with a knowing smile.

With a heavy sigh, Jake grabbed his notepad and camera, heading out to Heartsville. As he drove, he rehearsed how he would approach the interview. He wasn't a believer in gimmicks, especially ones that involved people's emotions and their pets. However, the journalist in him knew there was a story here, whether it was about hope, delusion, or just plain old capitalism, and he was going to uncover it.

Arriving at the clinic, Jake was immediately struck by the quaint charm of the building and the vibrant activity around it. Pets and their owners congregated around the entrance, chatting amiably. He pulled out his notepad, his gaze critical, and his mind alert for any signs of the absurdity he was convinced he'd find.

Stepping through the doors of the clinic, Jake was greeted by a blast of air conditioning and the faint smell of antiseptic mingled with dog shampoo. The receptionist, a young woman with a bright smile, noticed him standing somewhat lost.

"Can I help you?" she asked, her voice friendly.

"Yes, I'm Jake Carter, from the Heartsville Herald. I'm here to see Dr. Flynn about her... matchmaking service," he said, the last words tinged with a hint of skepticism.

"Of course! Dr. Flynn mentioned you'd be coming. She's just finishing up with a patient but should be free in a moment. Feel free to take a seat, Mr. Carter," the receptionist directed him to the waiting area.

As Jake sat down, he took in the scene around him: pets interacting with each other, owners exchanging stories, laughter and barks filling the air. It was a lively, heartwarming scene that, to his annoyance, began to soften his skepticism slightly.

After a few minutes, Nora Flynn appeared. She extended her hand, her smile genuine and welcoming. "Mr. Carter, I'm Nora Flynn. Thanks for coming out today. I understand you're curious about our little community project here?"

"Yes, Dr. Flynn. Curious and a bit skeptical," Jake admitted, shaking her hand. "I hope you can prove me wrong."

Nora's smile didn't waver. "Well, I'll certainly try. Shall we?" she gestured towards her office, and as they walked, Jake readied his notepad, his mind racing with questions. This was his element, and no amount of charming scenery or enthusiastic pet owners would deter him from his mission to dig beneath the surface.

- - - - - - - - -

As Jake followed Dr. Nora Flynn into her office, his gaze swept over the small, well-organized room adorned with photos of animals and certificates of veterinary excellence. It was clear this was a place of deep care and professionalism, challenging his preconceived notions about the frivolity of the clinic's matchmaking aspect. He settled into a chair across from Nora's desk, notepad ready, his demeanor still guarded but slightly less rigid.

Nora took her seat, her expression open and inviting. "So, Mr. Carter, what would you like to know about our work here?"

Jake started with a direct approach. "Dr. Flynn, you run a veterinary clinic, which is straightforward enough. But this added element of matchmaking—how does that factor into your practice? Isn't that a bit out of the ordinary for a vet?"

Nora nodded, her response thoughtful. "It is unusual, I'll give you that. But here's the thing—we're not just about treating animals; we're about making lives better. Pets have a unique way of bringing people together, and we found that facilitating that can really enhance the well-being of both pets and their owners."

Jake scribbled down her words, his skepticism not fully abated. "Can you give me an example of how this matchmaking works exactly?"

"Certainly," Nora replied. "Take, for instance, our 'Mutt Mixer Mondays.' We invite single pet owners to come with their pets and participate in group activities. It's casual, just a fun way to meet other animal lovers. What often happens is people connect over their shared experiences and interests. It's about community building."

"And you think that's effective? People actually form lasting relationships through these events?" Jake asked, his tone laced with a hint of incredulity.

Nora smiled slightly, not offended by his skepticism. "We've seen friendships formed, yes, and more. For some, it's just about finding camaraderie, but for others, it's led to meaningful relationships. There's a lot of research on the social support pets provide. We're just extending that concept."

Jake paused, considering her words. He changed tack slightly, "What about the pets themselves? How do they benefit from this setup?"

"That's a great part of it," Nora explained enthusiastically. "Socialization is crucial for pets. These events help them interact in a controlled, safe environment, which can help reduce anxiety and improve their behavior at home and in public spaces. Plus, they get a lot of affection and attention, which is always a good thing."

The journalist in Jake appreciated the logic, but he still held on to his reservations. "It sounds well-intentioned, Dr. Flynn, but isn't there a risk of trivializing the serious work of veterinary care? How do you balance the two?"

Nora leaned forward, her eyes earnest. "It's all integrated, Mr. Carter. The core of our practice is veterinary care—always has been, always will be. But we believe in holistic approaches. If we can create a happier, more connected community around us, that's going to reflect positively on the pets and their health. It's all connected."

Jake took a moment to jot down more notes before looking up again. "And what about you, Dr. Flynn? What drives you to expand your practice into these less traditional areas?"

Her answer was immediate, a reflection of her passion. "I grew up with pets, and I saw firsthand how they can bridge gaps between people. If I can foster that in my community, why wouldn't I? Plus, it makes our clinic a happier place. You should come to one of our events, see it for yourself."

Jake's pen paused over his notepad. Her invitation was genuine, a challenge to his skepticism. "Maybe I will, Dr. Flynn. Maybe I will."

As their interview wrapped up, Jake couldn't deny the intrigue Nora's words had sparked. Despite his initial doubts, he found himself considering her points more seriously than he had anticipated. Walking out of the clinic, the journalist felt an unexpected curiosity stirring within him, the kind that made him reconsider his angles and the depth of the story unfolding in Nora Flynn's unique veterinary practice.

Following the interview, Nora invited Jake to observe a day's activities at the clinic, hoping to give him a firsthand experience of the communal atmosphere she cherished so much. It was an opportunity for Jake to gather more material for his article, though his innate skepticism still cast a long shadow over his perceptions.

The clinic was a hive of activity, with pet owners arriving for appointments or just stopping by to say hello. Nora navigated these interactions with a practiced ease, her genuine affection for each animal and owner apparent. Jake, notebook in hand, maintained a professional distance, observing quietly, his eyes occasionally narrowing as he watched exchanges that, to him, seemed overly sentimental.

He watched as Nora consulted with a young couple who had recently adopted a nervous greyhound. "He's been skittish around our friends," the woman explained, worry creasing her forehead.

Nora listened attentively, then suggested, "Why not bring him to one of our social events? It could help him get used to being around more people in a controlled setting."

The couple seemed relieved at the suggestion, their faces brightening. As they left, Nora turned to Jake, her expression curious. "What do you think, Mr. Carter? Could you see the benefit in that?"

Jake shrugged noncommittally, his response measured. "It's a nice idea. But isn't it a bit of a stretch to expect a social event to fix behavioral issues?"

Nora's smile faltered slightly, her commitment to her methods undeterred by his skepticism. "It's not a fix, but a part of a broader approach. We work in conjunction with training and behavior specialists. It's all interconnected."

As the day progressed, Jake's observations formed a complex tapestry of doubt interwoven with reluctant fascination. He noted how the owners interacted, some sharing stories of their pets like proud parents, others seeking advice from Nora or even from each other. The atmosphere was undeniably warm, the community spirit palpable, yet Jake couldn't fully surrender his doubts about the efficacy of what he considered to be Nora's unconventional methods.

Later, as they walked through the clinic, Nora pointed out the bulletin board filled with photos of pets and their owners, notes of thanks, and announcements for upcoming events. "See, it's not just about the pets. It's about the people, too," she explained.

Jake took a moment to consider her words, his gaze lingering on a photo of an elderly man and a small terrier. "People are certainly buying into it," he conceded, his tone still laced with skepticism.

Nora, picking up on his tone, stopped to face him. "Isn't it possible, Mr. Carter, that there's something to this after all? Something worthwhile that goes beyond conventional veterinary practice?"

Jake paused, the journalist in him battling with the critic. "Perhaps," he finally said, his voice reflecting a crack in his skeptical armor. "But it will take more than a day's observation for me to be convinced."

The remainder of the day saw Jake speaking with several pet owners, his questions probing, seeking to uncover their true feelings about the clinic's community-oriented approach. While responses varied, the underlying theme was clear: they valued the clinic not just for the care it provided their pets, but for the sense of belonging it fostered among them.

As the sun began to set, casting long shadows across the clinic's front porch, Nora and Jake stood watching a small group of pet owners chatting animatedly. The sight seemed to soften Jake's perspective slightly, the edges of his skepticism blurred by the evident happiness of the people and their pets around him.

Walking back to his car, Jake felt a mixture of emotions. The journalist in him was intrigued, his article already forming in his mind with a more nuanced view than he had anticipated. Yet, the skeptic remained, his critical eye still questioning the depth of what he'd seen. This tension, between curiosity and doubt, would shape his reflections and, ultimately, his writing, as he mulled over the day's rich tapestry of interactions, both human and animal.

- - - - - - - - -

As the day wound down, Nora invited Jake to stay for the evening's event, a monthly gathering dubbed "Pet Parents' Night Out." It was designed as a relaxed meetup for pet owners, providing a space for community support and sharing pet care tips, often turning into informal storytelling sessions about the joys and challenges of pet ownership.

Jake agreed, his journalistic curiosity piqued despite his lingering skepticism. As pet owners began to filter in, their faces alight with anticipation, Jake took a position near the back of the room, his notepad ready, his gaze observant and somewhat critical.

Nora started the evening with a warm welcome, her voice carrying over the murmur of conversations. "Thank you all for joining us tonight. As always, this is your time to relax, share, and learn from each other. Let's start with something fun—does anyone have a particularly memorable pet story they'd like to share?"

A woman in the middle of the crowd raised her hand, standing up as the room quieted. "I do," she said, her voice strong yet warm. "It's actually about how I met my best friend here at one of Dr. Flynn's events." She proceeded to tell a touching story about her and her Labrador, Max, and how their frequent visits to the clinic led to an unexpected and deep friendship with another pet owner.

As the woman spoke, Jake watched the reactions of the audience, noting the nods and smiles, the occasional laughter, and the shared looks of understanding. He scribbled notes, the words 'community', 'connection', and 'support' underlined several times.

When the woman finished her story, Nora facilitated a short discussion about the social benefits of pet ownership, weaving in her professional observations and anecdotes from her practice.

"Seeing relationships like these form and grow among you all truly highlights the power of pets not just as companions, but as bridges between us," Nora commented, her eyes scanning the room, meeting those of her clients with a genuine affection.

Jake found himself reluctantly drawn into the discussions. A part of him wanted to dismiss it all as emotional exaggeration, yet another part—the part trained to observe and report human interest stories—recognized the genuine emotional resonance the evening held for the attendees.

As the event continued, Jake decided to engage more directly. He approached a small group, introducing himself as a journalist. "I'm curious," he began, his tone friendly yet probing, "do you really find these events beneficial, beyond just a social aspect? Do they make a difference in how you manage pet care?"

A man in the group, holding a sleepy French Bulldog, answered first. "Absolutely. I've picked up so many tips here that have helped me with Bruno's training and health. It's like crowd-sourcing pet care advice."

A woman next to him chimed in, "And it's not just the pets. It's a huge emotional support too. We share a lot, and knowing you're not alone in the challenges can be really comforting."

Their answers provided Jake with a deeper insight into the community Nora had built. His skepticism was still there, but it was now tempered with an understanding of the emotional and practical value these gatherings provided.

As the night drew to a close, Nora found Jake again, her expression curious. "Well, Mr. Carter, what did you think?"

Jake paused, choosing his words carefully. "It's more impactful than I expected," he admitted. "Seeing the interactions, the connections—it's given me a lot to think about."

Nora's smile was gentle, knowing. "I'm glad to hear that. Sometimes, seeing is believing—or at least the beginning of it."

Driving back to his apartment, the lights of Heartsville blurred past him. Jake's mind was a swirl of thoughts, his usual clear-cut conclusions muddled by the heartfelt stories and sincere testimonies he'd heard. Tonight had planted a seed of doubt in his skepticism, a glimmer that suggested there might be more to Nora's methods than he had initially believed. This feeling, unfamiliar and unsettling as it was, promised to lead his writing down new avenues, exploring the nuanced intersections of community, companionship, and the human-pet bond.

Chapter 3
A Town with Secrets

The clinic was abuzz with preparations for the evening's "Date Night with Dogs" event, a signature affair meant to foster connections not just between pets but their owners as well. Nora was in her element, decorating the space with playful, pet-friendly themes, her excitement palpable. As guests started to arrive, she checked each detail with a practiced eye, ensuring everything was perfect.

Jake arrived, notebook in hand, his skepticism shadowed by the intrigue kindled in the previous chapter. He watched Nora, noting the careful attention she gave to each arriving guest and their pet. It was clear she was passionate about her work, her enthusiasm infectious, even to someone as typically reserved as Jake.

"Good evening, Dr. Flynn," Jake greeted as he approached her, his tone polite but still carrying a hint of his usual reserve.

"Jake! I'm glad you could make it," Nora responded with a bright smile, wiping her hands on her apron before extending one to shake his. "I hope tonight gives you a deeper insight into what we do here."

Jake nodded, his expression one of professional curiosity. "That's the plan. I'm interested to see how this all plays out."

Nora gestured to a table laden with name tags and dog treats. "Everyone, including the dogs, gets a name tag. Helps with introductions and, well, it's part of the fun."

As they spoke, a young couple approached, their Dalmatian pulling eagerly on its leash towards a bowl of water set out for the canine guests. "Nora, we're so excited for tonight," the woman said, her voice bubbling with enthusiasm.

"I'm glad to hear that, Emily," Nora replied, turning to greet them. "I think you'll enjoy the activities we have planned. And it looks like Max is ready to make some friends!"

Emily laughed as Max lapped up water, splashing it around. "He's always the social butterfly."

Jake watched the exchange, his notebook open. "Do you find that events like these change people's perceptions of what a vet clinic can be?"

"Absolutely," Nora answered, still keeping an eye on the arriving guests. "It turns a place that can sometimes be associated with stress for pets and owners into a community spot, a place for positive experiences."

"That's an interesting approach," Jake remarked, scribbling in his notebook. "Turning the clinic into a community center, in a way."

Nora nodded. "Exactly. It's about more than just medical care. It's about building relationships and supporting each other."

As more guests arrived, the atmosphere grew lively with the sound of barking dogs and chatting owners. Nora introduced Jake to several attendees, explaining his presence as a journalist interested in the clinic's community impact.

"Jake's doing a story on our little matchmaking venture," Nora told a group, her tone light but proud.

One of the attendees, a man with a friendly Labrador, turned to Jake. "It's more than matchmaking for pets here. It's about connecting us, the owners. You come to one of these, and you see your neighbors in a new light."

Jake responded with a nod, his demeanor slowly warming. "That's what I'm beginning to see. It's quite a unique setup."

Throughout the evening, Jake's initial skepticism was challenged by the genuine displays of community and care. He engaged more openly with the guests, his questions becoming less about confirmation and more about understanding. This shift was subtle but significant, marking a departure from his earlier distance.

As the sun set and the clinic's lights cast a warm glow over the event, Nora could see the change in Jake's approach. His interactions were less guarded, more curious. It was a promising sign, one that hinted at the possibility of his perspective shifting, or at least expanding, to appreciate the full scope of her vision for the clinic and its role in the community.

The night continued, filled with laughter and the sounds of happy pets, the clinic transformed into a vibrant hub of

Heartsville's pet-loving community, with Jake at its heart, observing, learning, and slowly integrating.

As the "Date Night with Dogs" event warmed up, Jake and Nora found themselves amid a bustling scene. The gentle glow of fairy lights strung across the ceiling lent a soft ambiance to the clinic, which had been transformed into a lively social venue. Nora, ever the gracious host, introduced Jake to more attendees, subtly trying to demonstrate the clinic's broader impact.

However, Jake's journalistic instincts were still at play, driving him to probe deeper. During one such introduction, he asked a couple, "Do you really find that having your pets involved brings you closer to other people, or could it just be a nice backdrop to what would be a typical social gathering?"

The question caught Nora slightly off guard. She watched the couple's reaction closely. The woman, holding a sprightly terrier on a leash, answered first, "Well, I think it does more than just set the scene. It gives us a common ground. We start with our pets, but we stay for the friendships."

Her partner chimed in, "Exactly. And it's not just superficial chatter. Last time we were here, we ended up talking about everything from pet behavior to our jobs. It breaks down walls, you know?"

Jake noted their responses, his expression thoughtful yet still skeptical. Turning to Nora, he posed another question, "But isn't there a risk that people come just for the novelty? How do you ensure it's genuinely beneficial and not just entertainment?"

Nora, maintaining her composure under Jake's scrutinizing gaze, replied, "It's all about fostering a supportive community. Yes, the novelty might draw them in initially, but what keeps them coming back are the genuine connections they make, both human and canine."

As the evening progressed, Jake's questions did not let up, each one pointed and tinged with disbelief. Nora answered each patiently, though the air between them crackled with a mix of challenge and curiosity.

At one point, observing a quiet corner where a few dogs were playing, Jake asked, "Do you think events like these could be misinterpreted as trivializing serious veterinary care?"

Nora, sensing the critical undertone, answered firmly, "Not at all. If anything, they complement the serious aspects of care. They highlight the joy and community spirit that are just as vital to wellness as medical treatment. We're caring for the emotional well-being of our clients and their pets, not just their physical health."

Their exchanges, while polite, were marked by an undercurrent of tension, each trying to understand the other's perspective without fully conceding their own. As they moved through the crowd, their dialogue continued, both probing and defensive.

Jake's approach gradually softened, influenced by the undeniable warmth and camaraderie around him, but his questions remained sharp. "So, you see this as a holistic approach to veterinary care? Integrating social aspects explicitly?"

"Yes, exactly," Nora responded, her voice gaining strength as she spoke. "It's holistic in every sense. The health of a pet and the happiness of its owner are interlinked. By supporting one, we support the other."

The evening wore on, and despite the initial friction, Jake found himself gradually drawn into the atmosphere. The genuine laughter, the pets playfully interacting, and the stories shared by attendees began to paint a richer picture than he had anticipated.

As they paused by a group laughing over a dog's playful antics, Nora looked at Jake, a small smile playing on her lips. "See, it's about more than just care. It's about creating moments like these."

Jake watched the scene, his notepad temporarily forgotten, as he pondered Nora's words. Perhaps there was more depth to this concept than he had initially given credit for. The friction between his skepticism and the unfolding reality created a dynamic tension, one that promised to deepen his understanding of Nora's work and its impact on the community.

As the evening unfolded, Jake continued to weave through the crowd, his journalistic instincts sharpening with each observation. The "Date Night with Dogs" was in full swing, and despite his reservations, he couldn't ignore the palpable sense of community and joy that seemed to permeate the room.

Nora, watching Jake's interactions, guided him toward a series of mini-dates where pet owners introduced their dogs to each other under the guise of finding compatible playmates. It was a clever setup, thoughtfully designed to foster interactions not just between the dogs but more importantly, between the people at the end of the leashes.

"Here we see more than just pets meeting; we see people stepping out of their comfort zones," Nora explained, gesturing towards a timid man who was hesitantly introducing his pug to a spirited beagle. "For many, their pets are a safe topic to break the ice, which can lead to more meaningful exchanges."

Jake watched the man relax as the woman with the beagle laughed softly at the dogs' antics. He raised an eyebrow, turning to Nora. "Do you often see relationships—friendships or otherwise—blossom from these interactions?"

"More often than you might think," Nora replied. "It's not instantaneous, of course, but over time, we see real connections forming. And it's not just about romance. It's about finding companionship, camaraderie."

With his notepad in hand, Jake approached the man after his interaction. "Excuse me, I'm Jake Carter from the Heartsville Herald. Could I ask how you found this experience?"

The man, slightly flushed from his interaction, smiled. "Oh, it's my first time doing something like this. I was nervous, but it was actually really nice. Daisy here," he gestured to his pug, "she's a good icebreaker. And it's easier to talk to someone when you're both focusing on the dogs."

Jake noted his response, his journalistic skepticism tempered by the genuine warmth in the man's voice. Turning back to Nora, he commented, "It's an interesting dynamic, I'll give you that. The pets do seem to take the edge off."

Nora nodded, pleased by his observation. "They do. And sometimes, that little edge is all that stands between us and a new friend."

Their next stop was a small group where an elderly woman and a young couple were laughing over the antics of a particularly charismatic spaniel. Nora introduced Jake, who asked, "What brings you all here tonight?"

The elderly woman, holding the spaniel gently by his collar, answered, "My granddaughter brought me. I lost my husband last year, and she thinks I need to get out more. I was skeptical, but it's been... actually quite lovely."

The young woman from the couple chimed in, "We come often. It's great social exercise for Benny here, and we meet a lot of nice people. It's become something of a highlight for us."

Jake listened, the stories adding layers to his understanding of the event's impact. Each story shared contributed to the narrative he was building—one that was increasingly complex and human.

As the evening drew to a close, Jake found himself at the refreshment table, observing the crowd. Nora joined him, her eyes reflecting the soft lights as she asked, "So, what do you think, Mr. Carter? Any less skeptical than when you arrived?"

He considered her question, his answer more thoughtful than she might have expected. "I'm seeing the appeal, certainly. There's something to be said for the way everyone seems to open up. It's... compelling."

Nora smiled, sensing a shift in his perspective. "That's all we can ask for—just a chance to see the potential."

The event wound down, and as people began to leave, many stopped to thank Nora, their expressions conveying a mix of gratitude and contentment. Jake watched, his notes now filled with more than just observations but reflections on the genuine happiness and connections he'd witnessed.

His report would need to capture not only the mechanics of the event but the spirit, something he now realized was at the heart of Nora's practice. As he left the clinic that night, the cool air felt refreshing against his skin, mirroring the subtle but undeniable fresh perspective he now carried with him.

- - - - - - - - -

As the "Date Night with Dogs" drew to a close, Nora took a moment to introduce a final, playful element to the evening. She suggested that everyone pair up randomly for a mock 'first meet' with their pets, aiming to simulate how first impressions between pets could help ease or spark initial human interactions. Despite his typical reserve, Jake found himself reluctantly agreeing to participate, curious about the practical application of Nora's theories.

Nora, noticing Jake's tentative agreement, paired him with a participant who hadn't brought a pet, offering instead that they share a brief interaction with a clinic therapy dog, a gentle golden retriever named Honey. The participant, a woman named Claire, was initially as hesitant as Jake, her shy smile belying a mix of excitement and nervousness.

"Okay, Jake, Claire, meet Honey. She's one of our best at getting people to relax," Nora introduced them, her tone encouraging.

As Honey nuzzled both Jake and Claire, Jake found himself smiling, a natural reaction to the dog's warmth. Claire laughed, her initial shyness fading a bit as she stroked Honey's fur. "She's beautiful. Does she always help with these events?"

"Yes, she does," Jake responded, finding himself more at ease talking to Claire as they shared the experience of interacting with Honey. "She seems to have a knack for calming people down."

"I can see that. It's a lot easier talking while petting her. Takes some of the pressure off, doesn't it?" Claire remarked, her voice steadier.

Jake nodded, his initial skepticism softening in the face of the genuine connection forming, facilitated by the calm old dog. "It does. I guess there's something to what Dr. Flynn is trying to do here, using pets as a bridge between people."

Their conversation continued, flowing more smoothly as they discussed their own experiences with pets, and gradually veering into more personal territories like their hobbies and interests. The simple act of sharing time with Honey allowed them to step past the awkwardness of a first meeting, showcasing the very phenomenon Nora hoped to highlight.

As the mock date concluded, Nora approached them, her eyes twinkling with a mix of amusement and inquiry. "How did it go? Did Honey do her job?"

"She did," Claire answered before Jake could, a smile playing on her lips. "It was one of the more relaxed conversations I've had at an event like this."

Jake agreed, his notebook forgotten on a nearby table. "I have to admit, it was less awkward than I expected. There's something disarming about having a dog like Honey around."

Nora smiled, pleased by their feedback. "That's the idea. Pets have a way of opening doors that we sometimes can't open ourselves."

As the participants began to leave, Jake found himself lingering, watching as Nora bid farewell to each guest. The evening had offered him a series of revelations, each encounter and shared story adding depth to his understanding of the clinic's community role.

Finally, as the last guest departed and Nora began tidying up, Jake approached her. "Thank you for the evening, Nora. It's given me a lot to think about."

Nora, picking up stray decorations, paused to face him. "I'm glad to hear that, Jake. I hope it gave you a different perspective on what we're trying to achieve here."

"It did," Jake admitted, his voice carrying a newfound respect for her work. "And it's made me reconsider the role of pets not just in their owners' lives but in broader social settings."

As Jake picked up his notebook and prepared to leave, he felt a subtle shift in his perception. The evening hadn't just been an assignment; it had been an experiential insight into a community that thrived on mutual support and shared love for pets. The drive back home was reflective, with Jake considering how best to convey the complexity and warmth of the connections he'd witnessed, acknowledging that his article would now need to capture more than just the mechanics of a veterinary clinic's day-to-day operations—it needed to tell the story of a community, brought together by the love of animals.

Chapter 4
Uncovering the Past

Jake Carter, seated at the wooden table of Heartsville's only diner, looked out through the glass window, the scene outside painting a picturesque view of small-town life. The sun bathed the streets in a warm, golden hue as townsfolk went about their daily routines. Children cycled past on their way to school, while shopkeepers opened their doors, greeting each passerby with a friendly wave. On the surface, Heartsville was the embodiment of quaint, rural charm. But Jake wasn't here to be charmed. He was here to uncover the truth.

His notebook lay open in front of him, pages filled with scribbled notes and observations from the past few days. A half-empty cup of coffee sat beside it, the steam long since dissipated. Jake flipped through his notes, brow furrowed, as he considered the conversations he'd had. Everyone seemed so eager to talk about Nora Flynn and her clinic, about the way she had transformed it into the heart of the community. But the more he heard, the more skeptical he became.

"Morning, Jake," came a cheery voice, breaking his train of thought. He looked up to see Mary, the diner's waitress, with a pot of fresh coffee in hand. "Another refill?"

"Sure, thanks," Jake replied, offering a polite smile as she poured the coffee. Mary, in her early forties with a motherly demeanor, had been serving him breakfast every morning since he arrived in town.

"Working hard, I see," Mary commented, nodding towards his notebook. "Writing that big article on our little town?"

"Something like that," Jake said, noncommittal. He wasn't ready to reveal his true thoughts. "People here seem really fond of Nora Flynn."

Mary's face lit up. "Oh, absolutely. She's done so much for Heartsville. You won't find a kinder soul around here."

Jake nodded, but his mind was already turning over the information. Everyone had the same story: Nora was a saint, the clinic was a beacon of hope, and the town was better for it. It was all too perfect, too neat. Jake had been a journalist long enough to know that stories like this usually had another side—a side people didn't talk about unless you dug deep.

"Has she ever... I don't know, had any issues with anyone in town? Maybe someone who didn't like the changes she made?" Jake asked, trying to keep his tone casual.

Mary's smile faltered just a bit, and she shook her head. "Not that I've heard. Sure, some folks were a little hesitant when she first took over the clinic, but she won them over quickly enough. Why do you ask?"

"No reason," Jake said quickly, sensing her unease. "Just curious."

Mary seemed to study him for a moment before offering a tight smile. "You won't find any dirt here, Jake. Nora's one of the good ones."

Jake forced another smile, nodding as she moved on to another table. But Mary's reaction only confirmed his suspicions. There was something everyone was keeping quiet about. No one was perfect, not even Nora Flynn. The question was, what was it?

He finished his coffee and packed up his things, leaving the diner and stepping out onto the sunlit street. He walked down the main road, past the general store and the post office, nodding to a few townsfolk as he went. They all knew who he was by now—the outsider journalist poking his nose into their business. Some were friendly, others more reserved, but there was always a sense of wariness in their eyes. It was subtle, but Jake noticed it.

As he made his way towards the clinic, Jake couldn't help but feel the growing tension in the air. People were nice enough, but he could sense that they didn't entirely trust him. Maybe they were right not to. He was here to find a story, and he had a feeling it wouldn't be the one they wanted to tell.

When he reached the clinic, he paused outside, looking at the well-maintained building. The clinic was bustling as usual, with people coming and going, chatting with one another as they waited for their appointments. Jake watched them, noting the smiles, the laughter, the casual ease with which they interacted. It was the kind of scene that could make you believe in the goodness of people. But Jake knew better. He had seen too much in his career to take things at face value.

He stepped inside, greeted by the familiar scent of antiseptic and the sound of soft, calming music playing in the background. Nora was at the reception desk, chatting with an elderly man who was holding a small, trembling dog. She smiled warmly at Jake as he entered.

"Good morning, Jake," she called out. "How are you today?"

"Good, thanks," Jake replied, forcing a smile. "Busy morning?"

Nora nodded, her attention still on the elderly man as she gave the dog a reassuring pat. "Always is. Mr. Williams here brought in little Daisy for her check-up. She's been a bit under the weather."

Jake watched the interaction closely. Nora was kind, attentive, and clearly cared about her patients. But there was something about the way everyone spoke of her, the almost reverent tone they used, that made him uneasy. It was as if they were all in on some unspoken agreement to keep up the façade.

He approached the desk as Mr. Williams left, and Nora turned her full attention to him. "What can I do for you, Jake?"

"I was hoping to ask you a few more questions, if you don't mind," Jake said, pulling out his notebook. "For the article."

"Of course," Nora replied, her smile never wavering. "Why don't we step into my office?"

As they walked towards her office, Jake couldn't shake the feeling that something wasn't right. He was determined to find out what it was, no matter how deep he had to dig.

- - - - - - - - -

Nora Flynn sat at her desk, absently twirling a pen between her fingers as she stared out the window of her office. The morning sun filtered through the blinds, casting soft lines of light across the room. Outside, the clinic bustled with its usual activity—clients checking in, pets being led into examination rooms, and the gentle hum of conversations. But Nora's mind was elsewhere.

Her thoughts kept drifting back to Jake Carter, the journalist who had been spending an increasing amount of time at the clinic. She had initially welcomed his presence, believing that an outsider's perspective on the work they were doing could be beneficial. But lately, she had begun to sense something in his demeanor—a skepticism that made her uneasy. His questions had grown more probing, his tone more critical, and it was becoming clear to Nora that Jake wasn't just here to write a feel-good story about a small-town vet.

She sighed, setting the pen down and pressing her fingers against her temples. The community had worked so hard to build something special here, and the thought that Jake might write something that could jeopardize that… it was unsettling.

There was a knock on her office door, pulling her from her thoughts. Before she could respond, the door opened, and Jake stepped inside, a polite but guarded smile on his face.

"Nora, do you have a minute?" he asked, holding up his notebook.

"Of course, Jake," she replied, gesturing for him to take a seat. "What's on your mind?"

Jake settled into the chair opposite her desk, flipping open his notebook. He seemed to hesitate for a moment, as if weighing his words carefully. "I've been doing some more interviews around town," he began, his tone measured. "Talking to people about the clinic, about you. Everyone has a lot of good things to say."

"I'm glad to hear that," Nora said, forcing a smile, though her concern lingered just beneath the surface. "We've worked hard to create a place where people feel supported, where they know their pets are cared for."

"Right," Jake nodded, scribbling something in his notebook. "But I've also noticed… well, it's almost like everyone's reading from the same script. It's all very positive, almost too positive. You know what I mean?"

Nora's smile faltered, and she leaned forward slightly, her hands clasped on the desk. "Jake, Heartsville is a close-knit community. People here value what we've built together. It's not about following a script—it's about genuinely caring for each other."

Jake looked up from his notes, meeting her gaze directly. "I'm not saying that's not true, Nora. But as a journalist, I have to look at every angle. And I guess what I'm asking is… is there anything I'm not seeing? Any conflicts, any pushback when you were setting all this up?"

Nora's concern deepened. She could sense where Jake was heading with this line of questioning, and it worried her. "Jake, no community is without its challenges," she said carefully. "But we've always worked through them together. The truth is, people here believe in what we're doing. They support it because they see the difference it makes."

Jake tapped his pen against his notebook, his expression thoughtful. "But surely, there must have been some resistance, right? Not everyone would be on board with the changes you've made, especially when it comes to the clinic becoming such a central part of the town."

"There were a few who were hesitant at first," Nora admitted, her voice steady. "Change can be difficult. But over time, they saw the benefits. The clinic isn't just a place for veterinary care—it's become a hub for the community, a place where people can connect, share their experiences, and find support. That's something we've all worked hard to achieve."

Jake's eyes narrowed slightly as he listened, his skepticism evident. "And there's nothing more to it than that?"

Nora resisted the urge to sigh. She could see that Jake wasn't satisfied with her answers, and that worried her even more. "Jake, I can tell you're looking for something more," she said, choosing her words carefully. "I understand that as a journalist, you have a job to do. But I'd like to ask you to consider spending more time here, really observing how things work. Talk to more people, see how they interact with each other, how they engage with the clinic. I think you'll find that what you're seeing is genuine."

Jake tilted his head, regarding her with a mix of curiosity and caution. "Are you inviting me to shadow you? To see the day-to-day operations up close?"

"I am," Nora said, her voice firm. "If you're going to write about us, I want you to have the full picture. Not just what you might perceive on the surface. Spend some time here, and then make up your mind."

Jake leaned back in his chair, his pen hovering over his notebook. "You're confident I'll see things differently?"

"I'm confident you'll see the truth," Nora replied, meeting his gaze without hesitation. "And then you can decide what story you want to tell."

There was a long pause as Jake considered her offer, his expression unreadable. Finally, he nodded, closing his notebook with a decisive snap. "Alright, Nora. I'll take you up on that. Let's see if spending more time here changes my perspective."

Nora smiled, though it was tinged with the weight of her concerns. "I appreciate that, Jake. I really do. Let's start tomorrow—come by early, and you can see how the day unfolds from the very beginning."

Jake stood, slipping his notebook into his jacket pocket. "Sounds good. Thanks, Nora."

As he left her office, Nora watched him go, her smile fading as soon as the door closed behind him. She couldn't shake the feeling that this was just the beginning of something that could either reinforce everything she'd worked for—or unravel it. She only hoped that by opening up her world to Jake, he'd come to see the community as she did: a place built on trust, care, and mutual respect.

But until then, the uncertainty lingered, and with it, a growing sense of unease.

The day was settling into a comfortable rhythm at Nora Flynn's clinic when the front door burst open, breaking the usual calm. A young girl, no more than ten years old, rushed inside, her face flushed with a mixture of fear and desperation. Her wild eyes scanned the room, landing on Nora, who was kneeling beside a Labrador, finishing up a routine checkup.

"Nora! Nora, please, I need your help!" the girl cried, her voice trembling.

Nora immediately looked up, recognizing the urgency in the girl's tone. She gently patted the Labrador's head, murmuring a soothing word to the dog's owner before standing and crossing the room to the distressed child.

"Emily, what's wrong?" Nora asked, her voice calm but filled with concern.

"My dog, Sparky—he's gone! I can't find him anywhere!" Emily's words tumbled out in a rush, her small hands clenched into fists. "I was playing with him in the backyard, and then... and then he just ran off. I don't know where he went!"

Nora's heart clenched at the sight of the girl's tear-filled eyes. Sparky, a scrappy little terrier, was well-known around Heartsville for his energetic antics. He was a beloved companion to Emily, who had grown up with him by her side. Losing him, even temporarily, would be devastating for her.

"Okay, Emily, take a deep breath," Nora said, kneeling down to meet the girl at eye level. "We're going to find Sparky, alright? I promise. But I need you to help me. Can you do that?"

Emily nodded, wiping at her eyes with the back of her hand. "What do we do?"

"We start by letting everyone know," Nora said, standing up and turning to her assistant, Lisa, who had been watching the exchange from behind the reception desk. "Lisa, can you call the other clinics and animal shelters in the area? Let them know we're looking for Sparky, a small terrier with a red collar."

"On it," Lisa replied, already reaching for the phone.

Nora then turned to the roomful of clients, who had all fallen silent, watching the scene unfold. "Everyone, if you could, please keep an eye out for Sparky. He's a small terrier with a red collar. If you see him, bring him straight here or call me immediately."

There was a chorus of nods and murmured agreements. Heartsville was a community that rallied together in times of need, and it was clear that finding Sparky was now everyone's priority.

Jake, who had been observing the situation quietly from the corner of the room, felt a tug of something unfamiliar—empathy, perhaps—as he watched the scene. He had seen the girl run in, her face pale with fear, and now he was witnessing the way the community responded without hesitation. It was a stark contrast to the guarded skepticism he'd been holding onto since arriving in town.

As the room began to buzz with activity, Nora noticed Jake standing by himself, notebook in hand but forgotten. She walked over to him, her expression a mixture of worry and determination.

"Jake, this is the kind of thing I was talking about," she said softly, glancing back at Emily, who was now being comforted by an older woman who had stepped in to help. "Heartsville isn't just a town—it's a family. When someone needs help, we all step up. No questions asked."

Jake nodded, unable to deny what he was seeing. The people in the clinic were already making calls, some heading out to search the surrounding areas. There was no hesitation, no sense of obligation—just genuine concern and a desire to help.

"What can I do?" Jake found himself asking, surprising even himself with the offer.

Nora's eyes softened, and she placed a hand on his arm, a gesture of both gratitude and trust. "Thank you, Jake. If you could help spread the word—maybe head down to the park and let people there know. Sparky loves that place, and if he ran off, it's possible he went there."

"Consider it done," Jake replied, tucking his notebook away. Without another word, he turned and headed out the door, feeling a sense of purpose that had been missing from his work in recent months.

As Jake walked through the streets of Heartsville, stopping to inform people of the missing dog, he couldn't help but notice the way everyone responded with the same level of care and urgency. It wasn't just a formality; these people genuinely cared about Emily and Sparky. The more people he spoke to, the more he realized that this town wasn't just putting on a show for his benefit—this was who they were.

By the time Jake reached the park, a group of teenagers had already gathered, spreading out to search the area for any sign of Sparky. Jake joined them, his eyes scanning the bushes and trees, his ears alert for the sound of barking. As he searched, he couldn't stop thinking about how easily he had assumed the worst about this town, about Nora. But what he was witnessing now was something real, something undeniable.

He was so lost in thought that he almost missed the faint yip coming from a cluster of bushes near the playground. Jake's heart leaped in his chest, and he quickly moved towards the sound, pushing aside the branches to reveal a small, trembling terrier tangled in the underbrush.

"Sparky!" Jake exclaimed, reaching down to gently untangle the dog from the brambles. The terrier whimpered but didn't resist, recognizing the kindness in Jake's touch. Once free, Sparky looked up at him with wide, grateful eyes.

Jake picked up the little dog, cradling him in his arms. "Let's get you back to Emily, buddy."

As Jake walked back towards the clinic, Sparky safe in his arms, he couldn't help but feel a shift within himself. For the first time since he arrived in Heartsville, he wasn't just an outsider looking in—he was part of something bigger, something that mattered. And as he stepped through the clinic doors, greeted by the sight of Emily's face lighting up with joy at the sight of her beloved Sparky, Jake knew that his perspective was beginning to change.

Jake Carter stood on the edge of Heartsville's town square, watching as the late afternoon sun cast long shadows across the cobblestone streets. The town had returned to its usual quiet, the earlier flurry of activity surrounding the search for Sparky now subsided. The terrier was back in Emily's arms, and the townspeople had slowly dispersed, returning to their daily routines with a shared sense of satisfaction.

Jake should have felt relieved, maybe even content, but instead, he was unsettled. The day's events replayed in his mind like a film on loop—the frantic search, the way everyone had dropped what they were doing to help, and the genuine relief and joy that had spread through the town when Sparky was found. It was a scene straight out of a small-town idyll, the kind of story that warmed hearts and inspired faith in humanity.

And yet, here he was, struggling with his own feelings.

Jake's job as a journalist was to remain objective, to observe without becoming emotionally involved. It was a rule he had lived by for years, one that had served him well in covering everything from political scandals to human interest stories. He had always prided himself on his ability to maintain distance, to report the facts without letting his own emotions color the narrative. But Heartsville was challenging that principle in ways he hadn't anticipated.

He paced slowly across the square, his thoughts a tangled mess. In his mind, he could hear the voice of his editor, Marlene, clear and sharp as always. *Stick to the facts, Jake. Don't get too close. The moment you lose your objectivity, you lose the story.*

But what was the story here? Was it the fact that Heartsville was a small town that rallied together to find a lost dog? Was it the unwavering dedication of Nora Flynn, who had managed to turn a simple veterinary clinic into the heart of a community? Or was it something deeper, something that couldn't be neatly packaged into a headline or a column?

Jake paused by the fountain in the center of the square, his reflection rippling in the water as he leaned against the cool stone. He had come to Heartsville with the intention of uncovering a story, but now he wasn't sure what that story was. Every instinct told him to dig deeper, to find the hidden truth that would justify his growing unease. But what if there was no hidden truth? What if everything he had seen today—the kindness, the unity, the genuine care—was just that: genuine?

He ran a hand through his hair, frustrated by the war waging within him. He had always been able to separate himself from the subjects of his stories, to look at them through a lens of detachment. But Heartsville was different. The more time he spent here, the harder it was to maintain that distance. And the more he got to know Nora, the more he realized that she wasn't just the subject of his next article—she was a person who genuinely cared about her town and the people in it.

Damn it, he thought, staring down at the water. *Why can't I just see this for what it is?*

He could feel himself being pulled in two directions. On one side, there was the part of him that had come to Heartsville as a skeptic, determined to find the cracks in the façade, to expose whatever truth lay beneath the surface. On the other side was the part of him that was beginning to see the town not as a story to be told, but as a place with real people, real emotions, and real connections.

And then there was Nora. She wasn't just a vet running a clinic—she was the glue that held this town together. The way she had responded to Emily's distress, the calm yet firm way she had rallied the community to find Sparky, the genuine relief she had shown when the dog was safely returned—it was clear that she was more than just a professional; she was a pillar of this community. But was it her sincerity that was getting to him, or something more?

Jake pushed himself away from the fountain and started walking again, his steps slow and deliberate. The setting sun bathed the town in a warm, golden light, the kind of light that made everything look softer, more inviting. He felt an ache in his chest, a nagging doubt that refused to be ignored. Was he here to tell the truth, or was he here to confirm his own preconceptions? And what if the truth wasn't what he had expected?

He found himself back at the clinic, standing just outside the front door. Through the windows, he could see Nora inside, talking to a client with her usual calm demeanor. She looked up and met his eyes through the glass, offering him a small, knowing smile. It was a smile that said she understood more than he realized, a smile that invited him in, not just physically, but emotionally.

Jake hesitated, his hand hovering over the door handle. He knew that if he stepped inside, it wouldn't just be as a journalist—it would be as someone who was beginning to care, maybe too much. He took a deep breath, his heart pounding in his chest. Objectivity was slipping away, and in its place was something else, something that scared him because it was so unfamiliar.

Finally, he let out a long sigh and pushed open the door. The bell above chimed softly, and Nora looked up, her smile widening as he stepped inside. There was no turning back now. The lines between observer and participant were blurring, and for the first time in a long time, Jake wasn't sure if that was a bad thing.

As he crossed the threshold, Jake knew that this wasn't just a story anymore—it was something much more complicated. And for better or worse, he was in it now.

Chapter 5
The Skeptical Journalist

The search for Sparky had become the talk of the town by the time the sun dipped below the horizon. Heartsville's quiet streets, usually winding down at this hour, were alive with activity. Groups of townsfolk, armed with flashlights and determination, gathered at the clinic, where Nora had set up a makeshift command center. The clinic's waiting room was crowded with people, young and old, all eager to help find the missing dog.

"Nora, what's the plan?" Mrs. Thompson, an elderly woman who had lived in Heartsville her entire life, asked as she huddled near the reception desk, her cane tapping anxiously on the floor.

Nora, who had been organizing search parties, looked up from her map of the town, which was spread out on the counter. "Mrs. Thompson, I need you and a few others to check the park again. Sparky loves that place, and he might have gone back there."

"Consider it done," Mrs. Thompson replied, her voice steady despite her age. She turned to the group of teenagers behind her, some of whom were her grandchildren. "Come on, kids. Let's go find that dog."

"Thanks, Mrs. Thompson," Nora called after her, watching as the older woman led the group out the door. She then turned her attention to the next group waiting for instructions.

"Nora, where should we go?" a middle-aged man asked, his hand resting on the shoulder of his young daughter, who looked up at Nora with wide, worried eyes.

"Mr. Harris, could you take your group to check the streets around Maple Avenue? It's a bit quieter there, and Sparky might be hiding in someone's yard," Nora suggested, her tone calm but authoritative.

"Maple Avenue, got it," Mr. Harris nodded, giving his daughter a reassuring squeeze. "Come on, sweetie. Let's find Sparky."

As they left, Jake entered the clinic, his face reflecting the same determination he'd seen in everyone else. He walked up to Nora, who was busy coordinating another group of volunteers.

"Nora, I just checked the woods on the outskirts of town—no sign of him there," Jake reported, his voice laced with both concern and frustration.

"Thanks, Jake. I was thinking of sending another group to the lake. Sparky might have gone there to get a drink," Nora suggested, her brow furrowing slightly as she considered the possibilities.

"Good idea. I'll head up that group," Jake offered without hesitation.

Before Nora could respond, the clinic's door burst open, and a group of children came rushing in, all speaking at once.

"We didn't find him by the school, Nora," one of the boys, Timmy, said breathlessly.

"We looked everywhere!" another chimed in, his face flushed from running.

Nora knelt down to their level, her voice gentle but firm. "You all did great. Now, I need you to help me with something else. Can you go door to door in the neighborhood and ask people if they've seen Sparky? And make sure to tell them to check their backyards."

The children nodded eagerly, glad to have another task. "We're on it, Nora!" they chorused before racing back out into the night.

Jake watched the scene unfold, his respect for Nora deepening with each passing moment. She was calm, collected, and knew exactly how to handle the situation, keeping everyone focused and motivated.

"Nora, how do you do it?" Jake asked, unable to keep the admiration out of his voice.

"Do what?" she replied, glancing up at him as she prepared to dispatch the next group of volunteers.

"Keep everyone so organized, so... hopeful," Jake said, his tone softer now.

Nora smiled, though it was tinged with the worry she was trying to suppress. "It's not just me, Jake. This is what Heartsville does. We take care of each other. Sparky is part of our community, just like Emily and everyone else. We're not going to stop until we find him."

Jake nodded, feeling a warmth in his chest that he hadn't expected. "You're right. This town... it's something special."

Before Nora could respond, the clinic's phone rang, and Lisa, Nora's assistant, quickly answered. After a brief conversation, Lisa turned to Nora with a hopeful expression.

"Nora, someone thinks they might have seen Sparky near the old mill," Lisa said.

Nora's eyes lit up with renewed hope. "That's great news. Jake, can you take a group and check it out?"

"Absolutely," Jake agreed without hesitation. He turned to the volunteers still in the clinic. "Alright, everyone. Let's head to the old mill and bring Sparky home."

As the group hurried out, Nora watched them go, her heart swelling with pride. She knew they wouldn't rest until Sparky was found, and neither would she. This was what Heartsville was all about—coming together in times of need, no matter how big or small the crisis.

Once the room had cleared, Nora finally allowed herself a moment to breathe. She leaned against the counter, closing her eyes for just a second. The weight of responsibility was heavy on her shoulders, but she bore it gladly. These were her people, and this was her town. She would do anything to protect them, to keep them safe, even if it was just by helping find a lost dog.

Nora opened her eyes as Lisa approached her, concern evident on her face. "Nora, are you okay?"

Nora smiled faintly, nodding. "I'm fine, Lisa. We're going to find Sparky. I just know it."

And as the night deepened and the search continued, that belief—Nora's unshakeable faith in her community—remained a beacon of hope for everyone involved.

The old mill loomed ahead, its silhouette stark against the deepening twilight. Jake Carter led a small group of townspeople, their flashlights bobbing in the dark like fireflies. The search for Sparky had taken them to the outskirts of Heartsville, where the quiet rustling of the trees and the distant chirping of crickets were the only sounds that broke the stillness.

Jake's thoughts, however, were anything but still. The events of the day played over and over in his mind, mingling with the soft voices of the townsfolk as they talked quietly among themselves. His skepticism, so firmly rooted when he had arrived in Heartsville, was beginning to unravel, and he wasn't sure what to make of it.

"Over here! Let's check by the old fence," one of the volunteers called out, breaking Jake from his reverie.

Jake nodded, gesturing for the others to follow. As they moved toward the fence, his gaze shifted to Nora, who was walking beside Mrs. Thompson, her flashlight illuminating the ground in front of them. He watched as Nora gently supported the elderly woman, guiding her over the uneven terrain.

"Nora, you sure you should be out here? It's getting late," Mrs. Thompson said, her voice filled with both concern and affection.

"I'm not going anywhere until we find Sparky," Nora replied, her tone gentle but resolute. "Besides, I wouldn't be able to sleep knowing he's still out here somewhere."

Mrs. Thompson patted Nora's arm, her expression softening. "You're too good to us, you know that? Always thinking of others."

"It's just who I am, Mrs. Thompson," Nora said with a small smile. "And it's who we are as a town. We look out for each other, don't we?"

Jake found himself listening intently to their exchange, feeling something stir inside him. This wasn't the Nora Flynn he had expected—the small-town vet who might be hiding something beneath her warm exterior. This was someone who genuinely cared, who was woven into the very fabric of Heartsville. And the people around her responded to that care with a deep and abiding trust.

As they reached the fence, Nora stopped, shining her flashlight into the surrounding brush. "Sparky! Here, boy!" she called out, her voice echoing through the trees. When there was no response, she sighed and looked back at the group. "Let's spread out a bit, but stay within sight of each other."

Jake watched as everyone nodded in agreement, dispersing to search the area. He stayed close to Nora, unable to shake the feeling that he was seeing the town—and her—in a new light.

"You know," he began, his voice quiet, "I didn't expect any of this when I first came here."

Nora glanced at him, curiosity in her eyes. "What do you mean?"

"I thought... I thought this was going to be just another assignment," Jake admitted, his words slower, more deliberate. "Small town, tight-knit community, everyone's too friendly to be real. I was sure there was something underneath it all, something that wasn't quite as perfect as it seemed."

"And now?" Nora asked, though there was no judgment in her tone—only a genuine interest in his perspective.

Jake paused, considering his words carefully. "And now, I'm not so sure. Watching everyone come together today, the way you've organized all of this... It's not what I expected. I see the way people look at you, Nora. They don't just respect you because you're their vet. They trust you because you've earned it. You're more than just a part of this town—you're its heart."

Nora looked down for a moment, her expression thoughtful. "Heartsville has given me so much, Jake. It's not just a place—

it's my home, my family. When I came here, I didn't know anyone, didn't have anything except my skills as a vet and a hope that I could make a difference. The people here welcomed me, trusted me, and over time, we built something together."

Jake nodded slowly, the weight of her words settling over him. "And you've never thought about leaving? About going somewhere bigger, somewhere you could make more money or have more... I don't know, opportunities?"

Nora smiled, a touch of amusement in her eyes. "You sound like my mother. She always wondered why I chose to stay in a small town instead of moving to a big city where I could have a more lucrative practice. But the truth is, this is where I belong. I don't need more than what I have here. Heartsville isn't just my job—it's my life. And that means more to me than any paycheck ever could."

Jake was silent, processing what she had said. It was the kind of sentiment that, just days ago, he might have dismissed as naïve or overly sentimental. But now, after everything he had seen—the unwavering support of the townsfolk, the way Nora led with both strength and compassion—he was starting to see the truth in it.

Nora turned to him, her gaze direct but kind. "Jake, I don't know what you're planning to write about Heartsville, or about me. But whatever it is, I hope you see what I see—a town that's far from perfect, but one that cares deeply for its people. And that's something worth protecting."

Jake met her eyes, and for the first time, he found himself nodding in agreement. "You're right, Nora. I think I'm starting to see it."

They continued the search in silence, the bond between them subtly shifting as Jake's perspective continued to evolve. He still had a job to do, still had a story to tell, but the narrative in his mind was changing. Heartsville wasn't just a subject anymore—it was a place that had begun to touch something deeper within him.

And as they called out for Sparky in the gathering darkness, Jake knew that his article wouldn't just be about a small-town vet or a missing dog. It would be about the kind of strength that only comes from a community that truly cares—something he was beginning to realize was far more real, and far more valuable, than he had ever imagined.

- - - - - - - - -

The darkness had deepened, and the chill of the night air was beginning to settle in, but the search for Sparky continued with undiminished vigor. The small group led by Jake had combed the area around the old mill, calling out the terrier's name, shining flashlights into every nook and cranny they could find. Each passing minute heightened the tension, but no one was ready to give up.

"Over here, by the creek!" one of the volunteers shouted, his voice cutting through the quiet night.

Jake turned sharply, his heart leaping in his chest. "What is it? Did you find something?" he called back, already moving in the direction of the voice.

The volunteer, a young man named Kyle, was crouched by the edge of the creek, his flashlight trained on a small bundle of fur huddled against the roots of a tree. As Jake drew closer, his breath caught in his throat—it was Sparky, trembling but unharmed.

"Is he okay?" Jake asked, dropping to his knees beside Kyle, his voice filled with concern.

Kyle nodded, relief washing over his features. "He's scared, but I think he's fine. Probably just exhausted and cold."

"Sparky, hey buddy, it's okay," Jake murmured softly, reaching out to gently stroke the dog's fur. Sparky looked up at him with wide, tired eyes, his little body quivering from the cold. "You're safe now, we're going to get you home."

As the rest of the group gathered around, murmurs of relief spread through the crowd. Nora, who had been coordinating the search from the clinic, arrived moments later, breathless and anxious.

"Did you find him? Is he alright?" she asked, pushing through the small crowd to kneel beside Jake.

"Yeah, he's okay," Jake replied, looking up at her with a faint smile. "Just scared and tired."

Nora's face softened with a mix of relief and gratitude as she reached out to gently cradle Sparky in her arms. "You poor thing," she whispered, her voice thick with emotion. "We've been so worried about you."

Sparky whimpered softly, snuggling into Nora's embrace as if finally feeling safe. Jake watched the scene unfold, a deep sense of warmth spreading through his chest. This wasn't just a lost dog being found—this was a community coming together, each person playing their part to protect one of their own, no matter how small.

"Let's get him back to the clinic," Nora said, standing up with Sparky securely in her arms. "He needs to be warmed up, maybe given some food and water."

Jake nodded, rising to his feet. "I'll come with you."

As they began the walk back to the clinic, the group around them started cheering and clapping, the sound echoing through the quiet streets of Heartsville. The celebration was spontaneous and genuine, a reflection of the collective relief and joy that had been building up throughout the night.

"We did it!" someone shouted from the back of the group.

"Heartsville never lets one of its own down!" another voice called out, and the crowd responded with a resounding cheer.

Jake glanced over at Nora, who was smiling broadly, her eyes glistening with unshed tears. "You see what I mean, Jake?" she said, her voice soft yet filled with pride. "This town... we take care of each other. We don't give up, not on anyone."

Jake nodded slowly, feeling a lump form in his throat. "Yeah, I see it now," he admitted, his voice low. "I came here looking for something, but I didn't expect to find this."

Nora looked at him, her gaze searching his face. "And what did you find, Jake?"

He paused, struggling to put his feelings into words. "I found... a community that's real, that actually cares. I've covered stories all over, but I've never seen anything like this. It's not just talk—it's action. It's love, in the truest sense."

Nora's smile deepened, and she reached out to touch his arm lightly. "I'm glad you see it, Jake. Because that's what Heartsville is all about. And that's what I hope you'll tell people."

Jake's thoughts swirled as they continued toward the clinic. The article he had planned to write felt suddenly inadequate, as if it couldn't capture the depth of what he had witnessed tonight. He realized that the story wasn't just about a small town with a missing dog—it was about something much bigger. It was about a way of life, about people who believed in something greater than themselves.

When they reached the clinic, the crowd began to disperse, each person offering words of congratulations and thanks as they left. Nora carried Sparky inside, setting him down gently on an examination table as Lisa rushed over with a blanket.

"We'll take good care of him, don't worry," Lisa assured, draping the blanket over Sparky, who was already starting to relax.

Nora sighed, her shoulders finally sagging with exhaustion. "Thank you, Lisa. And thank you, Jake. I don't know what we would have done without everyone coming together like this."

Jake shook his head, a small smile playing on his lips. "You would have done exactly what you always do—rally the town, find a solution, and bring everyone home safe."

Nora chuckled softly, her eyes meeting his. "Maybe. But it helps to have good people by your side."

Jake's smile widened, and for the first time since he had arrived in Heartsville, he felt like he belonged. He wasn't just an outsider anymore, observing from a distance. He was part of something now, something that mattered.

As he left the clinic that night, Jake knew one thing for certain: his article would be different. It would tell the real story of Heartsville—not just a place on a map, but a community built on trust, resilience, and an unwavering belief in each other. And maybe, just maybe, it would help others see what he had come to understand—that there was something truly special about this little town.

Jake Carter sat at the small wooden desk in his rented room at the Heartsville Inn, staring at the blank screen of his laptop.

The room was quiet, save for the occasional creak of the old building settling for the night and the distant hum of a car passing by on the main road. He had been back from the clinic for over an hour, but his thoughts were still tangled in the events of the day.

He rubbed his hands over his face, feeling the weight of exhaustion, both physical and mental. Normally, after a long day in the field, Jake would have no trouble diving into his writing. The words would flow easily, his observations sharp and precise, painting a picture of the town or person he was investigating. But tonight was different. Tonight, the words wouldn't come.

With a sigh, Jake leaned back in his chair and glanced at the notes scattered across the desk. Pages filled with scribbles about Heartsville, Nora, the search for Sparky, and the people he had met since arriving in town. There was plenty of material here, enough to craft a compelling narrative. But the story that was forming in his mind wasn't the one he had expected to write.

He picked up his notebook, flipping through the pages slowly. His handwriting, usually neat and controlled, had grown more erratic as the day progressed. What he saw on those pages surprised him—positive observations, small moments of kindness, the unspoken bonds between the townspeople. There were no hidden scandals, no dark secrets waiting to be uncovered. Just a community that genuinely cared about each other.

This isn't what I came here to write, he thought, frowning. But even as the thought crossed his mind, he knew it wasn't true. He had come here looking for a story, and he had found one. It just wasn't the one he had anticipated.

Jake set the notebook down and turned his attention back to the laptop. His fingers hovered over the keyboard, hesitant. How could he write something critical when all he could think about was the way the people of Heartsville had come together today? How could he remain objective when his own perspective was shifting so dramatically?

He let out a frustrated breath and began to type, his words slow and deliberate.

Heartsville is a town like many others in America, small and seemingly ordinary at first glance. But spend just a day here, and you'll see that there's something extraordinary about this place. It's not the picturesque streets or the quaint charm of its buildings. It's the people—their resilience, their unwavering support for one another, and the deep, genuine connections that bind them together.

Jake paused, reading over what he had written. It was far from the hard-hitting piece his editor, Marlene, was expecting. There was no controversy, no hidden agenda to expose. Instead, it was the truth—at least, the truth as he was beginning to see it.

He thought back to the search for Sparky, the way the town had rallied together without hesitation. He remembered the look on Emily's face when she was reunited with her dog, the relief and joy that had spread through the crowd as if Sparky belonged to all of them, not just the little girl. And then there was Nora, leading the charge with quiet determination, her every action rooted in a deep love for her community.

Jake typed a few more lines, his thoughts coming more easily now.

Nora Flynn isn't just a veterinarian—she's the heart of this town. Her clinic is more than a place for treating animals; it's a gathering point, a symbol of what makes Heartsville special. The people here trust her, not just because she's skilled, but because she cares. And that care extends beyond the animals she treats to every person who walks through her doors.

He stopped again, feeling a twinge of uncertainty. Was he getting too close? Was he losing the objectivity that was so crucial to his role as a journalist? But even as he questioned himself, Jake knew that this story was different. It wasn't about maintaining distance; it was about capturing the essence of what made this town unique.

He leaned back in his chair, staring at the screen. The narrative was taking shape, but it was softer, more reflective than anything he had written before. It wasn't the story he had planned to write, but it was the one that felt right.

The truth was, Heartsville was starting to get under his skin. And more than that, so was Nora. She wasn't just a subject for an article—she was someone who had shown him a different way of seeing the world, a way that valued community and connection over cynicism and detachment.

Jake's fingers hovered over the keyboard once more, but this time, he hesitated. How would Marlene react to this? Would she push back, demand something more sensational? And what about his reputation as a hard-nosed journalist—would it suffer if he wrote something so unabashedly positive?

He shook his head, clearing the doubts from his mind. There would be time to worry about Marlene and the reception of his article later. For now, he had to write what he felt, what he knew was true.

In Heartsville, you won't find the typical small-town secrets or scandals. What you'll find is something far rarer—a genuine sense of community, a place where people come together in times of need, where every life, no matter how small, is valued. And in today's world, that's a story worth telling.

Jake sat back, reading over his words. They were simple, honest, and for the first time in a long time, he felt satisfied with what he had written. The article wasn't finished, but it was a start—a start that reflected the shift happening within him.

As he closed his laptop, Jake couldn't help but smile. He still had a job to do, but he knew that this story was going to be different. It was going to be real, just like the people of Heartsville. And for the first time in his career, that felt like enough.

Chapter 6
Nora's World

In the tranquil early hours of a crisp fall morning, Nora's clinic began to stir with activity, heralding a significant day: the annual Heartsville Pet Parade, a beloved community event that Nora had spearheaded several years ago. This year, however, the parade was not just a fun gathering but also a fundraiser for local animal shelters. The clinic's front yard, transformed into a registration and starting point for the parade, buzzed with excitement.

Nora, clipboard in hand, was in her element, orchestrating the setup with an infectious enthusiasm. Jake, now more a friend to the clinic than merely a journalist, arrived with coffee in hand, greeted by the sight of Nora directing volunteers and participants.

"Good morning, Nora! This looks like it's going to be bigger than last year," Jake remarked, handing her a cup of coffee.

"Good morning, Jake! Thanks for this," she said, taking the coffee. "Yes, we've got a great turnout already, and there's still an hour before we start. I think the fundraiser aspect has really resonated with people."

As they spoke, a family approached with a trio of festively dressed pugs, each sporting a tiny, colorful hat. Nora greeted them warmly, "Hello, Hendersons! Look at these adorable outfits!"

Mrs. Henderson laughed, "We thought we'd go all out this year. After all, it's for a good cause, isn't it?"

"It sure is," Nora agreed, checking them in on her clipboard. "Every bit helps. Thanks for coming out and supporting the shelters."

The Hendersons moved along, and Nora turned back to Jake. "It's amazing to see the community come together like this. Not just for fun, but to help out."

"It's impressive," Jake replied, scanning the growing crowd. "It seems like the whole town shows up for this."

"They pretty much do," Nora chuckled. "And it's not just about the parade. There's a deeper connection. People really care about these animals and each other."

As they chatted, a young man with a camera approached them. "Dr. Flynn, do you have a moment for a few questions? I'm covering the parade for the Heartsville Gazette."

"Of course, Jeremy," Nora responded, turning to the reporter with a friendly smile. "What would you like to know?"

Jeremy, ready with his notepad, asked, "What inspired you to link the parade with a fundraiser this year?"

Nora explained, "Well, we've always tried to foster a sense of responsibility in our community towards pets, not just our own but those in need. Linking the parade with a fundraiser seemed like a natural step. It's about fun, but it's also about giving back, making a tangible difference."

Jeremy nodded, jotting down notes. "And how do you see this event evolving in the future?"

"We're hoping to expand the scope, maybe include more educational components, workshops on pet care, things like that," Nora detailed. "It's about building a knowledgeable, caring community."

As Jeremy thanked them and moved on, Jake and Nora continued their walk through the crowd. They stopped by a booth where local veterinarians were offering free check-ups for pets.

"Events like this really highlight the ties that bind this community," Jake observed, watching a vet interact with a nervous spaniel and its equally anxious owner.

Nora nodded, her gaze following the vet's gentle assurance to the pet owner. "It's all connected, Jake. The health of the pets, the well-being of the owners, the vibrancy of the community—it's all part of the same fabric."

Their conversation was briefly interrupted by the arrival of another participant, an elderly woman with a large German Shepherd. "Dr. Flynn, we're ready to go whenever you are," she declared with a smile.

"We'll be starting soon, Mrs. Bradley," Nora assured her, then turned to Jake. "Ready to help me get this parade moving?"

"Absolutely," Jake agreed, feeling a part of something much larger than just an event. It was a manifestation of community spirit, a tapestry woven from countless threads of individual stories, all coming together in a celebration that symbolized much more than just a parade. It was a celebration of the ties that bound them all, nurtured and strengthened by Nora's endless dedication.

- - - - - - - - -

As the parade commenced, a colorful procession of pets and their owners wound its way through the streets of Heartsville, drawing smiles and cheers from onlookers. Jake walked alongside Nora, observing the interactions and the evident joy of the participants. Each pet, from the smallest guinea pig to the largest Great Dane, was adorned with ribbons, hats, or festive costumes, making a vibrant spectacle against the backdrop of the town's quaint shops and fall-decorated homes.

Nora watched the parade unfold with a proud, contented smile. "Every year, I'm amazed at how creative everyone gets," she remarked to Jake, who nodded in agreement, his eyes capturing the scene for his next article.

The route led them back to the clinic, where the parade concluded in the parking lot, now transformed into a fairground with booths for local artisans, pet supply vendors, and food trucks serving both human and canine treats. As people mingled and enjoyed the festivities, Nora took the opportunity to engage more deeply with several community members, reinforcing the bonds she had cultivated over the years.

She approached a booth where a local artist was selling handmade pet accessories. "Barbara, these are beautiful," Nora commented, picking up a delicately sewn dog bandana.

"Thank you, Nora. It's great to be involved in this event. It's not just good for business; it's a fun day for the community," Barbara responded, her booth busy with customers looking over her wares.

Jake, meanwhile, found himself in conversation with a family new to Heartsville, who had heard about the parade through Nora's clinic. "It's our first time at something like this," the mother explained, her twin daughters clinging to a pair of kittens recently adopted from the shelter. "We wanted the girls to feel part of the community, and this has been a perfect introduction."

As the afternoon wore on, Jake and Nora reconvened near a food truck offering gourmet dog treats. They watched as dogs and their owners lined up to try various flavors. "It's about more than just the treats," Nora observed. "Look at how everyone is chatting, sharing stories about their pets. It's these small interactions that really help to knit the community together."

Jake nodded, appreciative of the insight. "I can see the layers now—the parade, the fair. It's not just fun; it's strategic, building a network of support and friendship."

"Yes," Nora agreed, "and it's important for us to facilitate that, to give back to the community that supports us."

Their discussion was interrupted by a gentle tap on Nora's shoulder. Turning around, they were greeted by Mrs. Bradley, the elderly woman with the German Shepherd from earlier. "Dr. Flynn, I just wanted to thank you for organizing this. Every year it gets better, and it's something I always look forward to."

"That means a lot, Mrs. Bradley," Nora replied warmly. "I'm glad you enjoy it. How is Max doing today?"

"He's loving it," Mrs. Bradley said, patting her dog who wagged his tail vigorously. "Aren't you, Max?"

As they parted ways, Jake reflected on the depth of the relationships Nora maintained. "You've really built something special here, Nora. It's more than just a clinic."

"It has to be," Nora responded thoughtfully. "A vet's job is to care for animals, but we also have a role in the community. These connections, they're the heart of what we do."

As the day began to wind down, Jake took one last look around the bustling fair. Families were settling on picnic blankets, kids played with their pets, and old friends chatted happily. This was the tapestry of community life that Nora had helped weave, each thread strengthened today by joy, care, and a shared love for pets.

This deepening of connections was not just the theme of the day but a testament to Nora's vision and dedication—a vision that Jake now fully appreciated and was eager to share in his upcoming feature. The ties that bound the community were visible here, palpable and vibrant, a powerful reminder of the roles we can all play in each other's lives.

- - - - - - - - -

As the Heartsville Pet Parade fair neared its conclusion, the community's energy remained high, buoyed by the day's success and the warm, early evening sun. Nora, standing by the main stage set up in the clinic's parking lot, prepared to make her closing remarks. Unbeknownst to her, however, a group of community members had organized a small surprise to show their appreciation for her years of dedication.

Jake, in on the plan, was bustling around with his camera ready, capturing the final moments of the fair and the setup for the surprise. He approached Nora, who was reviewing her notes. "Looks like you've got quite a crowd waiting for your speech," he remarked, a hint of mischief in his tone.

Nora glanced up, smiling. "It's been an incredible day, Jake. I hope this brings us closer to our fundraising goal for the shelters."

As they chatted, the murmurs in the crowd grew louder, and Jake saw that it was time. He gave a subtle nod to Mr. Henderson, who was orchestrating the surprise. Mr. Henderson promptly guided his family, carrying a large, framed photo collage of various community events hosted by Nora over the years, towards the stage.

"Dr. Flynn," Mr. Henderson called out, catching her attention as he and his family approached with the framed collage. The crowd quieted, turning to watch the scene unfold.

Nora looked surprised, her hand covering her mouth as she realized what was happening. "What is this?" she asked, her voice choked with emotion.

"We wanted to do something special for you, Nora," Mr. Henderson explained as he presented the collage to her. "This is a thank you from all of us here in Heartsville. Each photo represents a moment you helped create, a life you touched. It's just a small token of our appreciation."

The collage was a patchwork of memories—pet adoption days, educational workshops, the previous year's pet parades, and candid moments of Nora interacting with community members and their pets. Each picture was a testament to her impact on the community.

Nora was momentarily speechless, her eyes glistening as she took in the collage. "I... I don't know what to say. This means so much to me. Thank you," she finally managed, her voice steady but deep with emotion.

The crowd erupted into applause, and Jake captured the moment, knowing it would be the perfect climax for his article. As the applause died down, Nora regained her composure and addressed the crowd.

"This community, all of you, have made this clinic what it is. These pictures, these moments, they're not just my doing—they're all of ours. We've built something special here in Heartsville, something that goes beyond just caring for animals. We care for each other, and that's the most important thing of all."

Her words resonated with the crowd, many nodding and a few wiping away tears of their own. Jake, watching from the sidelines, felt a profound sense of respect for Nora and the community she nurtured. This was more than just a news story; it was a powerful example of community spirit and collective care in action.

As the event wrapped up, Nora mingled with the crowd, many coming up to express their personal thanks or to share a quick story of how the clinic had helped them. Jake, observing these interactions, knew that his article would capture not just the day's events but the spirit of a community united by compassion and respect, led by one extraordinary veterinarian.

The surprise gesture, a simple yet powerful acknowledgment, underscored the deep bonds Nora had forged with Heartsville—a fitting end to a day that celebrated the ties that bind a community together.

As the last of the day's light faded into twilight, the fairgrounds began to empty, leaving Nora and Jake in a quiet, contemplative atmosphere. They sat on the same bench they had occupied earlier in the day, now watching the stars begin to pepper the darkening sky. It was a perfect moment for reflection after the bustling activities of the Heartsville Pet Parade and fair.

"You know, Nora," Jake began, breaking the comfortable silence, "today was more than just successful. It was inspirational. Seeing everyone come together like that, it really drives home the impact you've made here."

Nora looked up at the stars, her expression thoughtful. "It's days like today that remind me why I started all this. It's not just about treating animals—it's about treating hearts, human and animal alike."

"I could see that," Jake agreed. "The way people spoke to you, the stories they shared, it's clear you're more than just their vet. You're a part of their lives, a part of their families."

Nora nodded, her eyes still on the stars. "It's a big responsibility, but it's also a privilege. To share in their joys, their losses... it's deeply fulfilling."

Jake watched her for a moment, then said, "And what about you? We talk so much about how you support everyone else. Who supports you?"

Nora turned to him, a faint smile on her lips. "I have my family, friends, and this community. And days like today, they fill me up, remind me that I'm on the right path. But it's not always easy."

"I can imagine," Jake said softly. "But it's important, Nora. What you do—it changes lives."

"That's the hope," Nora replied. "Every pet, every person who walks through our doors—they're all looking for something. Healing, companionship, understanding. If we can provide that, if we can be that place of solace, then we're succeeding."

Jake nodded, his thoughts turning to his own role as a journalist. "You've given me a lot to write about, Nora. Not just the events of today, but the stories, the emotions, the community spirit. It's a powerful narrative."

"I'm glad to hear that," Nora said, her gaze returning to the sky. "If your articles can spread the word, maybe inspire others to foster community in their own ways, then that's another way we can make a difference, isn't it?"

"It is," Jake agreed. "Your story is one of connection and compassion. It's a reminder of the good that can be accomplished when people come together with common purpose."

As they sat in silence for a few more moments, both reflecting on the day and their conversations, the sounds of the night settled around them—the distant bark of a dog, the soft rustle of leaves in the gentle night breeze, and the occasional laughter of someone lingering near the fairgrounds.

Finally, Nora stood, stretching slightly. "It's been a long day, but a good one. Thank you, Jake, for being here, for sharing our story."

"Thank you, Nora, for letting me in," Jake responded, rising to join her. "I've learned a lot, not just about what you do, but about why you do it. It's been truly eye-opening."

As they walked towards the parking lot, the stars overhead bright and clear, both felt a sense of accomplishment and anticipation. For Nora, it was looking forward to continuing her work with renewed vigor; for Jake, it was the excitement of sharing Nora's story, hoping to capture the essence of Heartsville's community spirit in his writing. The night ended not just with a farewell, but with a mutual understanding and respect, a bond strengthened by shared experiences and the stories that had unfolded under the stars.

Chapter 7
The Unexpected Assignment

The new day dawned over Heartsville, bringing with it a soft, misty morning that hung like a veil over the town. Nora arrived early at the clinic, her steps slower than usual, her mind burdened with worries that hadn't been there the day before. The recent successes and the joy of the community fair still lingered, but they were now overshadowed by a lingering concern about the future sustainability of her community programs.

Jake, arriving to follow up on some details for his article, found Nora sitting quietly in her office, staring out the window at the waking day. He knocked gently on the open door, announcing his presence. "Good morning, Nora. Everything okay?"

Nora turned, managing a small smile. "Good morning, Jake. Yes, well, mostly. Just thinking about everything we need to do here. Yesterday was wonderful, but today the reality of running a clinic with so many extra activities hits home again."

"Sounds like you're feeling a bit overwhelmed," Jake observed, taking a seat opposite her. "Want to talk about it?"

Nora sighed, her gaze returning to the window. "It's just that, sometimes, I worry we're trying to do too much. The events, the community outreach—it's all great, but it's a lot to manage on top of the clinic's regular responsibilities."

"Do you think it's becoming too much?" Jake asked, his tone gentle, encouraging her to open up.

"Sometimes, I do," Nora admitted. "I wonder if we can keep all these programs running without sacrificing the quality of care we provide. The community expects a lot, and I don't want to let them down."

"That's a valid concern," Jake said, nodding. "But you've built a strong foundation here. Maybe there's a way to streamline or get more help?"

"It's possible," Nora conceded. "We've been relying a lot on volunteers and my staff, who are already stretched thin. Perhaps it's time to consider hiring more help or finding more sustainable funding sources."

"That sounds like a sensible approach," Jake suggested. "Have you thought about applying for grants or partnering with local businesses for sponsorships?"

"We've looked into it a bit," Nora replied, turning her chair to face Jake directly. "But I need to devote more time to it, to really focus on making sure we have the resources we need to keep everything going."

"Maybe this is also something to share with the community," Jake offered. "If they understand the challenges, they might step up even more. Your transparency could actually strengthen their commitment to the clinic's missions."

"That's an interesting point," Nora considered, her brow furrowing thoughtfully. "I've always tried to be open with our community. Maybe it's time to be open about our needs too, not just our successes."

"Exactly," Jake said. "People love this place, they value what you offer. Letting them know what it takes to keep it going could rally even more support."

Nora nodded, a flicker of determination lighting her eyes. "You're right, Jake. It's worth a try. We can't do this alone, and maybe we don't have to."

"Exactly," Jake echoed. "You've done a lot for this community. It's okay to let them know you need a bit back to keep it all going."

Their conversation shifted then to the specifics of how Nora might begin to engage the community in this new dialogue, discussing potential outreach strategies and the framing of her needs in a way that inspired further support rather than concern.

As Jake left the clinic that morning, Nora felt a renewed sense of purpose. The doubts were still there, but so were paths to potential solutions. With Jake's insights and her own experience, she was ready to face the challenges ahead, supported not just by her staff and volunteers but by the entire community that had come to rely on her clinic not just as a place of healing but as a beacon of communal spirit.

After her morning conversation with Jake, Nora spent the day mulling over her options and the potential pathways she could take to secure the future of her community projects. By late afternoon, as the clinic began to quiet down from the day's appointments, Nora had reached an unexpected decision.

She called a meeting with her staff in the small break room, where posters of pet care tips and community event flyers lined the walls. As her team gathered, the sense of anticipation was palpable.

"Thanks for joining me, everyone," Nora began, her voice steady but carrying an undercurrent of serious resolve. "I've been doing a lot of thinking about our clinic and all the extra activities we've been managing."

Her staff exchanged curious glances, sensing the gravity in her tone.

"I've realized that if we want to continue growing and providing these valuable community services, we need to make some changes," Nora continued. "We can't keep stretching ourselves thin. It's not sustainable, and I don't want our core mission to suffer."

"What kind of changes are you thinking about, Nora?" asked Liz, one of the veterinary technicians, her expression a mix of concern and interest.

Nora took a deep breath before answering. "I've decided to look for a co-director for the clinic. Someone who can share the load of managing our day-to-day operations and help expand our outreach efforts."

The room was silent for a moment as the team digested the news. It was a significant shift, one that could alter the dynamics they were all accustomed to.

"Why a co-director?" Thomas, the senior vet, finally asked. "Isn't it risky bringing in someone new at this level?"

"It is a risk," Nora acknowledged. "But it's a calculated one. I believe bringing in fresh energy and possibly even new ideas will help us do more without compromising the quality of care we're known for. I'll still be here, but I'll be able to focus more on the community and outreach side, which you all know is incredibly important to me."

"How will you choose this person?" Maria, the receptionist, chimed in. "It has to be someone who understands what we're all about."

"That's my top priority," Nora reassured her. "I want someone who not only has the credentials but who shares our vision and passion for community engagement. I'll involve all of you in the process, too. This will affect everyone, and I value your input."

The team nodded, the initial shock giving way to a sense of opportunity. The discussion that followed was lively, with team members expressing their thoughts on potential candidates, the qualities they felt were essential, and how they envisioned the transition.

"I think this could really be good for us," Liz finally said, a note of optimism in her voice. "It might be just what we need to keep moving forward without burning out."

Nora smiled, grateful for the support. "I'm glad to hear you say that. I believe this is the right step, not just for me or for our clinic, but for our community. We have the chance to turn our challenges into opportunities for growth."

As the meeting ended and her staff dispersed, Nora felt a weight lift from her shoulders. The decision was made, and while the path ahead would surely hold its challenges, she was ready to face them with the support of her team.

Later that evening, Nora shared her decision with Jake, who had stopped by to see how she was holding up after their morning talk.

"That's a bold move, Nora," Jake said, clearly impressed. "It shows a lot of foresight."

"I hope so," Nora responded, her gaze steady. "I think it's the best way to ensure that we continue to serve our community in the best way possible."

The day closed on a note of quiet resolve. Nora's unexpected decision had set in motion a new chapter for the clinic, one filled with potential for renewal and growth. As the clinic lights dimmed and Nora locked up for the night, the future seemed filled with as much promise as it did uncertainty. But one thing was clear: the clinic, under Nora's guidance, would continue to be a vital heart of the Heartsville community.

- - - - - - - - -

The next morning brought a sense of renewal to Nora's clinic. As the early sun filtered through the windows, casting a warm glow across the reception area, Nora prepared for a special appointment. Today, she was meeting with a family interested in adopting a rescue dog that had recently been brought to the clinic. The dog, a gentle but shy terrier mix named Toby, had been found wandering near a busy street and had quickly captured her heart.

Nora was in the middle of reviewing Toby's health records when the Martins walked in. The family of four—parents Alan and Jessica, and their two children, Lily and Noah—looked around excitedly. Nora greeted them with a warm smile.

"Good morning, Martins! Thanks for coming in. I've got someone I'd like you to meet," Nora said, leading them toward the area where Toby was waiting.

"Is it the dog we saw on your website?" Lily asked, her voice filled with anticipation.

"Yes, that's Toby," Nora replied as they approached the enclosure where Toby was patiently sitting, watching the newcomers with cautious interest.

"He's smaller than I thought," Noah observed, kneeling down to get a better look at Toby.

Nora opened the gate and invited Toby out. "Toby's a bit shy at first, but he warms up quickly, especially with kids."

As if to prove her point, Toby tentatively approached Noah and Lily, sniffing gently before giving Noah a small lick on his outstretched hand. The boy laughed, and the initial ice was broken.

"He seems really sweet," Jessica noted, watching her children interact with Toby. "How has he been doing here?"

"He's been good, a little quiet, adjusting to the shelter environment," Nora explained. "He was quite nervous when he first arrived, but he's made a lot of progress. He's ready for a loving home."

Alan, who had been quietly observing, finally spoke. "What kind of care will he need going forward? Any special considerations?"

Nora nodded, appreciating the question. "He's healthy, thankfully. He'll just need the usual—regular check-ups, vaccinations, and lots of love. Given his shy nature, he might benefit from some gentle socialization training to help him build confidence."

"We can definitely provide that," Jessica assured her, as Lily gently petted Toby, who was now more relaxed and wagging his tail. "We want to make sure we're fully prepared to give him a good home."

"That's wonderful to hear," Nora said, feeling a swell of satisfaction knowing Toby would be well cared for. "If you decide to go ahead with the adoption, I'm here to support you every step of the way. And if you have any questions or need advice, just give me a call."

"We've talked it over quite a bit," Alan replied, looking at his wife and children, who were already enamored with Toby. "And we think Toby would be a great addition to our family."

"That's great news!" Nora exclaimed. "I think Toby's going to be very happy with you all."

As the Martins filled out the adoption paperwork, Nora watched, her decision to bring a co-director on board reaffirmed. This would allow her more moments like this—personal interactions that made a real difference in the lives of animals and the people who loved them.

The appointment concluded with plenty of smiles and thanks. Nora helped the Martins prepare to take Toby home, providing them with a starter kit of care supplies and some parting advice.

As the family left, Toby in tow, looking happier and more confident than Nora had ever seen him, she felt a deep sense of accomplishment. This was what her work was all about—not just healing, but making lasting connections that improved lives. Her role in these moments, facilitated by her dedication to both animal and community care, was a source of profound professional and personal fulfillment.

After a fulfilling day at the clinic, Nora decided to take a leisurely walk through Heartsville. The town, with its quaint shops and tree-lined streets, always had a way of soothing her thoughts, especially after making big decisions like she had recently. As she strolled, she ran into Jake, who was out capturing some local scenery for his article.

"Hey, Nora! Fancy meeting you here," Jake greeted her with a friendly smile. "How's the day been?"

"Hi, Jake! It's been good, actually. Very fulfilling," Nora replied, her mood visibly brightened by the successful adoption earlier. "I just needed some fresh air to clear my head."

"Mind if I join you?" Jake asked, his camera slung over his shoulder.

"Not at all," Nora said, welcoming the company. As they walked, their conversation naturally drifted to the clinic and the changes Nora was considering.

"I've been thinking a lot about our talk," Nora shared, her eyes taking in the familiar, comforting sights of the town. "Bringing someone new into the clinic, it's a big step. But today reinforced why it's necessary. I need to ensure the clinic continues to thrive, not just survive."

"It sounds like you're really taking a strategic approach to it all," Jake commented, adjusting his camera settings as they paused near a picturesque view of the town square. "How do you feel about it?"

"Optimistic, mostly. It's about more than just dividing responsibilities. It's about growing our capability to serve this community," Nora explained, watching a couple of children playing in the park. "Heartsville has given so much to the clinic, and I want to keep giving back, maybe even more than before."

"That's a great way to look at it," Jake said, snapping a few photos before turning his attention back to Nora. "And today's adoption must have been a reminder of the impact you're already making."

"It was," Nora admitted with a nod. "It's those moments that remind me why I started all this in the first place. They're not just pets; they're family members, and they bring people together. That's what I love about this job."

Their walk led them to a small café, and they decided to stop for a coffee. As they sat at an outdoor table, Nora continued, "I want those success stories to keep coming. And I think having a co-director will help ensure they do."

"It sounds like you're really thinking about the future," Jake observed, sipping his coffee. "It's good to see. And it's something I want to highlight in my article—the vision behind the clinic, not just the day-to-day."

"I appreciate that, Jake," Nora said, a sincere smile crossing her face. "It's important to me that people understand our mission is about the community as much as it is about animal care."

As they finished their coffee, the conversation turned to lighter topics, but Nora's thoughts remained focused on her plans for the clinic. The walk through Heartsville, coupled with Jake's supportive presence, had given her a renewed sense of purpose and determination.

"I'm glad we bumped into each other today," Nora remarked as they stood to leave. "It's nice to have someone who understands what I'm trying to do."

"And I'm glad to be able to tell that story," Jake replied, adjusting his camera bag. "Let's just say, I think the next few chapters of Heartsville's story are going to be pretty exciting."

With that, they parted ways, Nora feeling energized and ready to face the challenges ahead. Her walk through Heartsville had not only provided her with a breath of fresh air but had also reaffirmed her commitment to her clinic and the community it served. As she headed back to close up the clinic for the day, her step was light, her mind clear, and her heart full of plans for the future.

Chapter 8
A Community in Crisis

The morning at Nora's clinic was charged with a palpable sense of anticipation. Today was not just another day of pet care; it was the day Nora had scheduled interviews for the co-director position. She had spent weeks preparing, sorting through applications, and selecting the most promising candidates who shared her vision for community engagement and animal care.

Nora was in her office early, organizing her notes and finalizing the questions she planned to ask. As she laid out her materials, Jake walked in, his presence a welcome sight.

"Good morning, Nora! Big day ahead, I see," Jake greeted her, placing his bag and notepad on a chair.

"Morning, Jake! Yes, it's a very important day," Nora replied, offering him a smile. "I'm a bit nervous, to be honest. This decision could really shape the future of the clinic."

"I can imagine," Jake said, pulling up a chair next to her desk. "Do you feel prepared?"

"I think so," Nora sighed, looking over her notes one more time. "I've got a clear idea of what I'm looking for in a co-director. It's just a matter of seeing who best fits that role."

"What are you looking for specifically?" Jake asked, genuinely curious about her criteria.

Nora leaned back in her chair, her eyes thoughtful. "I need someone who's not just skilled in veterinary medicine but who also understands and is passionate about community outreach. They need to be personable, driven, and creative. And, of course, they must mesh well with our team and the community."

"That's quite a list," Jake commented with a smile. "But given what you've built here, it's important to find the right match."

"Exactly," Nora nodded. "Today's interviews will tell me a lot about each candidate, not just through their answers, but how they interact with the staff and handle themselves in this environment."

"How many candidates are you interviewing today?" Jake inquired, ready to jot down details for his ongoing story about the clinic.

"Three," Nora replied. "Each of them comes highly recommended, with strong backgrounds in veterinary practice and some experience in community work. I'm hopeful."

"Would you mind if I sit in on the interviews? It could provide some interesting insights into your decision-making process for the article," Jake suggested, his tone tentative.

Nora considered his request for a moment. "I think that would be fine, Jake. It could be good to have another perspective, and I trust your discretion."

"Thank you, Nora. I appreciate being included," Jake said, his voice conveying his gratitude.

As the clock neared the time for the first interview, Nora and Jake prepared the conference room. They arranged chairs and laid out water bottles, creating a welcoming yet professional atmosphere.

"Just one more thing," Nora said as they finished setting up. "I want to ensure the candidates not only share our vision but are also ready to innovate and drive us forward. This clinic isn't just my project; it's a community pillar. Whoever takes this role needs to be ready to uphold that."

"I'll keep that in mind while I'm observing," Jake assured her, noting down her last-minute thoughts.

As the first candidate arrived, Nora took a deep breath, steadying herself. She greeted the candidate warmly, introducing Jake as part of the interview process.

With everything in place, the interviews began. Each candidate brought their own strengths and ideas to the table, discussing their experiences, visions, and why they felt they were a good fit for the role. Nora listened intently, her questions probing not just for professional competency but for a deeper understanding of each candidate's commitment to the clinic's dual mission of excellent animal care and community engagement.

As the day progressed, Nora's nervousness gave way to a cautious optimism. The candidates were impressive, and she felt hopeful about the possibilities each could bring to the clinic. With Jake's quiet support and the thoughtful responses from the interviewees, Nora felt confident that she was on the right path to finding a co-director who could help her continue to grow and nurture the clinic and its community.

- - - - - - - - -

After the interviews, Nora took Jake on a walk around the clinic, where he had arranged to speak with several of the clinic's long-time clients. His goal was to capture their stories and testimonials about what the clinic and Nora's efforts meant to them and their pets. These stories were to form a vital part of his feature article, highlighting the personal impact of Nora's work.

Their first stop was with Mrs. Allen, who was at the clinic with her sprightly Cocker Spaniel, Rosie. As Rosie underwent a routine check-up, Mrs. Allen shared her story with Jake, who recorded her words carefully.

"Nora has been a godsend to us," Mrs. Allen began, her eyes following Rosie as the dog wagged her tail on the examination table. "When Rosie here was diagnosed with diabetes, Nora guided us through everything. She even called after hours to make sure Rosie was adjusting to her new diet and medication."

"That's incredible," Jake responded, genuinely moved. "It sounds like she goes above and beyond."

"Oh, she does," Mrs. Allen confirmed, nodding emphatically. "And it's not just the medical care. She's created a community here where everyone feels supported. It's like a family."

Jake made a note of her words, recognizing the emotional depth they conveyed. "Thank you, Mrs. Allen. Your story really helps illustrate the community aspect here."

Next, they spoke with Darren, a young man with a rescue dog named Max. Darren had struggled with personal issues until he found companionship and responsibility through pet ownership, which Nora had encouraged.

"Max has changed my life, and I owe a lot of that to Nora," Darren told Jake, patting Max affectionately. "She didn't just help me find him; she supported me through some tough adjustments. She's more than a vet; she's a mentor."

"How would you describe the clinic's impact on your life?" Jake asked, intrigued by the depth of the relationship.

"It's been transformative," Darren replied. "I've learned so much here, not just about pet care but about being part of a community. Nora has built something special here."

As Jake wrapped up his conversation with Darren, they moved on to speak with an elderly couple, the Harrisons, who had brought in their cat, Whiskers, for a check-up. The couple shared their appreciation for the clinic's senior pet care program, which Nora had initiated to help older pets and their owners manage age-related health issues.

"The program has been a blessing for us and Whiskers," Mr. Harrison explained. "Nora always has time to answer our questions, no matter how busy she is. It's comforting to know she's here for us."

Mrs. Harrison added, "She treats every pet as if it were her own. We've seen her at community events, too, always spreading knowledge and kindness."

"Thank you both," Jake said, concluding his interviews for the day. "Your experiences really highlight the personal touch Nora brings to her work."

After saying their goodbyes, Nora and Jake strolled back to her office. Jake shared his reflections on the interviews. "Hearing directly from people about how you and the clinic have touched their lives—it's been inspiring. It's clear you've built much more than just a veterinary practice."

Nora smiled, a mix of humility and pride in her expression. "These stories remind me why I do this, even on the hard days. It's about making a difference, one pet and one person at a time."

As they reached her office, Jake thanked her for the opportunity to capture these heartfelt testimonies. "This article is going to be special, Nora. Thank you for letting me tell your story."

"And thank you, Jake, for telling it with such care," Nora replied, her eyes reflecting the deep connections she had forged in Heartsville.

As Jake left, notebook full of rich, emotional content, he felt more connected to Nora's mission than ever. The day had not only provided material for his article but had deepened his understanding of the profound impact one dedicated individual could have on a community.

Back at her clinic, as the day wound down, Nora sat quietly in her office, reflecting on the interviews and the testimonials that had been shared. She felt a renewed sense of purpose, but also a profound responsibility. It was during these quiet moments of contemplation that she realized how significantly her role had evolved from a veterinarian to a community leader.

The door to her office creaked open, and her assistant, Maria, peeked in. "Nora, do you have a minute?"

"Of course, Maria. Come in," Nora replied, gesturing to the chair across from her desk.

Maria closed the door gently behind her and sat down, her expression a mixture of enthusiasm and seriousness. "I've been thinking a lot about what you've been saying about expanding the team and bringing in a co-director," she began. "And I've seen how much you do, how much this place means to everyone."

Nora nodded, encouraging her to continue.

"I just want to say that I think it's a great idea," Maria continued. "I know change can be scary, but the clinic has grown so much, and your vision for it—it's just inspiring. Not just to me but to everyone here."

Nora listened, touched by Maria's words. "Thank you, Maria. That means a lot. I've had some doubts, wondering if it's the right move."

"It definitely is," Maria reassured her. "You've created a space here that's more than a clinic. It's a part of the community, a part of people's lives. Bringing someone else in to help manage it all can only make it stronger."

Nora considered Maria's perspective, feeling the weight of her decision lighten slightly. "I hope you're right. I want to ensure that we continue to provide not just excellent veterinary care but also maintain our commitment to the community."

"You will," Maria said confidently. "And you're not alone in this. We all believe in your vision, and we're here to support you, no matter what."

Their conversation shifted to the specifics of how the staff could assist in the transition, discussing potential responsibilities they could take on to smooth the integration of a new co-director into the clinic.

As they talked, Nora felt a shift in her perception of the situation. What had once seemed like a daunting change now felt more like a natural evolution of her practice. She began to see the decision not as a necessity borne of overextension but as an opportunity to deepen the clinic's impact and expand its capabilities.

"Thanks, Maria," Nora said as they wrapped up their discussion. "Your support, and everyone else's, it's what keeps me going. It's good to know I have such a strong team behind me."

"Always," Maria replied with a smile. "And I think everyone will be excited about what's ahead."

After Maria left, Nora sat alone for a few more minutes, her thoughts clear for the first time in days. The interviews earlier had not just been for Jake's article but had served as a reminder of the many lives her clinic had touched. Each story was a testament to the clinic's role in the community, and now, with the support of her staff and the potential addition of a co-director, she felt ready to take on whatever challenges lay ahead.

Feeling more confident, Nora stood up, her determination renewed. She was ready to move forward, to continue building on the foundation she had laid, ensuring that her clinic remained a vital part of the Heartsville community. As she left her office to close up the clinic for the day, her stride was purposeful, her mind set on the future. This turning point in her perception marked a new chapter for both Nora and the clinic, filled with potential and promise for continued growth and deeper community engagement.

As evening descended over Heartsville, Nora found herself at the local park, a place she often visited to clear her mind and gather her thoughts. The park was quiet at this hour, with only a few distant joggers and dog walkers enjoying the cool, gentle breeze of the early night. Seated on a familiar bench that overlooked a small, tranquil pond, Nora was joined by Jake, who had become not just a chronicler of her professional life but a trusted confidant.

"Quiet evening," Jake remarked, taking a seat beside her.

"It is," Nora agreed, drawing in a deep breath of the fresh air. "It's nice to step away from the clinic sometimes, reflect on everything outside the confines of those walls."

"I can imagine," Jake said, turning slightly to face her. "You've had a lot on your plate lately. How are you feeling about everything—the clinic, the interviews, the changes coming up?"

Nora paused, her gaze fixed on the gentle ripples in the pond caused by a light breeze. "Honestly, it's a mix of emotions. I'm excited about the future and what we can achieve with someone new to share the load. But there's also a part of me that's apprehensive about handing over part of what I've built."

"That's completely understandable," Jake sympathized. "Change is never easy, especially when it involves something you've poured so much of yourself into."

"Yes, but today's conversations at the clinic... they've reinforced that this is the right step—not just for me but for the community we serve," Nora reflected. "Hearing Maria and the others express their support made me realize how much we can all benefit from this change."

"It sounds like you've got a great team behind you," Jake noted, his tone encouraging.

"I really do," Nora said, a smile touching her lips as she thought of her staff. "Their support is what makes this possible. I couldn't ask for a better group to work with."

Jake nodded, then shifted the conversation slightly. "And what about you, personally? Outside of the clinic, how are you holding up?"

Nora considered his question for a moment. "It's been challenging to balance everything, but moments like this—quiet, reflective—they help a lot. They remind me why I started this journey. It's not just about the day-to-day operations; it's about the impact we have on lives, human and animal alike."

"That's a powerful motivator," Jake acknowledged, looking out over the pond. "The stories you've shared, the lives you've touched—it's clear you've built something special."

"Thanks, Jake," Nora said, her voice soft but filled with determination. "I hope to continue building on that, no matter what changes come our way."

As they sat in comfortable silence for a few moments, both lost in their thoughts, the tranquility of the park provided a perfect backdrop for introspection. Finally, Nora stood, feeling rejuvenated by their conversation and the peaceful setting.

"I should get going," she said, glancing at Jake. "But thank you for this, for the chat. It's exactly what I needed."

"Anytime, Nora," Jake replied, standing with her. "And if there's anything you need, you know where to find me."

As they walked back towards the town, the park behind them softly disappearing into the evening shadows, Nora felt a renewed sense of purpose. The path ahead might be fraught with challenges and changes, but with the support of her team and the community, she felt ready to face them head-on. This reflective downtime had not only provided her with much-needed peace but also reaffirmed her commitment to her life's work and the community she cherished.

Chapter 9
Rising Doubts

In the cool, bustling morning at Nora's clinic, a new figure stepped through the doors, her presence marking a significant turn in the clinic's journey. Bethany, a young, enthusiastic veterinarian with a passion for community service, was there for her first day as the new co-director. Her arrival was anticipated with a mix of excitement and curiosity by the clinic staff and Nora herself.

Nora greeted Bethany at the entrance, her demeanor a blend of professionalism and warmth. "Bethany, welcome! We're so glad to have you join us. I hope your move here was smooth?"

"Thank you, Nora. Yes, everything went well, and I'm excited to start," Bethany replied, her eyes scanning the familiar bustle of the clinic with a keen interest. "I've been looking forward to working with you and learning more about the community here."

"As we are to have you," Nora said, leading Bethany into the clinic. "Let me give you a quick tour and introduce you to everyone."

As they walked through the various areas of the clinic, Bethany met with staff members who were eager to learn more about her. Each introduction was an opportunity for Bethany to share her background and her aspirations for the clinic.

"I've spent the last few years working in urban animal hospitals, focusing on not just treatment but also preventive care and education," Bethany explained to Liz, one of the veterinary technicians. "I'm particularly interested in how we can extend our community programs to reach more people and pets in need."

"That sounds fantastic," Liz responded, clearly impressed. "We have a lot of initiatives here, but there's always room to grow and improve. Your experience will definitely be an asset."

"I hope so," Bethany said, her tone both humble and hopeful. "I'm particularly interested in your outreach programs. Nora's told me a lot about the impact you've had."

Nora smiled, pleased with the exchange. "Bethany also has a strong background in grant writing and has worked on several successful fundraising campaigns. I'm looking forward to seeing how we can leverage that experience here."

"That's excellent," Thomas, another veterinarian, chimed in. "Funding is always a challenge, but it's crucial for the sustainability of our programs."

"Yes, I've seen the difference that solid funding can make not only to the quality of care but also to the scope of what's possible," Bethany added. "I'm eager to dive into that here."

As the tour continued, Nora and Bethany discussed more detailed aspects of the clinic's operation and future plans. They stopped by the recovery room where a few pets were comfortably resting after treatments.

"Nora, I've been really impressed with how integrated the clinic is with the Heartsville community," Bethany remarked, observing a cat being gently cared for by a nurse. "It's clear there's a lot of love and dedication here."

"It's what drives us," Nora affirmed. "Our community is at the heart of everything we do. Each animal, each person who walks through our doors becomes part of our extended family. And now, so do you."

"I'm honored to be a part of it," Bethany said, her voice sincere. "I've always believed that veterinary care should go beyond the clinic. It's about building relationships and supporting the community in meaningful ways."

As they concluded the tour back at Nora's office, both felt a renewed sense of excitement about the possibilities ahead. Bethany's fresh perspective and Nora's seasoned experience promised a dynamic partnership.

"I'm really looking forward to working together, Nora," Bethany said as they sat down to discuss her first week's schedule. "I think we can do great things."

"I believe so too," Nora replied, her initial apprehension about bringing in a co-director now replaced by optimism. "Welcome aboard, Bethany. Let's make a difference together."

As Bethany settled into her new role, her enthusiasm and fresh ideas breathed new life into the clinic, promising new horizons for both the team and the community they served.

- - - - - - - - -

Bethany's first week at the clinic was a whirlwind of activity. As she acclimated to her new role, she spent a significant amount of time observing the daily operations, getting a feel for the pace and the personal touch that Nora had infused into the practice. This observation period was crucial, not only for her to understand the workings of the clinic but also to gain insight into the community dynamics that were so central to Nora's mission.

During one particularly busy afternoon, Bethany stood back and watched as Nora interacted with a long-time client, Mrs. Peterson, who had brought in her aging Golden Retriever, Sandy, for a check-up. Bethany's attention was caught by the ease and warmth with which Nora communicated.

"Nora, I've been so worried about Sandy. She's not eating much these days," Mrs. Peterson expressed, her voice tinged with concern.

Nora, examining Sandy gently, responded reassuringly, "Let's see what might be causing that. Sometimes, as dogs age, their dietary needs can change. We might need to adjust her diet to make it more appealing and easier to digest."

"That makes sense," Mrs. Peterson said, watching Nora carefully. "You always have a way of making things clearer. What would we do without you?"

"It's my job to help, and I'm here whenever you need," Nora replied, giving Sandy a gentle pat. "Let's try a few things, and we'll keep an eye on her together."

Bethany noted the interaction with interest, seeing the trust and relief on Mrs. Peterson's face. Later, she approached Nora to discuss what she had observed.

"Nora, watching you with Mrs. Peterson was really enlightening," Bethany began. "The rapport you have with your clients—it's something special. How do you build such trust?"

"It's all about consistency and care," Nora explained as they walked towards the staff room for a quick break. "Many of our clients have been with us for years, and they've come to know that we're here for them, no matter what. It's about more than just medical care; it's about being a part of their lives, understanding their challenges, and providing support."

Bethany nodded, absorbing every word. "I noticed that. It's almost like you're part of their family."

"That's exactly it," Nora agreed. "We see our clients through many stages of their lives and their pets' lives. We celebrate with them, and sometimes we grieve with them. It creates a bond that goes beyond the typical client-service provider relationship."

As they reached the staff room, Bethany reflected on her own experiences and how they might blend with the clinic's ethos. "I've worked in places where the focus was almost exclusively on the medical side. This approach, focusing on community and emotional support as much as on health, it's different."

"It's challenging but incredibly rewarding," Nora said, pouring them both a cup of coffee. "I think your experience and fresh perspective can really add to what we've built here. I'm looking forward to seeing how you integrate your ideas with our mission."

"I have a lot to learn from you, but I'm also excited to contribute," Bethany replied, her enthusiasm evident. "I think there's a lot we can do together."

Their conversation shifted to more practical matters—upcoming community events, ongoing cases, and Bethany's ideas for new initiatives. It was clear that Bethany was not just observing from the sidelines; she was gearing up to be an active participant in the life of the clinic and the community.

As they returned to the hustle of the clinic, Bethany felt more determined than ever to embrace Nora's approach and make a meaningful impact. Her initial observation period had provided valuable insights into the compassionate, community-oriented ethos of the clinic, and she was ready to contribute her part to its ongoing story.

- - - - - - - - -

A few weeks into her role, Bethany felt more integrated into the clinic and Heartsville's community. One sunny afternoon, she took the initiative to join Nora at a local community event aimed at promoting pet health awareness. It was a perfect opportunity for Bethany to see the clinic's community engagement efforts in action and to play a more active role herself.

As they set up their booth, complete with educational pamphlets, free samples of pet food, and a sign-up sheet for a free clinic visit, Bethany watched Nora interact with event-goers with a mix of professionalism and genuine friendliness.

"Nora, I'm really impressed with how you engage with the community. It's seamless," Bethany remarked as they arranged the last of their materials.

"It's taken years to build these relationships, Bethany," Nora replied, smiling as she greeted a passing family with a dog. "But it's worth every effort. Each interaction is a chance to educate, to help, and to build trust."

Bethany nodded, taking in the scene—families, children, pets of all sizes, all mingling and enjoying the day. "I can see the impact already. It's like you're a celebrity here."

Nora laughed lightly. "Well, I don't know about that. But it's important that the community knows we're here not just to treat their pets, but to be part of their lives."

As the day progressed, Bethany took a more active role at the booth, answering questions from pet owners, discussing the importance of regular check-ups, and even helping a few children understand how to care for their pets. Nora watched her with pride and satisfaction, seeing her new co-director's confidence and care for the community shining through.

"How do you feel it went today?" Nora asked Bethany as the event wound down.

"I loved it," Bethany exclaimed, her enthusiasm unabated despite the long day. "It's different from what I've done before, but it's incredibly rewarding. Seeing the direct impact of our work, interacting with the community this way—it's powerful."

"It is," Nora agreed, beginning to pack up their booth. "And it's these interactions that often remind us why we do what we do. It's not just about the animals; it's about the people behind them."

"I'm beginning to understand that more deeply now," Bethany said, helping Nora fold a tablecloth. "Today was about more than just sharing information. It was about being visible, accessible, and part of a larger community dialogue about pet care."

"Exactly," Nora responded, placing the folded tablecloth in a bin. "And every question answered, every piece of advice given, it adds up. It strengthens the community's knowledge and their relationship with us."

Bethany paused, reflecting on the day's interactions. "I think I'd like to get more involved in these types of events. Maybe even spearhead a few initiatives that could further our reach, especially in parts of the community we see less often."

"I think that's a fantastic idea," Nora said, clearly pleased. "Your fresh perspective and drive are exactly what we needed. Let's sit down next week and brainstorm some ideas. We can look at what's worked in the past and explore new possibilities."

As they finished packing up and prepared to leave, Bethany felt a profound sense of belonging and purpose. The event had not only allowed her to observe and learn from Nora but had also provided a platform for her to engage directly with the community she was now a part of. This experience solidified her commitment to the clinic and its mission, marking a significant step in her journey as co-director.

Driving back to the clinic, both women discussed plans for future events and community engagement strategies. The afternoon had been a defining moment for Bethany, capturing the essence of the community spirit that Nora had cultivated and that Bethany was now eager to help foster and expand.

- - - - - - - - -

The day had been long and fulfilling, and as it drew to a close, Bethany found herself in Nora's office, reflecting on her first significant interaction with the Heartsville community. The walls of the office, adorned with pictures of community events and thank-you notes from clients, served as a testament to the impact the clinic had made under Nora's guidance.

Sitting across from Nora, Bethany felt a mixture of exhaustion and exhilaration. "Today was more eye-opening than I expected," she began, her voice filled with a mix of wonder and resolve. "Seeing you in action, understanding the real depth of your connection with the community—it's inspiring."

Nora, who was tidying up some files on her desk, looked up and smiled. "I'm glad you felt that way. It's one thing to hear about our community work; it's another to be a part of it."

"It's more than just medical care, isn't it?" Bethany asked, leaning forward, her eyes eager for affirmation.

"Absolutely," Nora replied, settling back in her chair. "We're not just looking after animals; we're caring for people and fostering a sense of community. Every pet we treat, every owner we help—they're all part of this larger family we're building here."

Bethany nodded thoughtfully. "I sensed that today. The way people spoke to you, their openness and trust—it's clear they see you as much more than their vet. You're a vital part of their lives."

"That's the goal," Nora said, her tone reflective. "And now, you're becoming a part of that. It's a big responsibility, but also a great opportunity to make a difference."

"I feel ready for it," Bethany said, her voice steady, despite the underlying nerves. "But I also feel the weight of that responsibility. I want to contribute, to build on what you've started."

"And you will," Nora assured her. "You bring fresh ideas and new energy. Together, we can expand our outreach and deepen our impact."

Bethany paused, considering her next words carefully. "I've been thinking about some of the programs we discussed starting. Like a community pet care workshop series and maybe setting up a fund for those who can't afford critical treatments."

Nora's eyes lit up. "Those are excellent ideas. The workshop series, especially, could really empower pet owners with knowledge and skills. And the fund— it could change lives."

"Could we really do it?" Bethany asked, the magnitude of the idea dawning on her.

"We can, and we should," Nora replied firmly. "Let's outline some initial plans and see where we need support or resources. I think you'll find the community is even more receptive and supportive than you might expect."

The conversation shifted to planning these new initiatives, both women animated with the possibilities. As they spoke, Bethany felt a profound connection to her new role and the community she now served.

As they wrapped up their discussion, Bethany felt a renewed sense of purpose. "Thank you, Nora, for trusting me with this. I truly believe we can do something special here."

"I believe that too," Nora said, standing to signify the end of their meeting. "I'm excited to see where we go from here. With your vision and drive, I know we're going to continue doing great things."

Bethany left Nora's office filled with a mixture of pride and anticipation. The path ahead was sure to be challenging, but she felt equipped and supported to take it on. Today had not only been about learning the ropes—it had been a profound shift in her understanding of what it meant to be a part of Nora's clinic and Heartsville's community.

As she walked through the quiet clinic, the responsibilities of her role seemed less daunting, framed by the real, tangible impacts she had witnessed that day. Bethany was not just a co-director; she was a key player in a story of community, care, and connection, ready to add her own chapters to the ongoing narrative of the clinic and its place in Heartsville.

Chapter 10
The Heart of the Town

The sun had just started to dip below the horizon, casting a warm, golden glow over the quiet streets of Heartsville. Jake and Nora walked side by side down Main Street, the air between them charged with the kind of unspoken tension that had been building for days. They had spent the afternoon together, visiting local businesses as part of Jake's research, but now the work was done, and the conversation had shifted into more personal territory.

"Do you ever miss the city?" Jake asked, glancing sideways at Nora as they strolled past the bakery, the scent of freshly baked bread wafting through the open door.

Nora smiled softly, her hands tucked into the pockets of her light jacket. "Sometimes," she admitted. "But not in the way you might think. I miss the energy, the constant movement. There's always something happening in the city, always something to do. But..."

Jake raised an eyebrow, sensing there was more. "But?"

"But it was never really home," Nora continued, her voice thoughtful. "I grew up in a small town, much like Heartsville. The city was exciting, sure, but it was also... lonely. You can be surrounded by people and still feel completely alone. Here, it's different. People know each other, they care. It's a community in the truest sense of the word."

Jake nodded, understanding more than he cared to admit. "I get that. The city can be overwhelming. I used to think that was what I wanted—big stories, big excitement. But now..."

"Now you're not so sure," Nora finished for him, her gaze meeting his.

"Yeah," Jake said, his voice quieter. "I guess you could say that."

They walked in silence for a moment, the only sound the soft crunch of their footsteps on the gravel. It was a comfortable silence, the kind that didn't need to be filled with words. But Jake couldn't shake the feeling that there was more to Nora's story, something she hadn't shared yet.

"Nora, what brought you here?" Jake asked, finally breaking the silence. "I mean, to Heartsville. Why leave the city?"

Nora paused, her steps slowing as she considered his question. "It's not something I talk about often," she began, her voice tinged with a hint of sadness. "But I suppose you've earned the right to know."

Jake's curiosity piqued, and he turned to face her, giving her his full attention. "I'm listening."

Nora took a deep breath, her eyes fixed on a distant point beyond the horizon. "My parents passed away when I was in college. It was sudden—an accident. One moment they were there, and the next... they weren't."

Jake's heart clenched at the raw emotion in her voice. "I'm so sorry, Nora."

She nodded, her expression distant. "Thank you. It was hard, but I had to keep going. I finished school, moved to the city, and threw myself into work. But no matter how hard I tried, I couldn't fill the void they left behind. That's when I realized that I needed something more, something that would give my life meaning. I needed to feel connected again."

Jake remained silent, letting her continue at her own pace.

"When I found Heartsville, it was like coming home," Nora said, her voice softening. "The people here reminded me of my parents, of the way they cared about others, about their community. I wanted to be a part of that, to build something meaningful. So I left the city and came here, and I've never looked back."

Jake swallowed hard, his respect for Nora deepening with every word. "That's... incredible, Nora. The way you've dedicated yourself to this town, to these people. It's not something you see every day."

Nora offered a small, bittersweet smile. "It's not always easy. There are days when I wonder if I'm doing the right thing, if I'm really making a difference. But then something happens—like the way everyone came together to find Sparky—and I remember why I'm here."

Jake nodded, his mind racing. He had spent his entire career chasing stories, trying to uncover the truth, but here was Nora, living her truth every day. And the more time he spent with her, the more he found himself questioning everything he thought he knew.

"Nora," he began, his voice hesitant, "I've met a lot of people in my line of work, but none like you. You're... you're different."

Nora looked at him, her eyes searching his. "Different how?"

"Different in a good way," Jake clarified, though he knew his words didn't quite capture what he was feeling. "You've got this way about you, this... I don't know, strength. It's like you've taken all the hard things in your life and turned them into something good. I admire that."

Nora blushed slightly, taken aback by his honesty. "Thank you, Jake. That means a lot, coming from you."

Jake shook his head, a small smile tugging at his lips. "I'm not the person I thought I was when I first came here. You've made me see things differently."

"And is that a good thing?" Nora asked, her tone light but her eyes serious.

Jake hesitated, the weight of his emotions pressing down on him. "I don't know yet. But I think it might be."

They continued walking, the conversation lingering in the air between them. Jake could feel the boundaries of their professional relationship blurring, the lines becoming less defined with each passing day. He wasn't just writing a story anymore—he was living it, and that terrified him.

But as they walked together into the fading light, Jake couldn't deny that he was drawn to Nora, not just as a subject for his article, but as a person. And that, more than anything, was what scared him the most.

The crisp morning air carried an unusual tension as Nora made her way to the clinic, the familiar sights of Heartsville offering little comfort today. Word had spread quickly, as it always did in a small town. The local mill, a cornerstone of the community's economy for generations, was facing closure. For years, the mill had provided steady employment for many of Heartsville's residents, but now, with a decline in business and the looming shadow of corporate competition, the owners had no choice but to shut it down.

Nora's heart was heavy with worry as she reached the clinic. She could already feel the undercurrent of fear and uncertainty that had begun to grip the town. Families depended on the mill, and its closure would mean more than just lost jobs; it would be a blow to the very spirit of Heartsville.

As she unlocked the clinic's door and stepped inside, Nora was met with the concerned faces of her staff. Lisa, her ever-reliable assistant, looked up from behind the reception desk, her eyes reflecting the anxiety that had settled over the town.

"Morning, Nora," Lisa greeted, though her usual cheerfulness was absent. "I suppose you've heard the news?"

Nora nodded, setting her bag down on the counter. "I have. It's terrible, Lisa. I can't stop thinking about the families who are going to be affected by this. We need to do something."

Lisa sighed, her shoulders slumping slightly. "I know. I've been talking to some of the clients, and everyone's worried. People are scared, Nora. They don't know what they're going to do if the mill closes."

Nora leaned against the counter, her mind racing. This was more than just an economic issue; it was about the very fabric of the community. The mill had been a part of Heartsville's identity for as long as anyone could remember. Without it, the town would be fundamentally changed, and not for the better.

"We need to come together," Nora said firmly, more to herself than to Lisa. "We need to find a way to help the people who are going to be affected by this."

Lisa nodded in agreement. "I think a lot of people would be willing to pitch in, but they're looking for direction. They're looking to you, Nora."

The weight of those words settled over Nora like a heavy cloak. She had always been a leader in the community, but this was different. This was a crisis that threatened the very survival of Heartsville as they knew it. The people were turning to her for guidance, and she knew she couldn't let them down.

"Alright," Nora said decisively. "We need to hold a town meeting, and soon. We need to get everyone together and start brainstorming solutions. If the mill closes, we have to figure out how to support the families who will be impacted, whether it's through finding new employment opportunities or offering financial assistance in the short term."

Lisa gave her a determined nod. "I'll start spreading the word. The sooner we can get everyone together, the better."

"Thank you, Lisa," Nora said, squeezing her arm briefly before turning towards her office. "I'm going to make some calls, see if we can get any outside help or advice on this. We can't face this alone."

As Lisa got to work, Nora retreated to her office, her thoughts a whirlwind of plans and possibilities. She sat down at her desk and reached for the phone, dialing the number of the mill's owner, Mr. Harper, a man who had always been fair and community-minded but who now found himself in an impossible situation.

"Mr. Harper, it's Nora Flynn," she said when he answered. "I just wanted to touch base with you about the mill. I know this isn't easy for you, but I wanted to see if there's anything the town can do to help—maybe some way to keep the mill open, or at least to mitigate the impact on the workers."

Mr. Harper's voice was heavy with regret. "Nora, I wish there were something we could do. Believe me, if there was any way to keep the mill running, I would. But the numbers just don't add up. The big corporations have undercut us at every turn, and we can't compete. I hate to say it, but I think it's time to face the reality that the mill's days are numbered."

Nora swallowed hard, the reality of the situation settling in. "I understand, Mr. Harper. But I'm not ready to give up just yet. We're holding a town meeting to discuss the situation, and I'd appreciate it if you could come. Your insight could help us find a way forward, even if it's just to support the workers during this transition."

"I'll be there, Nora," Mr. Harper promised. "I owe it to the people who have worked at the mill all these years to be part of the solution, whatever that may be."

After ending the call, Nora sat back in her chair, her gaze unfocused as she considered the enormity of the challenge before them. This was more than just a leadership test for her; it was a test of the entire community's resilience. Could Heartsville survive without the mill? Could they find a way to reinvent themselves in the face of such a devastating loss?

As the day wore on, Nora made more calls, reaching out to local businesses, community leaders, and even the state representative's office, looking for any possible avenues of support. But as she spoke to one person after another, the enormity of the task ahead became increasingly clear. There were no easy answers, no quick fixes. It would take all of Heartsville's strength and ingenuity to navigate this crisis.

By the time the sun was setting once more, casting long shadows across the town, Nora felt both exhausted and invigorated. The meeting was set for the following evening, and she knew that it would be the first step in a long, difficult journey. But she also knew that Heartsville was not a town that backed down in the face of adversity. They had faced challenges before, and they had always come through stronger on the other side.

As she left the clinic that evening, Nora couldn't help but glance down the street, where the mill's tall, imposing structure stood against the darkening sky. It was more than just a building; it was a symbol of everything Heartsville had built over the years. But now, it was a symbol of the fight they had ahead of them—a fight for their community, for their way of life, and for the future they all wanted to protect.

- - - - - - - - -

The Heartsville Town Hall was packed to the rafters. Every seat was taken, with people standing along the walls and spilling out into the hallway. The usual hum of polite conversation was absent, replaced by a low murmur of anxiety and uncertainty. The town's future was at stake, and everyone knew it. Nora Flynn stood at the front, her presence commanding but calm, as she prepared to address the gathered crowd.

Jake Carter, standing near the back of the room, watched the scene unfold with a sense of growing unease. He had attended countless town meetings in his career, but this one felt different. The stakes were personal, and the weight of his responsibility as a journalist pressed heavily on his shoulders. He had a job to do, but for the first time, he wasn't sure how to do it.

His notebook, usually filled with confident, objective observations, lay closed in his hands. The story he had come here to write—the potential downfall of a small town, the economic struggles that threatened to tear it apart—now felt incomplete, even misleading. Heartsville wasn't just another town on the brink of collapse; it was a community fighting tooth and nail to save itself. And Jake was starting to see that the story wasn't about defeat, but about resilience.

Nora's voice cut through the murmur of the crowd, drawing Jake's attention back to the front of the room. "I know everyone is worried, and I know that the news about the mill has shaken us all," she began, her tone steady but filled with emotion. "But we've faced challenges before, and we've always come through. This time will be no different. We just need to come together, as we always have, and find a way forward."

A few murmurs of agreement rippled through the crowd, but there was also a palpable tension, the kind that comes from fear and uncertainty. Jake could feel it, too—a gnawing doubt that maybe this time, things wouldn't turn out alright. The mill's closure was a heavy blow, one that could cripple Heartsville's economy and force families to leave in search of work. It was the kind of story his editor, Marlene, would jump on—a narrative of decline, of a small town crushed by the weight of progress.

But as Jake looked around the room, at the faces of the people who had welcomed him into their lives, his resolve began to waver. He had seen the strength of this community firsthand—the way they had come together to find Sparky, the way they supported one another in times of need. How could he reduce all of that to a story of defeat?

His phone buzzed in his pocket, a sharp reminder of the world outside this small town. He glanced at the screen: a message from Marlene.

Jake, need an update. What's the angle here? Don't hold back—we need something gripping.

Jake's stomach tightened. He could already imagine the conversation that would follow. Marlene would want drama, conflict, a story that would draw in readers with its bleakness. But what if that wasn't the truth? What if the real story was about hope, about a community refusing to give up?

Nora continued speaking, her voice unwavering as she outlined possible solutions: reaching out to nearby towns for job opportunities, organizing fundraisers to support affected families, and even exploring the possibility of a community-owned cooperative to keep the mill running. Her ideas were met with cautious optimism, but also with the harsh reality that nothing was guaranteed.

Jake's dilemma deepened with each word. He had a choice to make: report the story as expected, focusing on the negative aspects, or take a different approach, one that might not be as sensational but would be true to what he had witnessed. But if he chose the latter, would Marlene accept it? Or would she demand the story she had anticipated, leaving him with no choice but to compromise his integrity?

His thoughts were interrupted by a man standing up in the middle of the room. "Nora, what if we can't save the mill? What happens to us then?"

The question hung in the air, heavy with the fear everyone was feeling. Nora didn't shy away from it. "If we can't save the mill," she said slowly, "then we find another way. Heartsville isn't just a town with a mill—it's a town with heart, with people who care about each other. As long as we stick together, we'll find a way to keep going. It might not be easy, but we'll make it through. We always do."

Jake's chest tightened at her words. This was the story he wanted to tell—the story of a town that wasn't defined by its struggles, but by its strength, by its willingness to fight for survival even when the odds were stacked against it. But he knew that wasn't the story Marlene would want to run. It lacked the bite, the sensationalism that sold papers and garnered clicks.

As the meeting continued, Jake's mind raced. Could he find a way to tell the truth without sacrificing his career? Could he convince Marlene to see the value in a story that highlighted resilience over defeat? And if he couldn't, what then?

By the time the meeting ended, Jake was no closer to an answer. The townspeople began to file out, their expressions a mix of hope and lingering fear. Nora stayed behind, talking quietly with a few of the town's leaders, her face a mask of determination.

Jake watched her, his decision weighing heavily on him. He knew he needed to talk to Marlene, to find a way to balance the demands of his job with the truth he had come to see. But as he left the town hall and stepped out into the cool night air, he couldn't shake the feeling that his life was about to change—one way or another. The question was, would it be for the better?

The town hall had emptied out, leaving behind an eerie quiet that contrasted sharply with the earlier buzz of anxious voices. Jake lingered near the front of the room, his mind a storm of conflicting thoughts. He had watched as the townspeople filtered out, their faces a mixture of hope and trepidation. Now, only Nora remained, gathering up papers and tidying up after the meeting.

Jake approached her slowly, his footsteps echoing in the now-empty space. "Nora," he called softly, not wanting to startle her.

She looked up, offering him a tired but genuine smile. "Jake, you're still here. I thought you might have left with the others."

He shook his head, hands shoved deep into his pockets as he stepped closer. "I wanted to talk to you. About... well, about everything."

Nora set down the papers she was holding, turning her full attention to him. "What's on your mind?"

Jake hesitated, searching for the right words. "The meeting tonight... it was intense. There's a lot at stake, and I can see how much you care about this town, about these people. It's... it's impressive."

Nora's smile softened, and she took a step closer, her expression serious. "Heartsville is more than just a place to me, Jake. It's my home, and the people here—they're like family. I can't just sit back and watch them struggle without doing something to help."

"I know," Jake replied, his voice low. "And that's exactly why I'm struggling with what to write. I came here with a certain story in mind, a certain angle, but now... now I'm not so sure."

Nora studied him, her gaze penetrating. "What do you mean?"

Jake let out a long breath, the weight of his dilemma pressing down on him. "My editor, Marlene—she wants something sensational, something that highlights the struggles, the drama. That's what sells, right? But after tonight, after everything I've seen, it just doesn't feel right. I don't want to write a story that paints Heartsville as a town on the brink of collapse, even if that's part of the truth. There's more to it than that, and I don't know how to balance it."

Nora nodded slowly, understanding dawning in her eyes. "Jake, I get it. You're torn between telling the truth and giving your editor what she wants. But you have to ask yourself—what kind of journalist do you want to be?"

Jake frowned slightly, his brow furrowing. "What do you mean?"

Nora took a deep breath, choosing her words carefully. "You have the power to shape the narrative, to decide how people will see Heartsville. You could write the story that's expected of you, focus on the struggles, the hardships, and that's a valid perspective. But is that the whole truth? Or is there more to this town, to these people, that deserves to be told?"

Jake was silent for a moment, her words sinking in. "I don't want to sensationalize their pain," he admitted, his voice quieter now. "But I also can't ignore what's happening. The mill closing is a big deal—it's going to affect a lot of people."

"Of course it is," Nora agreed, her tone gentle but firm. "But it's not the whole story. The whole story is about how this community comes together, how we fight for each other, how we find a way to survive even when the odds are against us. That's the truth, Jake. It's not just black and white—it's complex, it's messy, and it's real."

Jake ran a hand through his hair, feeling the frustration bubbling up. "But how do I tell that story? How do I write something that captures all of that, without it being too... I don't know, too optimistic? Marlene isn't going to go for a feel-good piece. She wants something that packs a punch."

Nora's eyes softened, and she reached out, placing a hand on his arm. "You're a good writer, Jake. I've read your work—I know you can tell a story that's both honest and compelling. You don't have to choose between truth and impact. You can have both, if you're willing to dig deep and really see what's happening here."

Jake looked down at her hand on his arm, the warmth of her touch grounding him. "I just don't want to let anyone down," he said, his voice barely above a whisper.

Nora smiled, a touch of sadness in her eyes. "You won't, Jake. Not if you stay true to what you know is right. Heartsville needs someone who can tell our story the way it really is, not just the way it's expected to be. And I think you're the one who can do that."

Jake swallowed hard, the lump in his throat making it difficult to speak. He had spent his entire career priding himself on his objectivity, his ability to tell the hard truths. But now, standing here with Nora, he realized that the truth wasn't always what it seemed. It wasn't just about facts and figures—it was about people, about their lives, their struggles, and their triumphs.

"Thank you, Nora," he said finally, his voice thick with emotion. "You've given me a lot to think about."

Nora squeezed his arm gently before letting go. "Just promise me one thing, Jake. Whatever you write, make sure it's something you can stand behind. Something you believe in."

Jake nodded, the weight of her words settling over him like a mantle. "I promise."

As they stood there in the quiet of the empty town hall, Jake felt a shift deep within him. This conversation had changed something—had pushed him to reconsider not just the story he was writing, but the kind of journalist, and person, he wanted to be. He wasn't sure where this journey would take him, but he knew one thing for certain: he couldn't go back to the way things were before. Not after seeing Heartsville, and Nora, for what they truly were.

When he finally left the town hall that night, the cool night air filling his lungs, Jake knew he had a decision to make. The story was still his to tell, but now, it was up to him to decide how it would be told. And for the first time in a long time, he felt ready to tell it right.

Chapter 11
The Turning Point

The morning at Nora's clinic began with an uncharacteristic chill, not from the weather, which was pleasantly mild, but from a palpable tension that seemed to have settled between the staff. Bethany arrived earlier than usual, her mind preoccupied with a conversation she'd had the previous day with one of the senior technicians, Anne, who had expressed some concerns about the new changes being implemented at the clinic.

As Bethany walked through the clinic's front doors, she sensed the shift in atmosphere immediately. Conversations paused slightly as she passed; smiles were polite, but they lacked their usual warmth. The clinic, usually buzzing with a harmonious energy, felt disjointed this morning.

Nora, noticing Bethany's early arrival and her concerned expression, approached her in the hallway. "Good morning, Bethany. You're in early today," she remarked, trying to gauge her new co-director's mood.

"Yes, I wanted to catch up on some paperwork and go over the feedback from yesterday's staff meeting," Bethany responded, her voice betraying a hint of the stress she felt. "It seems there are some concerns about the pace of changes since I've come on board."

Nora nodded, understanding the delicate nature of leadership transitions. "Change can be challenging. It's important we address any concerns head-on, make sure the team feels heard and supported."

Bethany appreciated Nora's calm demeanor. "I plan to do just that. I think it's crucial we clear the air, ensure everyone is on the same page moving forward."

As the morning progressed, Bethany made a point to engage more with the staff, asking about their current projects and any issues they were facing. Her approach was gentle, aiming to rebuild the camaraderie that had always been a cornerstone of the clinic's culture.

Meanwhile, Nora continued her rounds, treating a young Labrador with a sprained leg and a cat with a dietary issue, her professional focus never wavering despite the underlying tensions. Each patient provided a momentary escape from the administrative challenges waiting for her.

In between appointments, Nora and Bethany convened briefly in Nora's office, a space filled with sunlight and lined with pictures of community events and thank-you notes from clients. Here, they discussed strategies to better integrate staff feedback into the clinic's daily operations.

"We might need to slow down a bit," Bethany suggested, taking a sip of her coffee. "Perhaps introduce changes more gradually, give everyone more time to adjust."

"That sounds reasonable," Nora agreed. "It's important that these changes are evolutionary, not revolutionary. We want to foster development, not disruption."

The rest of the morning saw Bethany taking a more hands-on approach in the clinic, assisting with treatments and sharing her expertise in a way that was both instructive and inclusive. Her efforts did not go unnoticed by the staff, who began to respond more positively to her presence, gradually dispelling the morning's tension.

As lunch approached, the clinic regained some of its usual rhythm. Conversations became more relaxed, and the morning's awkwardness gave way to a cautious optimism. Bethany's willingness to listen and adapt, coupled with Nora's steady leadership, reminded the team of the clinic's core mission: to serve their community and care for its pets with compassion and excellence.

The day's early tensions had highlighted the challenges of transition, but they had also opened up important dialogues about growth, leadership, and the value of maintaining a supportive and collaborative workplace culture. As Nora and Bethany stepped out for a brief lunch together, they did so with a clearer understanding of the path forward, both committed to navigating it together for the betterment of their team and the many lives they touched.

After lunch, Bethany decided to address the morning's tensions directly. She invited Anne, the senior technician who had voiced concerns the previous day, to join her for a private chat in one of the clinic's small conference rooms. Bethany knew that clearing the air was crucial, not just for her relationship with Anne but for the overall morale of the clinic.

"Anne, thank you for meeting with me," Bethany began, her tone sincere. "I've been thinking a lot about our conversation yesterday, and I wanted to apologize if the changes I've introduced have felt overwhelming."

Anne, who had seemed a bit reserved at first, relaxed slightly at Bethany's words. "Thank you for saying that, Bethany. I appreciate it. We're all here because we care about the clinic and the animals, but it has been a lot to adjust to."

"I can understand that," Bethany acknowledged. "I might have been too eager to implement new ideas without fully considering how they would affect everyone. I'm here to learn, and I value your experience and input."

"That means a lot," Anne replied. "We do see the value in your ideas. It's just the pace and some of the processes that have been a bit jarring."

Bethany nodded, taking in Anne's feedback. "Let's work together on this. Maybe you can help me understand better ways to integrate changes that don't disrupt our workflow but still move us forward?"

"I'd like that," Anne said, a hint of a smile appearing. "I think if we could have more frequent check-ins during the transition, it would help. It gives everyone a chance to be heard and to clarify things before they become issues."

"That's an excellent suggestion," Bethany agreed, feeling a sense of relief as the conversation progressed positively. "I'll set up a weekly meeting for the next couple of months. We can review upcoming changes, discuss any concerns, and make adjustments as needed."

Anne seemed pleased with the proposal. "That sounds perfect. It'll make everyone feel more involved and perhaps ease the transition a bit."

As their meeting concluded, Bethany felt grateful for Anne's openness and willingness to collaborate. She extended her hand, and Anne shook it firmly, the gesture marking a renewed understanding between them.

Returning to her duties, Bethany felt more confident in her ability to lead with sensitivity to her team's needs. The rest of the afternoon passed smoothly, with Bethany taking the time to engage with other staff members, reinforcing her commitment to openness and teamwork.

Later, Bethany shared the outcomes of her conversation with Nora, who listened intently and nodded in approval. "Well done, Bethany," Nora said. "These are the kinds of conversations that build trust and respect. You're learning the ropes, and you're doing it with grace."

"Thanks, Nora," Bethany responded, feeling reassured by her mentor's praise. "It's a learning curve, but I'm not in this alone. Having your support and the team's input makes all the difference."

As the day neared its end, the clinic regained its familiar sense of unity and purpose. Bethany's proactive approach to addressing the concerns head-on had not only mitigated the morning's tensions but had also strengthened her leadership position within the team. She looked forward to the weekly meetings, viewing them as an opportunity to further meld her vision with the practical, day-to-day realities of the clinic's operation.

Reflecting on the day's events as she prepared to close up the clinic, Bethany felt a deep satisfaction. The path ahead would undoubtedly hold more challenges, but she was ready to meet them with a clear mind and an open heart, guided by the knowledge that open communication and mutual respect were key to navigating any change.

The clinic was closing for the day, and as the last patient left, Nora invited Bethany to join her for a quiet cup of tea in her office. It had been a day of emotional highs and lows, and Nora felt it was a good moment to share her own experiences and vulnerabilities with Bethany, hoping to strengthen their bond as co-directors.

As they settled into the comfortable chairs in Nora's office, Nora began, her tone reflective. "Bethany, I've been thinking about how today unfolded. You handled everything with such poise, especially your conversation with Anne. It reminded me of my early days here."

Bethany, sipping her tea, was attentive. "It was a challenging day, but I felt it was important to address things directly. How did you manage when you first started?"

Nora smiled, remembering her initial struggles. "It wasn't easy. I had big ideas just like you, and I wanted to change everything at once. But I learned that change has to be a conversation, not a decree. Sharing that journey with my team, being open about my uncertainties—it helped us grow together."

"That makes sense," Bethany nodded, feeling comforted by Nora's openness. "I guess part of me was worried about showing any uncertainty. I thought I needed to appear fully confident to be effective."

Nora leaned forward, her expression earnest. "I've found that sharing vulnerabilities can actually strengthen leadership. It shows your team that you're human and that you value their support. It builds real trust."

Bethany considered this, the weight of her earlier anxieties easing somewhat. "I see what you mean. It's about balance, isn't it? Being strong but also being open."

"Exactly," Nora agreed. "And it's a learning process. Each challenge, each misunderstanding, is an opportunity to learn and adapt. The fact that you're open to doing that will make you an incredible leader here."

The conversation shifted to discuss more about their visions for the clinic. Bethany shared some of her ideas, and Nora provided insights from her years of experience. This exchange not only deepened their professional relationship but also established a mutual respect based on shared vulnerabilities and common goals.

"Nora, thank you for sharing that with me," Bethany said sincerely as they wrapped up their discussion. "It really helps to know that it's okay to not have all the answers right away."

Nora stood, placing her teacup on the desk. "You're welcome, Bethany. Remember, leadership is as much about listening and learning as it is about guiding. We're all in this together."

As Bethany left Nora's office, she felt a renewed sense of purpose and a deeper connection to her role. The day's events had provided her with valuable lessons in leadership, particularly the power of openness and the strength found in shared vulnerabilities.

Reflecting on their discussion, Bethany felt more equipped to face future challenges. She was determined to continue fostering an environment where open communication was the cornerstone of their success. As the clinic's lights dimmed and the doors locked behind her, Bethany felt confident in her path forward, supported by the trust and guidance of her mentor and the resilience of her team.

In the days following the tense encounters and heartfelt discussions, Bethany dedicated herself to rebuilding and reinforcing trust within her team at the clinic. She knew that her early actions had unsettled some staff, but she was also aware that time and consistent effort would be key to smoothing over those initial bumps.

On a bright Wednesday morning, as the clinic began to buzz with the day's early appointments, Bethany took proactive steps to engage with her team more openly. She started by organizing a brief meeting before the clinic opened, intended to provide everyone with an update on current projects and an opportunity to voice any concerns or suggestions.

"Good morning, everyone," Bethany began, standing at the front of the staff room, her posture relaxed but confident. "I want to take a few minutes to talk about where we are with some of our initiatives and hear your thoughts on how things are going."

As she outlined the status of several ongoing programs, including the new community outreach plans, she made it a point to ask for feedback directly. "I value your input, and I'm here to support you, just as much as you support our patients and their families," she stated clearly, her eyes meeting those of her colleagues.

After the meeting, as the day progressed, Bethany made rounds through the clinic, stopping to assist where needed and engaging in casual conversation with the staff. Her approach was hands-on, aimed at not just overseeing but participating in the day-to-day activities that kept the clinic running.

During a quieter moment, Bethany found herself helping Anne, the senior technician, with organizing the supply room. The task was mundane, but it provided a perfect opportunity for a more personal conversation.

"Anne, I really appreciated your input last week," Bethany said, handing her a box of syringes to shelve. "It's helped me adjust my approach, and I hope it's made a difference."

Anne nodded, placing the box on the shelf before turning to face Bethany. "It has, and thank you for taking it to heart. We all want what's best for the clinic and the community. Seeing you so open to feedback—it's made a lot of us feel more comfortable."

Bethany smiled, grateful for the acknowledgment. "I'm learning every day. It's important to me that we all feel like we're moving forward together."

This interaction was a small but significant indicator of the improving dynamics within the team. Bethany's efforts to integrate herself more fully and her genuine commitment to the clinic's ethos were becoming evident to everyone.

As the week continued, Bethany's presence in the clinic began to feel more natural, and the staff's initial wariness gave way to a collaborative spirit. The change didn't happen overnight, but each day brought small victories in trust and teamwork.

By the end of the week, during the staff's regular lunch gathering, Nora quietly observed the changes from across the room. She noticed the laughter and relaxed exchanges between

Bethany and the rest of the team. It was clear that Bethany was no longer an outsider trying to find her place but was becoming a respected and integral part of the clinic family.

Later that day, as Nora and Bethany reviewed the week's progress, Nora felt compelled to express her thoughts. "Bethany, I've seen how you've grown into your role here, and how the team has responded to your leadership. It's a testament to your dedication and empathy."

Bethany, feeling a mix of relief and pride, acknowledged Nora's praise. "Thank you, Nora. It's been a journey, but I feel like we're heading in the right direction. Your support has been invaluable."

As they planned for the following week, both leaders were aware that while challenges would inevitably arise, the foundation of trust and mutual respect they were building would sustain them through future obstacles. The clinic was more than just a place of work; it was a community of care, and Bethany was now truly a part of it.

Chapter 12
A Call for Unity

On an unassuming Tuesday that started like any other at the Heartsville Veterinary Clinic, a routine appointment took an unexpected turn, leading to revelations that would deepen the staff's understanding of their impact on the community they served.

Nora and Bethany were in the midst of examining a Bernese Mountain Dog named Bernie, who had been brought in by Mrs. Thompson for a limp that had recently worsened. While Nora gently manipulated Bernie's leg, Bethany reviewed his medical history.

"Looks like Bernie here might be dealing with early signs of arthritis," Nora noted, her tone professional yet comforting as she addressed Mrs. Thompson. "We'll need some x-rays to confirm, but we can manage it with the right treatment plan."

Mrs. Thompson nodded, her expression a mix of concern and gratitude. "Thank you, Nora. I don't know what we'd do without you and your team. You've helped not just Bernie, but all of us, through so much."

As they prepared Bernie for his x-rays, Mrs. Thompson shared more about the role the clinic had played in her family's life, revealing the depth of the bond she and many others felt with Nora and her team. "When my husband was ill last year, coming here with Bernie was a bright spot in very tough days," she confessed.

Nora paused, touched by her words. "We're more than just a clinic to our patients and their families. We're part of their support system," she reflected aloud, more to herself and Bethany than to Mrs. Thompson.

Bethany, handing over the x-ray lead vests, agreed. "It's these stories that remind us why we do what we do. It's not just about treating animals; it's about caring for the people who love them, too."

The rest of the day seemed to underscore that sentiment. Later, as they treated a series of routine check-ups and minor emergencies, each patient came with a story, each interaction laced with personal connections and shared histories that spanned years.

In the afternoon, a young couple came in with a new puppy, nervous and seeking guidance. The couple, Tim and Marla, were first-time pet owners and had chosen the clinic based on glowing recommendations from neighbors.

"We've heard so much about this place," Tim explained as Bethany showed them how to hold the squirming puppy for a vaccination. "People don't just talk about the great medical care; they talk about how coming here feels like visiting family."

Bethany smiled, ensuring the puppy was comfortable. "We hope you'll feel the same. We're here to make sure you and your puppy have all the support you need."

As the day wound down, Nora and Bethany took a moment in Nora's office to reflect on the revelations of the day. The walls, adorned with photos of community events and thank-you cards, seemed to echo the sentiments shared by their clients.

"It's been quite a day," Bethany remarked, sinking into one of the chairs. "Hearing how deeply we touch the lives of those we serve—it's profound."

Nora nodded, her gaze settling on a photo from a recent community pet fair. "It's these connections that build the foundation of our practice. Each story, each thank you—it's a reminder that what we do here extends far beyond medical care."

The conversation lingered on the many ways they could continue to foster these connections, perhaps through more community outreach or by hosting workshops for pet owners like Tim and Marla. Both knew that the revelations of the day were more than just affirmations; they were a call to deepen their commitment to the community.

As they left the office to head home, both Nora and Bethany felt a renewed sense of purpose. They were reminded that at the heart of their work were not just the animals they treated but the human lives they touched and improved, making every day a meaningful endeavor in the heart of Heartsville.

- - - - - - - - -

The next day at the clinic began with a steady stream of appointments, but between the regular check-ups and vaccinations, Bethany took time to observe and reflect on the deeper aspects of her interactions with the clients. Her recent conversations had opened her eyes to the nuances of community veterinary practice, and she was eager to apply these insights to improve service further.

During a lull in the schedule, Bethany sat down with Nora in the staff lounge, both enjoying a rare quiet moment to discuss their observations from the previous days.

"Bethany, I've noticed you've been quite thoughtful lately," Nora started, her tone inviting. "Any new insights from your interactions with our clients?"

"Yes, actually," Bethany replied, eager to share her thoughts. "I've been thinking about how each client interaction not only helps the pet but also supports the pet owners. It's more than healthcare; it's about providing peace of mind and a sense of community."

Nora nodded, pleased with Bethany's perceptiveness. "Exactly. Our work has a ripple effect. By helping the pet, we help the owner, and this in turn strengthens the community's fabric. It's all interconnected."

Bethany continued, "I was particularly struck by what Mrs. Thompson shared about how much this clinic meant to her during her husband's illness. It made me realize that we could perhaps do more to support our clients who are going through difficult times, beyond just medical care for their pets."

"That's a wonderful insight," Nora responded warmly. "Perhaps we could think about a support group or a workshop series? Something that allows pet owners to connect not just with us but with each other."

"I was thinking along those lines too," Bethany agreed. "A support group for pet owners could be beneficial. It could provide a space for sharing experiences and advice, not just about pet care but about coping with the challenges they face."

"It's important that we keep finding ways to extend our care beyond the clinic," Nora added. "Let's put some ideas down on paper and see what resources we would need to make it happen."

As their discussion continued, they outlined potential formats for the support group and other community-engagement activities. They considered guest speakers, topics for sessions, and even partnerships with local counselors or therapists who could provide additional support.

Their conversation was interrupted by the arrival of their next appointment, but the ideas sparked in that brief meeting stayed with them. Later in the afternoon, as Bethany treated a young spaniel with an ear infection, she shared some of the plans with the dog's owner, Mrs. Gilmore.

"We're thinking about starting a support group for pet owners," Bethany mentioned casually as she examined the spaniel. "It could be a place to discuss not just pet-related issues but also the joys and challenges of pet ownership."

Mrs. Gilmore looked intrigued. "That sounds wonderful. It can be tough, especially when you're dealing with an illness or behavioral issues. Having a community to talk to and share with would make a big difference."

Encouraged by Mrs. Gilmore's response, Bethany felt even more convinced of the value such initiatives could bring. "We hope it will help strengthen the bonds within our community," she explained. "And provide additional support where it's needed."

By the end of the day, Bethany and Nora reconvened to discuss the positive feedback from Mrs. Gilmore and other clients. They agreed to move forward with planning the support group, motivated by the clear need and potential impact it could have.

Their day of observations and insights had confirmed the vital role their clinic played in the community, not just as a provider of veterinary services but as a cornerstone of support and connection. As they locked up the clinic for the night, both felt a deep sense of fulfillment and anticipation for the new initiatives they were about to introduce.

- - - - - - - - -

Later in the week, Bethany and Nora planned an informal after-hours meeting at the clinic for the staff. The idea was to gauge the team's interest in the proposed support group for pet owners and gather any additional feedback on how best to implement such a program. As the staff gathered in the cozy break room, the air was filled with a mix of curiosity and enthusiasm.

Nora took the lead in starting the conversation. "Thank you, everyone, for staying a bit late today. We've been thinking about starting a support group for our clients—a place where they can share their experiences and challenges in pet ownership, not just with us but with each other."

Bethany, standing beside Nora, added, "We believe it could really strengthen the community support aspect of our work. But we want to hear from you all. What do you think about this idea, and how do you see us making it work?"

Thomas, one of the veteran veterinarians, was the first to respond. "I think it's a great idea. We've all seen how much our clients rely on us for support beyond just medical care. A formal group could really formalize that support."

Liz, a veterinary technician, chimed in with a practical concern. "It sounds wonderful, but who would run these sessions? We're all pretty stretched as it is."

"That's a valid point," Bethany acknowledged. "We were thinking about perhaps sharing the responsibility among us, maybe rotating the leadership. And we could also look into bringing in outside experts or counselors to lead some sessions."

Anne, who had initially been skeptical of some of Bethany's earlier changes but had since warmed up to her leadership, now voiced a supportive suggestion. "Maybe we could also have some themed sessions, based on common issues we see here at the clinic. Things like dealing with anxiety in pets, or managing chronic illnesses."

"That's an excellent idea," Nora replied, visibly pleased with the team's engagement. "It could make the sessions even more relevant and beneficial for our clients."

The discussion continued with team members proposing various ideas, from logistics like scheduling and space allocation to potential outreach methods to ensure clients knew about and felt welcome to participate in the group.

As the meeting drew to a close, Bethany felt a profound sense of collaboration and community. She turned to Nora, expressing her gratitude. "This conversation has been incredibly insightful. It's clear we have a team that cares deeply not just about the animals, but about the people we serve."

Nora nodded in agreement. "It's one of the things that makes our clinic special. We're not just a team; we're a community. And this support group could be an extension of that."

After everyone had left, Nora and Bethany stayed behind to consolidate the ideas that had been shared. They drafted a preliminary plan for the support group, incorporating the feedback from the staff.

As they worked together, a conversation unfolded about their personal motivations and the deeper connections they'd developed with their work.

Bethany shared a personal anecdote, "You know, when I first considered moving to Heartsville and working here, I never imagined how deeply this job would affect me. It's more than a career; it's a calling."

Nora smiled, her eyes reflecting a mix of pride and empathy. "I've felt that way many times over the years. It's what keeps us going, even on the tough days. And it's what drives us to keep finding new ways to help, like this support group."

The day ended with both women feeling invigorated by the potential of their new project and the solid support of their team. They knew that the road ahead would have its challenges, but the conversation that evening had revealed a shared commitment to the clinic's mission and a collective eagerness to see it succeed in new ways.

- - - - - - - - -

In the days that followed the staff meeting about the support group, there was a noticeable shift in the clinic's atmosphere. The air of anticipation and enthusiasm was palpable as the team began to see the potential impact of their collaborative effort on the community. For Bethany, it was gratifying to witness the change in morale and the increasing involvement of every staff member.

One late afternoon, as the clinic began to wind down from the day's appointments, Nora and Bethany found a moment to discuss the progress in implementing the support group. They sat in Nora's office, where the golden light of the setting sun filtered through the blinds, casting a warm glow over their plans laid out on the desk.

"It's incredible to see how everyone is coming together on this," Bethany remarked, her voice tinged with relief and happiness. "There's a real sense of purpose that I think we were missing before."

Nora nodded, her expression thoughtful. "It's a testament to your leadership, Bethany. You've managed to turn uncertainty into opportunity. The team's enthusiasm is a direct reflection of their trust in you and their belief in our mission."

Bethany appreciated Nora's words. "It was a team effort, Nora. Your guidance has been invaluable to me. This whole experience has changed how I feel about my place here. I feel more connected, not just to our goals, but to the people we work with."

As they spoke, the topic shifted to the logistical aspects of the support group. "We'll need to finalize the schedule and get the word out to our clients," Nora pointed out, reviewing the list of tasks they had drafted.

"Yes, I've drafted a newsletter update, and I thought we could also use social media to reach out," Bethany suggested, showing Nora the content on her laptop.

"That sounds perfect," Nora agreed, pleased with the initiative. "Let's make sure the messaging is clear—we want everyone to feel welcome."

The conversation flowed easily, with both leaders contributing ideas and solutions. It was a productive session, ending with a detailed plan of action for the next few weeks.

After Nora and Bethany left the office, they paused by the front desk where Anne was finishing up some administrative tasks. "We're moving forward with the support group," Bethany shared, a smile spreading across her face. "Thanks for your suggestions—they've been really helpful."

Anne looked up, her face breaking into a smile. "I'm glad to hear that. It's a great initiative. I think it's going to make a big difference."

The positive feedback was reassuring, and as Bethany and Nora said their goodbyes and left the clinic for the evening, there was a shared sense of accomplishment and excitement. The drive to improve and expand their community support had invigorated their professional relationship and deepened their mutual respect.

Walking to her car, Bethany reflected on the day's discussions and the progress they had made. The initial resistance and her own uncertainties seemed like distant memories now. The shift in her feelings—from doubt to determination, from feeling like an outsider to being an integral part of the clinic—was profound. She knew there would be challenges ahead, but she also knew that she and the team were ready to meet them head-on.

As the clinic's lights dimmed and the doors locked behind her, Bethany felt a deep connection to her work and the community. The support group was just the beginning, and she looked forward to the continued impact they would make, not just in the lives of pets, but in the lives of everyone they touched. The evening ended not just with a sense of closure for the day, but with a renewed commitment to the heart of their mission.

Chapter 13
The Search for Truth

The day at Heartsville Veterinary Clinic began under the typical hustle of early morning appointments, but a simmering issue between two staff members soon escalated, threatening the harmonious work environment that Nora and Bethany had worked hard to foster.

The conflict arose over the treatment plan for a particularly difficult case involving a rescue dog with multiple health issues. Mark, one of the newer veterinarians, believed a more aggressive treatment was necessary, while Susan, a seasoned veterinary technician, argued for a conservative approach, citing the dog's fragile state.

As voices raised slightly in the treatment room, Bethany stepped in before the disagreement could disrupt the workflow further.

"Let's take a step back for a moment," Bethany interjected, her voice firm yet calm, as she entered the room. "Can we discuss this in my office, please?"

Once in the office, Bethany facilitated the discussion, encouraging open communication. "Mark, Susan, I know you both have the best interests of the dog at heart. Let's talk through your perspectives."

Mark, slightly flustered, began, "I've reviewed the latest studies on this condition, and I think a more aggressive approach might give us a better chance at managing his symptoms."

Susan, clearly frustrated but trying to remain professional, countered, "I understand where you're coming from, but I've seen cases like this go downhill fast with aggressive treatments. This dog has been through a lot already. We might do more harm than good."

Bethany listened attentively, nodding. "Both approaches have their merits. Mark, your research is invaluable, and Susan, your experience gives you a unique insight into the practical side of these treatments."

Mark looked at Susan, his expression softening. "I didn't mean to dismiss your experience, Susan. I just think we should consider all options."

Susan sighed, her demeanor relaxing slightly. "I get that, Mark. I'm just worried about the risks. Maybe there's a middle ground?"

Bethany smiled, pleased with the shift towards compromise. "That sounds like a constructive approach. How about we start with a modified version of Mark's suggestion, monitor closely, and if there are any signs of distress, we revert to a more conservative regimen?"

Both nodded in agreement, relieved to have reached a resolution. "Thank you, Bethany, for helping us find common ground," Susan said as they stood to leave.

Bethany's handling of the situation not only prevented further conflict but also reinforced the clinic's values of respect and collaboration. After Mark and Susan left her office, Bethany took a moment to reflect on the incident.

Realizing the importance of preemptively managing such disagreements, Bethany decided to propose regular team meetings focused on treatment strategies, especially for complex cases. She shared this idea with Nora when they met for a quick coffee break.

"Nora, the disagreement today between Mark and Susan made me think. Maybe we should have regular strategy meetings where we can discuss complex cases as a team before deciding on a treatment plan. It could help preempt these conflicts and ensure everyone feels heard," Bethany suggested.

Nora sipped her coffee, considering the proposal. "I think that's an excellent idea. It aligns perfectly with our collaborative approach. Let's schedule the first meeting for next week. We can review upcoming cases and discuss them as a group."

Pleased with Nora's support, Bethany felt confident that this new approach would strengthen the team's unity and improve their collective decision-making.

As the day continued, the earlier tension dissipated, replaced by a renewed sense of teamwork. The clinic staff went about their duties, reassured by the leadership's commitment to maintaining an open and supportive work environment. This incident, though initially a spark of conflict, ultimately served to ignite a deeper understanding and appreciation among the team, highlighting the importance of communication and respect in navigating the complexities of veterinary care.

- - - - - - - - -

Later in the week, another incident tested the newly reinforced bonds within the clinic team. During a casual lunch break in the staff room, a conversation about upcoming community events led to an unexpected misunderstanding that momentarily disrupted the team's harmony.

Bethany, excited about the success of recent community outreach programs, shared her thoughts with the team gathered around the lunch table. "I'm really impressed with how everyone has stepped up for these events. It's making a huge difference. We just need to keep the momentum going."

Tom, a veterinary assistant, chimed in with enthusiasm. "Absolutely, it's been great. But you know, it would be even better if we could get some more modern equipment to show off at these events. Some of the stuff we have is pretty ancient."

Bethany laughed, assuming Tom was joking. "Ancient? Now, let's not exaggerate. But point taken, updating some of our equipment could definitely be on the agenda."

However, Tom's comment, initially meant in a light-hearted manner, was overheard by George, the clinic's longest-serving technician, who was passing by the staff room. George, who had been instrumental in maintaining and often repairing the clinic's equipment over the years, took the comment more personally than intended.

George stopped in his tracks, visibly upset. "Ancient, huh? I spend a lot of time keeping our 'ancient' equipment running smoothly. It's not as easy as it looks."

Bethany, realizing the impact of the conversation, immediately addressed George's concern. "George, I'm sorry, that came out wrong. We all appreciate how hard you work to keep everything in top shape. Tom was just making a light comment, and I didn't mean to dismiss all your efforts."

Tom, looking apologetic, quickly added, "George, I didn't mean to offend. You do amazing work here. I was just thinking about how some new tech could enhance the great stuff we're already doing, especially for the public events."

George, though slightly mollified, still seemed hurt. "I understand, but maybe we could talk about these things more directly next time. It feels a bit off to hear about it this way."

Bethany nodded, her leadership instincts kicking in. "You're right, George. Communication is key, and we should have brought this up differently. How about we set up a meeting to discuss potential upgrades and how we can implement them? Your input would be invaluable, given your experience with our current setup."

George considered this for a moment, then agreed. "Alright, that sounds fair. I'd like to be involved in that conversation."

Bethany was quick to arrange the meeting, ensuring it was scheduled at a time when George could attend. "Let's make sure we're all on the same page and moving forward together," she affirmed, her tone inclusive and conciliatory.

As the lunch break ended and the team dispersed to return to their duties, the incident served as a reminder of the delicate balance required in maintaining team morale and respect. Though the comment had been innocent and without malice, it highlighted the importance of how words could be perceived differently depending on the context and the audience.

Bethany reflected on the situation as she prepared for the afternoon appointments. The quick resolution and her proactive approach had helped avert a deeper conflict, but the lesson was clear: maintaining a positive and supportive team environment required constant vigilance and sensitivity to each team member's contributions and feelings.

The day continued without further incident, and the clinic's atmosphere slowly returned to its usual supportive and collaborative mood. Bethany's handling of the situation reinforced her role as a leader who was not only approachable but also capable of navigating the complexities of interpersonal dynamics within a busy veterinary clinic.

- - - - - - - - -

As the clinic closed for the day, Bethany and Nora found themselves last to leave, a common occurrence given their responsibilities. They used this quiet time to reflect on the events of the past week, particularly focusing on the misunderstandings that had arisen, highlighting areas where communication could be improved.

In Nora's office, surrounded by the soft hum of the computers powering down, they settled into their chairs, each with a cup of coffee in hand. Bethany initiated the conversation, her tone contemplative.

"Nora, this week has been a real eye-opener for me," Bethany began, looking slightly weary but resolved. "I've realized just how delicate the balance is within our team. Even offhand comments can have a bigger impact than expected."

Nora nodded, her expression understanding. "It's part of the learning curve in leadership. The important thing is how we handle these situations. You've done well to address things directly and compassionately."

Bethany sighed, absorbing Nora's affirmation. "I appreciate that, Nora. I guess what's been most revealing is seeing how deeply our team cares—not just about the animals, but about how they contribute to our clinic. George's reaction was a powerful reminder of that."

"Yes, George takes great pride in his work, as he should," Nora responded. "We rely heavily on his skills. It's crucial that we all acknowledge and respect each other's contributions, no matter how seemingly small."

The conversation shifted towards strategies for preventing similar issues in the future. "Do you think regular team meetings focused not just on operational issues but also on interpersonal communication could help?" Bethany proposed, hopeful.

"Absolutely," Nora agreed, her eyes brightening with the suggestion. "A regular forum where everyone can voice concerns, offer suggestions, or even share personal achievements could strengthen our team dynamics. It's about building a culture where everyone feels valued and heard."

Bethany nodded, making a mental note to organize the first of these meetings. "I'll put together an agenda and circulate it by the end of this week. I think this could be a step towards fostering a more open and supportive workplace."

As they wrapped up their discussion, Nora shared a piece of advice that had guided her through her own years of leadership. "Remember, Bethany, the strength of a leader is not just measured by how you celebrate successes but by how you handle challenges. You're proving to be very capable on both fronts."

Grateful for Nora's mentorship, Bethany felt reassured. "Thanks, Nora. It means a lot to hear that from you. I'm committed to making this work, for our team and our community."

They finished their coffee in companionable silence, each lost in their thoughts about the future. As they stood to leave, a mutual sense of understanding and resolve filled the room. The challenges of the week had not only tested but ultimately strengthened their leadership and the clinic's internal community.

Walking out of the clinic together, Bethany felt a renewed sense of purpose. The missteps of the week had led to valuable realizations about the importance of communication and respect within their team. With these lessons in mind, she was ready to help guide the clinic into a future where every team member felt empowered and appreciated.

This day of reflection and realization marked a significant point in Bethany's journey as a co-director, underscoring the complexity and the profound rewards of her role. The clinic, under her and Nora's guidance, was not just a place of healing for animals but a nurturing environment for all who worked there.

The following morning, Bethany arrived at the clinic with a clear plan to solidify the newfound understanding within the team. She wanted to not only address recent tensions but also celebrate the clinic's collaborative spirit. Her first order of business was to formally apologize to George and to ensure such misunderstandings were less likely in the future.

Bethany found George in the back room, meticulously organizing the clinic's medical supplies. She approached him with a friendly, albeit serious, demeanor.

"George, do you have a moment?" she asked, as he turned to greet her.

"Sure, Bethany. What's up?" George replied, his tone open but cautious.

"I wanted to apologize again for the other day—the comment about the equipment. It was thoughtless, and it didn't reflect my appreciation for all the hard work you do here," Bethany began earnestly.

George nodded, acknowledging her apology with a slight smile. "I appreciate that, Bethany. I know you didn't mean anything by it, and I might have reacted too hastily."

Bethany was relieved by his response but wanted to ensure the air was completely clear. "Thank you for understanding, George. I value your expertise and dedication greatly. I'm also putting in place a new protocol where we can all discuss any updates or changes in equipment collectively. I want everyone's input, especially from those of you who use it daily."

"That sounds like a good idea," George responded, visibly pleased with the proactive approach. "I think that will help everyone feel more involved and valued."

Encouraged by the positive interaction, Bethany moved on to her next task. She gathered the entire team in the break room later that morning to announce the implementation of regular team meetings and to openly discuss the importance of communication and respect in their work environment.

"As a team, we've faced a few challenges recently, and I believe these have been learning opportunities for us all," Bethany addressed the group. "I want to ensure we all feel supported and valued here. Starting this month, we'll have regular team meetings to discuss any issues and share successes. It's a chance for everyone to have a voice."

The team listened intently, and many nodded in agreement, pleased with the new initiative. Tom, whose comment had inadvertently sparked the initial tension, added, "I think these meetings are a great idea. It's a good way to keep everyone in the loop and feeling connected."

With the meeting coming to a close, Bethany felt a genuine sense of accomplishment. "Thank you all for your hard work and for your commitment to our clinic and our community. Let's continue to support each other and work together to provide the best care possible."

As the staff dispersed, returning to their duties, the atmosphere in the clinic was noticeably lighter. The team seemed more cohesive, and the morning's meeting had evidently strengthened their collective resolve to work harmoniously.

Bethany spent the rest of the day reflecting on the positive changes that had taken place. She realized that leadership was not just about guiding others but also about listening, learning, and adapting. The day's events had not only helped mend fences but had set the clinic on a path toward a more inclusive and supportive work environment.

By the end of the day, as Bethany reviewed patient files and prepared for the next day, she felt more connected to her team than ever before. The steps taken to address and amend recent missteps had not only restored harmony but had also deepened her own understanding of what it meant to lead with empathy and integrity. The clinic, under her and Nora's guidance, was not just a workplace but a community, each member integral to its success and wellbeing.

Chapter 14
Jake's Dilemma

The morning at Heartsville Veterinary Clinic started quietly, with the soft hum of computers and the distant sound of morning traffic filtering through the open windows. It was a slow start to the day, giving Bethany time to sit in her office, a cup of coffee in hand, lost in thought. Today, unlike most, she had time to reflect on her journey at the clinic, the lessons learned, and the future that lay ahead.

Bethany gazed out the window, watching the early rays of sunlight dance on the leaves of the trees lining the street outside. Her mind replayed the many conversations she had with Nora, the stories of the clinic's early days, the challenges faced, and the victories celebrated. Each story was a building block in her understanding of the clinic's core mission and her role in its continued evolution.

The phone rang, briefly pulling her from her thoughts. It was a routine check-in from one of the technicians about the day's schedule. After confirming a few details, Bethany returned to her reflections, considering how far the clinic had come and the role she now played in its story.

As the morning progressed, the clinic began to buzz with activity. Pets and their owners arrived, each greeted by the friendly staff with a warmth and professionalism that Bethany had helped to foster. Between appointments, she continued her contemplations, pondering the balance between innovative growth and maintaining the warm, community-focused ethos that Nora had established.

Later, as she reviewed patient files, Bethany's thoughts were interrupted by a gentle knock at her office door. It was Nora, coming in with her usual warm smile and a second cup of coffee for Bethany.

"I thought you might need a little refill," Nora said, placing the cup on Bethany's desk.

"Thank you," Bethany smiled, appreciating the gesture. "I've just been thinking about everything we've been through and where we're headed. It's quite a journey we're on."

Nora nodded, taking a seat opposite Bethany. "It is. Reflection is an important part of growth. Taking the time to consider our actions and their impacts helps us guide the clinic in the right direction."

Bethany shared some of her thoughts with Nora, discussing the integration of new practices with the traditional values of the clinic. "I want to make sure we continue to evolve without losing the personal touch that makes this place so special," she expressed.

"That's the key," Nora agreed. "Balancing innovation with tradition. We've always been about more than just medical care; we're a part of the community. Whatever changes we implement, they need to enhance that, not overshadow it."

Their conversation delved deeper into potential initiatives that could further embed the clinic into the fabric of the community. They discussed partnering with local schools for educational programs and creating more interactive community health events.

As the morning turned into afternoon, Bethany felt grounded and inspired by the conversation. The contemplative start to her day, combined with the meaningful dialogue with Nora, had reinforced her commitment to her role and to the clinic's mission. She was more certain than ever that their work touched lives in profound ways, and she was determined to ensure it continued to do so.

Nora stood to leave, her presence always a reassuring constant. "Keep thinking, keep reflecting," she advised as she walked out. "It's how we make sure we're doing the best we can."

Bethany took a final sip of her coffee, her mind clear and focused. The morning of contemplation had provided a valuable pause, a moment to align her goals with the clinic's ethos. As she prepared to step back into the flow of her day, she felt ready to face the challenges ahead, armed with a deeper understanding of the past and a clear vision for the future. The clinic, under her and Nora's stewardship, would continue to thrive as a beacon of care and community connection.

One quiet afternoon at the clinic, as Bethany was sorting through old files in the archive room, she stumbled upon a collection of photographs and documents that chronicled the clinic's early years. Each picture and note painted a vivid picture of the struggles and triumphs that had shaped the clinic into the community cornerstone it was today.

As Bethany flipped through these memories, Nora walked in, her curiosity piqued by the old albums spread across the table. "Ah, you've found our little clinic museum," Nora remarked with a chuckle, pulling up a chair beside Bethany.

Bethany smiled, holding up a photograph of a much younger Nora standing in front of the clinic's first location, a modest building much smaller than their current space. "It's fascinating to see all this history. What was it like back then?"

Nora took the photo, her eyes softening with nostalgia. "It was a different time. We were a small team with big ambitions. Resources were tight, and every day brought new challenges. But there was a sense of adventure, too. We were doing something meaningful."

Listening intently, Bethany could see the pride in Nora's expression. "It looks like you've always been dedicated to the community."

"Absolutely," Nora replied, handing the photo back to Bethany. "From the very beginning, our mission was to not just treat animals, but to educate and support their owners. Much like what we strive for today, but on a much smaller scale."

Bethany picked up another photograph, this one of a community event similar to those the clinic still hosted. "It seems like some things haven't changed much. The community events, the focus on education."

Nora nodded. "Those elements have always been at the core of what we do. They're what bind us to the community. Over the years, we've just gotten better at it, more organized. And now, with your fresh ideas and energy, we're taking it even further."

The conversation turned to a particularly worn document, a proposal for the first major expansion of the clinic. Nora explained the risks they had taken, the uncertainty of that time, and how it had been a turning point for the clinic.

"It was a leap of faith," Nora said. "We weren't sure it would work, but we believed in our mission. Seeing how far we've come, I'm reminded that sometimes, taking a big risk is necessary."

Bethany absorbed every word, realizing that the challenges she faced now were not so different from those Nora had encountered. "Hearing about your experiences, I feel less daunted about the steps we need to take for the future. You've shown that it's possible to evolve and grow, no matter the obstacles."

Nora smiled, clearly pleased with Bethany's insight. "That's exactly right. Every challenge is an opportunity for growth, both for the clinic and for us as individuals. You're doing a wonderful job, Bethany. Just keep believing in the work we do."

As they finished reviewing the archives, Bethany felt a renewed connection to the clinic's history and a deeper appreciation for

Nora's guidance. The past, with its challenges and victories, was not just a record of what had been but a blueprint for what could be.

The day ended with Bethany more inspired than ever. The insights from the past had not only provided perspective but had also steeled her resolve to continue the work with confidence and creativity. As she locked up the archive room, she felt a profound sense of continuity and purpose, ready to add her own chapter to the clinic's enduring legacy.

After their exploration of the clinic's historical records, Nora found herself reflecting more deeply on her journey as the clinic's founder and how it had evolved with the addition of Bethany. Later that week, she invited Bethany to join her for a late afternoon walk in a nearby park, a place where Nora often went to think and unwind.

As they strolled along the path, lined with the vibrant colors of early fall, Nora began to share more about her personal experiences and the evolution of her thoughts over the years.

"When I started the clinic, it was out of a pure love for animals and a desire to serve this community," Nora started, her voice tinged with reminiscence. "But over the years, that mission grew. It became about creating a space where people could learn, find support, and feel connected."

Bethany listened intently, appreciating the rare opportunity to gain insight into Nora's personal motivations. "It's amazing to hear how your vision has expanded. What do you think was the turning point for you?"

Nora paused, considering the question. "There were many, but one significant moment was when we first started hosting community events. Seeing the impact of those events made me realize that our work could reach beyond medical care. It was about community, about building relationships."

"That sense of community is stronger than ever," Bethany noted, linking the past to the present. "It's something I admire deeply and hope to continue and build upon."

"I have no doubt that you will," Nora said with a warm smile. "You've brought fresh ideas and a new perspective that have invigorated the clinic. It's been a joy to see."

The conversation shifted as Bethany asked more about the challenges Nora had faced. "What were some of the toughest challenges, and how did you manage them?"

"Every step of growth brought its challenges," Nora explained. "Financial hurdles, staffing issues, even personal doubts. What helped me through was a strong support network, a clear vision, and sometimes, just the determination to keep going no matter what."

"Your resilience is inspiring," Bethany responded genuinely. "It's comforting to know that it's normal to face such wide-ranging challenges and still find a way through."

As they turned back toward the clinic, Nora shared one last piece of advice. "Always remember why you started. Keep that at the heart of your decisions, and you'll find your way through the toughest times. And remember, you're not alone. You have a team that believes in the vision and in you."

Bethany felt a surge of gratitude for Nora's mentorship. "Thank you, Nora. These conversations mean a lot to me. They help me see the larger picture and my role within it."

Nora nodded, pleased with the mutual understanding and respect that had developed between them. "I'm glad. I see so much of my own journey in yours. It's a pleasure to share these insights with you."

Their walk ended as they approached the clinic, both feeling more connected and committed to their shared goals. Nora felt reassured about the future of the clinic under Bethany's co-leadership, while Bethany felt empowered by Nora's trust and the shared history of their work.

As they parted ways, both carried with them a renewed sense of purpose and the comforting knowledge that their partnership was built on solid ground, enriched by shared experiences and a deep understanding of the clinic's foundational mission. The day closed not just with the setting sun but with an affirmed commitment to continuing the legacy of care and community that Nora had begun.

- - - - - - - - -

As the week drew to a close, Bethany and Nora organized a small gathering for the clinic staff in the late afternoon to discuss the integration of everyone's ideas and insights into the future planning of the clinic. It was an opportunity to ensure that the thoughts and reflections of the entire team were aligned and moving forward together.

The staff gathered in the spacious break room, where Bethany started the meeting with an open invitation for dialogue. "I want to thank everyone for coming together today. This is a chance for us to share our thoughts about where we are and where we're headed as a team and a community."

Nora added her perspective, reinforcing the purpose of the gathering. "We've all been part of this clinic's journey, and your insights and experiences are invaluable as we plan our path forward."

Tom, who had been with the clinic for several years, was the first to speak. "I've been thinking a lot about how we manage patient flow during peak times. I believe we could streamline our processes to reduce wait times and stress for both the pets and their owners."

"That's a great point, Tom," Bethany responded, noting down his suggestions. "Improving efficiency is definitely on our radar, and incorporating direct feedback from your experiences on the floor is crucial."

Liz, a veterinary technician, shared her thoughts on customer engagement. "I've noticed that many of our clients are interested in more than just medical advice. They often need guidance on behavioral issues, dietary needs, and general wellness."

Bethany was quick to acknowledge this. "Absolutely, Liz. Providing holistic care and advice can set us apart and deepen our relationships with the community. Maybe we can think about workshops or even casual meet-ups where clients can discuss these topics."

As the conversation continued, George, the senior technician, brought up the topic of continuing education for the staff. "If we're going to keep up with the latest developments and maintain our high standards, we need to ensure that our team is continually learning and growing."

Nora nodded in agreement. "Investing in our team's education is investing in our clinic's future. We could set up a regular schedule of training sessions and maybe even bring in specialists for advanced topics."

Each team member had something to contribute, from innovative ways to improve day-to-day operations to ideas for community outreach programs. Bethany and Nora listened, engaged, and acknowledged each contribution, making everyone feel heard and valued.

As the meeting drew to a close, Bethany summarized the key points discussed. "Today's conversation has been incredibly productive. We've identified areas for improvement in our operations, client engagement, and professional development. Let's put these ideas into a plan of action."

Nora concluded the meeting with words of encouragement. "This clinic isn't just a workplace; it's a community. Each of you plays a vital role in making it what it is. Let's keep this spirit of cooperation and growth going."

The staff left the meeting feeling motivated and united in their shared goals. Bethany and Nora stayed behind to discuss how best to prioritize and implement the ideas raised.

Reflecting on the convergence of thoughts from the day, Bethany felt a profound sense of fulfillment. "Nora, today really highlighted the strength of our team. With everyone's input, I believe we can make meaningful improvements that will benefit not just our clients and their pets, but all of us here at the clinic."

Nora smiled, satisfied with the progress. "I agree, Bethany. It's clear that when we all work together, reflecting on our past and planning for our future, we can achieve great things."

As they left the clinic that evening, the sunset cast a warm glow over the day's end. The meeting had not only been a discussion of practical steps but a reaffirmation of the clinic's mission and values, a testament to the power of shared goals and mutual respect.

Chapter 15
The Pet Parade

The evening at Heartsville Veterinary Clinic was setting up to be one unlike any other. Tonight, the clinic was hosting its annual appreciation dinner for the staff and their families, a tradition that Nora had started years ago as a heartfelt thank you to her team for their dedication and hard work. This year, however, there was a special twist; the event was also celebrating the clinic's 20th anniversary, making it a milestone event in the clinic's history.

As the sun began to set, casting a golden hue over the clinic, the staff transformed the usual space of consultation rooms and treatment areas into a warmly lit banquet hall. Tables were draped in rich blue tablecloths, candles flickered softly, and photographs from the clinic's history lined the walls, telling the story of decades of community service and animal care.

Bethany, who had been deeply involved in planning the event, took a moment to stand back and take it all in. The clinic had never looked more inviting. As guests began to arrive, she greeted each one with Nora by her side, both sharing their gratitude for the team's hard work and dedication.

"Thank you for coming tonight," Bethany said to one of the clinic's longest-serving technicians as she welcomed him at the door. "This evening is a celebration of all that we've achieved together, and it's all thanks to the efforts of people like you."

Nora, ever the gracious host, echoed Bethany's sentiments. "We wouldn't be where we are without each and every one of you. Tonight is about celebrating our past and looking forward to our future together."

As the evening progressed, the clinic buzzed with laughter and lively conversations. A delicious dinner was served, featuring a menu that Nora had carefully selected to include something for everyone. During the meal, a short video was played, showcasing some of the clinic's most memorable moments and achievements, which brought smiles and even a few tears to those in attendance.

After the video, Nora stood to give a brief speech. "Twenty years ago, I could not have imagined that we would grow into the family we are today," she began, her voice filled with emotion. "This clinic is more than just a place of work. It is a community, a family, and a home to many. Tonight, we celebrate not just what we have accomplished, but who we have become together."

Bethany followed, her own speech reinforcing Nora's message and highlighting the vision for the future. "As we look forward, we see endless opportunities to grow, to learn, and to serve our community. We are committed to innovation and compassion, just as we have always been."

The speeches concluded with a toast, glasses raised high as everyone joined in celebrating the clinic's past achievements and future aspirations. The rest of the evening was filled with music, dancing, and shared stories, deepening the bonds among the team members.

As the event wound down, Bethany found herself reflecting on the significance of the evening. It was more than just an anniversary celebration; it was a reaffirmation of the clinic's values and a renewal of their commitment to each other and the community they served.

The clinic, so often filled with the sounds of barking dogs and the hustle of busy days, was tonight filled with the sound of unity and celebration. As the last guests departed and the lights dimmed, Bethany and Nora shared a quiet moment of satisfaction, knowing that the evening would be remembered as a pivotal moment in the clinic's history—a beautiful night that had perfectly encapsulated the depths of the heart that defined Heartsville Veterinary Clinic.

- - - - - - - - -

As the evening unfolded at Heartsville Veterinary Clinic's 20th-anniversary celebration, the atmosphere was alive with the sharing of stories that painted a vivid picture of the clinic's history and impact. After the formalities and dinner, small groups formed around the room, each buzzing with conversation. Bethany moved from group to group, engaging with the team members and their families, each person eager to share their personal experiences.

In one corner, Bethany found herself listening intently to an animated discussion between some of the clinic's original staff members, including George, who had been with Nora from nearly the beginning.

"It's amazing to think about how much we've grown," George was saying, his eyes twinkling with nostalgia. "I remember when we first opened, and we had just two small treatment rooms. Now look at us!"

Bethany smiled, prompting him to continue. "What's one of your most memorable moments from those early days?"

George laughed, "Oh, there was this one time we had a litter of puppies who had gotten into some mischief, and we spent the entire day chasing them around the clinic. They were hiding under desks, jumping into supply closets, you name it. Nora was just about ready to declare it a puppy holiday."

The group chuckled, and another long-time staff member, Helen, added her own story. "And don't forget the cat that Nora personally rescued from a tree. She climbed right up there in her vet scrubs. Became quite the local hero for that one."

Bethany listened, fascinated by the tales that wove the rich tapestry of the clinic's legacy. "These stories are incredible. It's this spirit and dedication that have built the foundation of our clinic."

Encouraged by Bethany's genuine interest, the group continued to reminisce, each story shedding light on the challenges and triumphs that had shaped their journey.

As the evening progressed, Bethany found herself in another group, this time with newer members of the team, who shared how the clinic's reputation had drawn them to join.

"I heard about the clinic from a conference where Nora spoke about community impact," one of the newer veterinarians, Lisa, shared. "The passion she had for not just animal care but really embedding into the community was what convinced me this was where I wanted to be."

Bethany nodded appreciatively. "It's wonderful to hear that the values Nora established continue to inspire and attract talent like yourself. What has been your most impactful moment since joining?"

Lisa thought for a moment before responding, "There was a case early on when I was here—a young boy and his dog had been in a car accident. The dog was pretty badly hurt, but we managed to save him. Seeing their reunion, knowing we made that moment possible, reaffirmed why I became a vet."

The stories continued, weaving a narrative of dedication, compassion, and community that defined Heartsville Veterinary Clinic. Each person's tale added depth and color to the evening, making it clear that the clinic was more than a workplace—it was a place where meaningful human and animal connections were made.

As the night drew to a close, Bethany stood with Nora, both watching as the staff shared laughs and the last few stories.

"Nora, hearing all these stories tonight, it's clear that your vision has created something truly special here," Bethany said, her voice full of admiration and gratitude.

Nora smiled, her eyes reflecting a deep sense of pride and accomplishment. "It's not just my vision anymore, Bethany. It's ours. And it's every person in this room who carries it forward. Tonight isn't just about looking back—it's about celebrating the present and looking ahead to all we still want to achieve."

Bethany felt a profound connection to everyone at the clinic and a renewed sense of purpose. The stories of the past and present had merged this evening, a vivid reminder of the deep bonds and shared mission that would guide them into the future. As they turned off the lights and locked the clinic doors, both leaders were filled with a sense of accomplishment and anticipation for the continued journey ahead.

- - - - - - - - -

As the evening celebration continued, the casual atmosphere allowed for spontaneous exchanges and heartfelt testimonies. Among the mingling staff and their families, one particular conversation stood out, highlighting the profound impact the clinic had on both its clients and their pets.

Late into the evening, as guests were enjoying desserts and light music played in the background, Bethany noticed a small group gathering around Mrs. Harrow, a long-time client of the clinic. Mrs. Harrow was holding court with a few of the newer staff members, her voice soft but clear in the quiet buzz of conversations.

Bethany approached the group, curious about the story being shared. As she drew closer, she heard Mrs. Harrow speaking about her late golden retriever, Max, who had been a beloved patient at the clinic.

"And there was this one time," Mrs. Harrow was recounting, "when Max fell terribly ill with a mysterious infection. It was Nora and her team who stayed up all night with him, trying every possible treatment until they found the right one. They saved his life that night, and gave us many more years with him. It wasn't just their knowledge, but their dedication that made all the difference."

Bethany joined the group, touched by the story. "Mrs. Harrow, thank you for sharing that. It's stories like yours that remind us why we do what we do every day."

Mrs. Harrow smiled warmly at Bethany. "I've always been grateful to this clinic. It's not just a place to get medical help—it's a place where you know everyone truly cares."

One of the newer veterinarians, Dr. Jensen, who had joined the group, asked, "Mrs. Harrow, what do you think makes this clinic different from others you've visited?"

Without hesitation, Mrs. Harrow replied, "It's the heart. Nora, and now Bethany, have created an environment that feels like family. When Max was sick, it wasn't just his health they were concerned about—it was how we were coping as a family."

The conversation opened up a wider discussion among the group about the role of veterinary clinics in supporting not just the physical health of pets but also the emotional well-being of the families they belong to.

As they talked, Nora joined the circle, having overheard the last part of the conversation. "Thank you, Mrs. Harrow. Your words mean a lot to us, and they reinforce the values we strive to uphold here."

Bethany, reflecting on the interaction, felt a deep sense of pride and responsibility. The unplanned testimony had not only validated the work being done at the clinic but also underscored the emotional depth of their mission.

The evening gradually wound down, with guests starting to say their goodbyes. Bethany and Nora took a moment to debrief and reflect on the testimonials and stories shared throughout the night.

"It's evenings like these that truly show the depth of our impact," Bethany remarked, helping Nora tidy up some of the remaining refreshments.

Nora nodded, "Indeed. And it's a reminder of the responsibility we carry, not just to heal but to comfort and support our community."

As the last of the guests departed and the lights of the clinic dimmed, Bethany and Nora left the building together. The unplanned testimonies and heartfelt exchanges from the evening had strengthened their resolve and commitment to their work.

Driving home, Bethany felt more connected to the clinic and its community than ever before. The stories and appreciations shared by clients like Mrs. Harrow were not just affirmations of the past but beacons for the future, guiding her and Nora as they continued to navigate the depths of the heart that defined their mission.

- - - - - - - - -

After the anniversary celebration, as the final guests departed and the staff began to clean up, Bethany and Nora decided to take a moment for themselves. They stepped outside the clinic into the cool night, where the stars were just beginning to pepper the dark sky, providing a serene backdrop for a moment of reflection.

They walked to a small bench near the clinic, a spot that offered a view of the night sky and a quiet space away from the day's activities. Sitting down, they each took a deep breath, absorbing the calm of the evening.

"That was quite a celebration," Bethany began, breaking the silence with a contented sigh. "It’s amazing to see how many lives we’ve touched, how many stories are interwoven with our own here at the clinic."

Nora nodded, her eyes reflecting the starlight. "It is. Every one of those stories is a reminder of why we do what we do. And hearing them from the people we've helped adds a whole new layer of meaning to our work."

Bethany turned to Nora, her expression thoughtful. "You know, Nora, hearing Mrs. Harrow and others speak tonight, it struck me just how much trust people place in us. It's a huge responsibility, but also a privilege."

Nora responded with a gentle smile. "It is a privilege. And you've embraced it beautifully, Bethany. You've brought so much to the clinic—your energy, your ideas, your compassion. It's rejuvenating, not just for the clinic but for me personally."

"I've learned so much from you, Nora. Your guidance has been invaluable," Bethany said, her tone full of gratitude. "The way you've melded a strong business with a heart for community service is inspiring. It's something I hope to continue and build upon."

The conversation shifted as they discussed the future—plans for the clinic, community initiatives, and ways to further enhance their service to the community. Nora shared some of her aspirations, things she hadn't yet started, and Bethany listened eagerly, excited about the possibilities.

"I've been thinking about starting a scholarship program for aspiring veterinarians in our community," Nora revealed, her eyes alight with enthusiasm. "I think it could make a real difference, opening doors for those who want to follow in our footsteps but might not have the resources."

"That sounds incredible," Bethany responded, visibly excited by the idea. "It's a perfect extension of our mission. Education, community support, animal care—it ties everything together."

As they spoke, the stars above seemed to shine a little brighter, mirroring the spark of inspiration and shared purpose between them. They discussed practical steps for the scholarship program, potential partnerships with local schools, and community outreach strategies to ensure the program's success.

Finally, as the night deepened, they stood up from the bench, feeling refreshed and reinvigorated. "These moments, these conversations under the stars—they're just as important as any work we do inside the clinic," Nora said as they began walking back.

Bethany agreed, "Absolutely. It's these moments that fuel our passion and remind us why we started. I'm looking forward to all we will accomplish together."

As they reached the clinic door, they shared a look of mutual respect and anticipation for the future. The night's reflections under the stars had not only deepened their bond but had also reaffirmed their commitment to the clinic and the community.

With a final glance at the night sky, they stepped back inside, ready to turn their reflections into actions, guided by the knowledge that they were making a real difference in the lives of both animals and people. The clinic, under their care, was not just a place of healing but a beacon of hope and a hub of community connection.

Chapter 16
A New Perspective

The day of the Heartsville Pet Parade dawned bright and clear, with the kind of crisp autumn air that made the town's colorful leaves seem even more vibrant. The parade was an annual tradition, a beloved event that brought the entire community together in a celebration of their furry companions. But this year, the stakes were higher. The parade had been transformed into a fundraiser, an effort to support the local businesses that had been hit hard by the mill's closure. The town needed this event to be a success, and from the moment Jake stepped onto Main Street, he could feel the energy crackling in the air.

Vendors had set up booths along the sidewalks, offering everything from homemade treats to handcrafted goods. The scent of popcorn and fresh-baked pies mingled with the crispness of the autumn leaves, creating an intoxicating blend that drew people in from all directions. The streets were already crowded, with families and their pets arriving early to find the best spots to watch the parade. Children ran ahead, clutching balloons shaped like their favorite animals, their laughter ringing out like music.

Jake stood near the center of the street, his camera slung over one shoulder and his notebook in hand. He had been to countless events like this, covered them with the detachment that came from years of experience. But today felt different. Today, he wasn't just an observer; he was part of something larger, something that went beyond the superficial details of a small-town parade.

As he looked around, Jake saw familiar faces everywhere. There was Mrs. Thompson, the elderly woman who had helped organize the event, her eyes sparkling with pride as she watched the preparations unfold. Nearby, a group of teenagers, led by Kyle, were busy setting up a game booth, their excitement palpable. And at the heart of it all was Nora, moving through the crowd with the grace and confidence of a natural leader, her smile warm and reassuring as she stopped to talk with each person she passed.

Jake watched her for a moment, admiring the way she seemed to bring out the best in everyone around her. She had been the driving force behind this event, rallying the town when they needed it most. And now, as the parade was about to begin, he could see the fruits of her labor—Heartsville was alive with hope and determination, a town refusing to be beaten by adversity.

The sound of a marching band tuning up in the distance signaled that the parade was about to start. Jake made his way to the edge of the street, where a line of children and their parents had gathered, their pets in tow. Dogs of all shapes and sizes were decked out in costumes, from regal lions to cuddly teddy bears, their tails wagging eagerly as they awaited their turn in the spotlight.

"Jake!" Nora's voice called out, drawing him out of his thoughts. She approached him with a bright smile, her own golden retriever, Max, trotting beside her, proudly sporting a red bandana. "What do you think? Quite the turnout, huh?"

Jake smiled, nodding in agreement. "It's incredible, Nora. You've really pulled this off."

"It wasn't just me," she replied, her eyes scanning the crowd with a mixture of pride and relief. "Everyone came together to make this happen. That's what makes Heartsville special."

Jake followed her gaze, taking in the scene around him with a renewed sense of appreciation. This wasn't just about the pets or the parade—it was about the resilience of a community that refused to give up, even when the odds were against them. As he watched the first floats start to move down the street, each one more colorful and creative than the last, he found himself focusing not on the surface details, but on the deeper meaning behind it all.

The parade was a riot of color and sound, with local businesses sponsoring floats that showcased their unique personalities. There was the bakery's float, shaped like a giant cupcake with frosting-covered children waving to the crowd. The general store had gone all out, creating a replica of Heartsville in miniature, complete with tiny figurines of the townspeople, including a tiny version of Nora standing proudly in front of her clinic.

The crowd cheered as each float passed by, but it wasn't just about the spectacle. Every cheer, every wave, every laugh that echoed through the streets was a testament to the strength of the community, to their collective determination to keep Heartsville alive and thriving. And Jake, standing in the midst of it all, felt a sense of connection that he hadn't experienced in years.

As the parade wound down and the fundraiser began in earnest, with auction items being displayed and raffle tickets being sold, Jake found himself walking through the crowd, capturing moments with his camera. He photographed the smiles, the small acts of kindness, the way people came together to support one another. And as he did, he realized that his article was already writing itself, not with the words of cynicism or detachment he had once relied on, but with the truth of what he was witnessing.

This was more than just a story about a pet parade. It was about a town that had faced hardship and responded with unity, creativity, and an unbreakable spirit. It was about people who believed in each other, who were willing to fight for their way of life. And it was about a journalist who had come to Heartsville expecting to find a story of decline, but who had instead found something far more powerful.

The day ended with the auction raising more money than anyone had anticipated, and the parade being hailed as the best in years. But for Jake, the real success of the day was the story he now knew he needed to tell—a story not just about a town in trouble, but about a town that refused to be defined by its troubles. A town that, against all odds, was determined to keep moving forward.

- - - - - - - - -

The Pet Parade had wound down, and the fundraiser was in full swing. Heartsville's Main Street had transformed into a bustling fairground, with stalls lined up along the sidewalks, each one offering something different—handmade crafts, baked goods, raffle tickets, and games. The energy was infectious, with laughter and lively conversation filling the air. Jake Carter walked through the crowd, his notebook in one hand and his camera in the other, capturing the day's events from every angle. But unlike before, today's work felt different.

"Jake, over here!" A cheerful voice pulled him from his thoughts, and he turned to see Kyle, one of the teenagers he'd met during the search for Sparky, waving him over to a booth filled with jars of homemade jam. "You've got to try some of this! Mrs. Thompson makes the best jam in town."

Jake smiled and made his way over, accepting a small spoonful of the sweet spread from Mrs. Thompson herself. "You weren't kidding, Kyle. This is amazing."

Mrs. Thompson beamed, her wrinkled face glowing with pride. "Thank you, Jake. You know, it's not just about the taste—it's about the tradition. My grandmother taught me how to make this jam, and now I pass the recipe down to anyone willing to learn."

Jake nodded, jotting down a few notes. But as he did, he couldn't help but notice the warmth in Mrs. Thompson's eyes, the sense of continuity and connection that she embodied. This wasn't just about jam—it was about the way the people of

Heartsville held onto their history, their shared identity, and how that identity was woven into every aspect of their lives.

He moved on, stopping to interview more participants. There was Mr. Harris, proudly showing off his woodworking skills at a booth displaying hand-carved furniture. "It's tough, losing the mill," Mr. Harris admitted, running a hand over the smooth surface of a wooden chair. "But I'm not giving up. None of us are. We've been through hard times before, and we'll get through this one, too."

Jake's pen hovered over his notebook, hesitating before he wrote down Mr. Harris's words. There was a determination in the man's voice that resonated with Jake on a level he hadn't expected. He had come here to document the struggles of a small town, but what he was finding was something far more complex, far more human. These weren't just stories of hardship—they were stories of resilience, of hope, of people refusing to let go of what mattered most to them.

As the afternoon wore on, Jake found himself increasingly conflicted. His editor, Marlene, had made it clear that she expected a critical piece, something that would capture the harsh realities of Heartsville's situation. But the more Jake immersed himself in the event, the more he realized that the narrative he had been sent to uncover didn't match the reality in front of him.

He made his way to the heart of the event, where Nora was overseeing the auction. She was in her element, effortlessly moving between conversations, offering words of encouragement, and ensuring that everything ran smoothly. Jake watched her for a moment, his heart tightening with a mixture of admiration and something deeper—something that made him question his role here.

"Nora, can I have a minute?" he called out, stepping up to her as she finished a conversation with one of the bidders.

She turned to him, her smile warm but tinged with exhaustion. "Of course, Jake. What's on your mind?"

He hesitated, unsure how to put his feelings into words. "I've been talking to people all day, getting their stories. And... it's not what I expected. I thought I'd be writing about a town on the brink, about how everyone's struggling to hold on. But that's not what I'm seeing. These people, they're not giving up. They're fighting back, in their own way."

Nora's smile softened, and she nodded. "That's Heartsville for you. We've never been the kind of town to roll over when things get tough. We come together, we find a way. That's what this fundraiser is all about—showing that we're not going anywhere, no matter what."

Jake looked down at his notebook, the pages filled with quotes, observations, and notes that all pointed to one thing: Heartsville was more than just a struggling town. It was a community with heart, with strength, with a spirit that couldn't be easily broken. And for the first time in his career, Jake found himself struggling to maintain the detachment that had always served him so well.

"What if my editor doesn't see it that way?" Jake asked, his voice low. "What if she wants something more... dramatic? More focused on the negative?"

Nora studied him for a moment, her expression thoughtful. "Jake, you're the one who's here. You're the one seeing it firsthand. Your job is to tell the truth as you see it, not as someone else expects it to be. If the story you're finding isn't what you thought it would be, that's okay. Sometimes the best stories are the ones we don't expect."

Her words hit home, resonating with the internal struggle that had been building inside him all day. "It's just... I didn't come here to get emotionally involved. I'm supposed to be objective."

Nora reached out, placing a hand on his arm. "Being objective doesn't mean being disconnected, Jake. It doesn't mean you can't care. In fact, caring might be what helps you tell the story in the most honest way. You've seen what this town is going through, but you've also seen how we're fighting to stay strong. That's the truth. And if you tell that truth, I think your editor will understand."

Jake looked into her eyes, feeling the sincerity of her words. He nodded slowly, the tension inside him beginning to ease. "You're right. I just... I need to figure out how to balance it all."

"You will," Nora said confidently. "You've got a good heart, Jake. Trust it. It'll guide you to the right story."

As she turned back to the auction, Jake watched her for a moment longer, feeling the weight of his decision settle over him. The truth was clear, even if it wasn't what he had expected. Heartsville wasn't just a town in trouble—it was a town with a fighting chance. And that was the story he needed to tell, no matter how complicated it might be.

He took a deep breath, flipping to a new page in his notebook, and began to write. This time, he wasn't just documenting facts—he was capturing the spirit of a place that had found its way into his heart. And in doing so, he realized that he had become part of the story, too.

Jake sat at the small wooden desk in his rented room at the Heartsville Inn, the glow of his laptop screen casting a faint light in the otherwise darkened room. Outside, the town was quiet, the excitement of the day having finally settled into a peaceful night. But inside, Jake's mind was anything but peaceful.

His fingers hovered over the keyboard, the cursor blinking on the blank page. He had spent hours jotting down notes, reflecting on the day's events, and now it was time to turn those thoughts into words. But the task felt heavier than it ever had before. This article was different. Heartsville was different.

With a deep breath, Jake began to type, the words coming slowly at first.

"Heartsville, a small town nestled in the heart of America, is facing a challenge that many similar communities know all too well—the closure of a local mill, the economic lifeblood of the town. But rather than succumbing to despair, the people of Heartsville are doing what they've always done: coming together, supporting one another, and finding hope in the face of adversity."

Jake paused, rereading the opening paragraph. It was a far cry from the sensational lead his editor, Marlene, would have expected. There was no mention of desperation, no focus on the potential downfall of a struggling town. Instead, the emphasis was on resilience, on community—on the very qualities that had drawn Jake in over the past few weeks.

He continued typing, the pace of his writing picking up as he recounted the events of the Pet Parade and fundraiser.

"The annual Pet Parade, which this year doubled as a fundraiser for local businesses, was a testament to the spirit of Heartsville. Despite the challenges ahead, the event was a resounding success, drawing in more participants than ever before. It wasn't just a parade; it was a celebration of what makes Heartsville special: the people. From the homemade jams of Mrs. Thompson to the handcrafted furniture of Mr. Harris, the town's talent and dedication were on full display. But more than that, the event showcased a community that refuses to give up."

As Jake wrote, he felt a growing sense of unease. This wasn't the hard-hitting, dramatic story Marlene had asked for. He could already hear her voice in his head, questioning the angle, pushing for something with more edge. But how could he write something that wasn't true to what he had seen, what he had felt?

His phone buzzed on the desk, the screen lighting up with a message from Marlene: *"Need a draft ASAP, Jake. Hope you've got something juicy."*

Jake stared at the message, his heart sinking. *Juicy.* That was the word she had used. But there was nothing juicy about Heartsville's story—at least not in the way Marlene wanted. It wasn't about scandal or sensationalism; it was about real people facing real challenges with a strength that was both humbling and inspiring.

He resumed typing, his fingers moving more deliberately now, as if each word carried the weight of his conviction.

"The true story of Heartsville isn't one of decline or defeat. It's a story of resilience, of a community that rallies together when times are tough. The people of this town have shown that they are more than the sum of their struggles. They are a testament to the power of unity and hope in the face of uncertainty."

Jake leaned back in his chair, reading over what he had written. It was honest, it was real, but it wasn't what Marlene would want. He could already predict her reaction—disappointment, frustration, maybe even a demand for a rewrite. But how could he betray the people of Heartsville by turning their story into something it wasn't?

A knock on his door startled him, breaking his concentration. Jake frowned, glancing at the clock—it was late, too late for visitors. He got up and opened the door to find Nora standing there, her expression a mix of concern and determination.

"Nora? What are you doing here?" Jake asked, surprised.

"I was just walking home and saw your light on," she said softly, stepping inside when he motioned for her to enter. "I figured you were working on your article."

"Yeah," Jake admitted, running a hand through his hair. "I'm trying to, anyway."

Nora glanced at the laptop screen, then back at him. "It's not going the way you thought it would, is it?"

Jake shook his head, frustration evident in his voice. "No, it's not. I'm trying to write what I believe is the truth, but I know it's not what my editor wants. She's expecting something... I don't know, more dramatic, more focused on the negatives. But that's not the story I want to tell."

Nora took a seat on the edge of the bed, her eyes never leaving his. "Then don't. Write the story that's true to you, Jake. You've seen what this town is about. You've been part of it, whether you realize it or not. That's the story people need to hear."

Jake sighed, sitting down next to her, his hands clasped together. "But what if it's not enough? What if she rejects it?"

Nora's hand found his, squeezing it gently. "You can't control what she'll do, but you can control what you write. If you believe in the story, if you know it's the truth, then you have to stand by it. Even if it means taking a risk."

Jake looked at her, feeling the weight of her words sink in. She was right. He couldn't compromise his integrity for the sake of sensationalism. The story of Heartsville was worth telling, even if it wasn't the one Marlene expected.

He nodded slowly, determination settling in. "You're right, Nora. I can't sell these people short. They deserve better than that."

Nora smiled, a warm, encouraging smile that made the tension in his chest ease. "I know it's not easy, but you've got this, Jake. Just tell the truth. That's all anyone can ask."

Jake squeezed her hand in return, feeling a renewed sense of purpose. "Thank you, Nora. I needed to hear that."

She stood, giving his hand one last squeeze before letting go. "You're welcome. Now, go finish that article. I have a feeling it's going to be something special."

Jake watched as she left, the door closing softly behind her. He turned back to his laptop, the cursor still blinking on the screen. With a deep breath, he resumed typing, pouring everything he had into the words. This wasn't just about Heartsville anymore—it was about his own integrity, about the kind of journalist he wanted to be.

The draft he submitted would be true, honest, and real. And whatever happened next, Jake knew he could stand by it.

- - - - - - - - -

Jake sat at the edge of Heartsville's small town park, the soft glow of the streetlights casting long shadows over the empty benches and quiet pathways. The eventful day had finally drawn to a close, and the town, after hours of celebration and community effort, had slipped into a peaceful stillness. Yet, peace was the last thing Jake felt. His mind was a whirlpool of thoughts, each pulling him in a different direction, making it impossible to find any clarity.

He glanced at the document on his laptop, the cursor blinking on the final sentence of his draft. It was a good article—honest, reflective of the day's events, and true to what he had experienced in Heartsville. But was it enough? Would Marlene accept a story that didn't fit the usual narrative of struggle and drama? Or would she push him to rewrite it, to focus on the more sensational aspects that she knew would sell?

The sound of footsteps on the gravel path pulled Jake from his thoughts. He looked up to see Nora approaching, her silhouette outlined by the dim light. She had changed out of the clothes she'd worn for the parade and fundraiser, now dressed casually in jeans and a sweater, but the warmth in her expression remained the same.

"Hey," she greeted softly as she reached him, taking a seat beside him on the bench. "Thought I might find you here."

Jake offered a faint smile. "Couldn't sleep," he admitted, closing his laptop. "Too much on my mind."

Nora nodded, her eyes searching his. "Want to talk about it?"

Jake hesitated, but the weight of his thoughts was too heavy to carry alone. "It's this article," he began, his voice low. "I wrote what I believe is the truth—about Heartsville, about today, about everything I've seen here. But I don't know if it's the story my editor wants. I'm afraid she'll ask me to rewrite it, to make it something it's not."

Nora listened quietly, her expression thoughtful. "And how do you feel about that?"

Jake ran a hand through his hair, frustration evident in his posture. "I don't want to compromise what I've written. But at the same time, I know I have a job to do. Marlene expects something that'll grab attention, something dramatic. I just... I don't know how to balance that with what I know is right."

Nora turned slightly, facing him fully. "Jake, I can't tell you what to do. This is your decision, and whatever choice you make, you'll have to live with it. But I can tell you this: you have to be true to yourself, to your values. If you don't believe in what you're writing, it's going to show. People can tell when something isn't authentic."

Jake looked at her, the sincerity in her words resonating deeply. "But what if staying true to myself costs me my job? Or damages my career?"

Nora smiled gently, a knowing look in her eyes. "You've got to ask yourself what's more important—your career or your integrity. Because at the end of the day, you have to live with the choices you make. If you compromise on this, it might seem like a small thing now, but it could lead to bigger compromises down the line. And soon, you might not recognize the person you've become."

Her words hung in the air, sinking into Jake's consciousness. He knew she was right, but that didn't make the decision any easier. "I just wish it didn't have to be this hard," he murmured, his voice heavy with the weight of the situation.

Nora reached out, placing a hand on his arm, her touch both comforting and grounding. "Life's full of hard choices, Jake. But those choices are what define us. I know you're struggling with this, but I also know you're a good man, with a good heart. Trust that. Trust yourself."

Jake met her gaze, the honesty in her eyes reflecting back at him. He had come to Heartsville as an outsider, someone who believed he could observe and report without getting emotionally involved. But now, as he sat beside Nora, he realized just how deeply he had become entangled in the lives of the people here. And maybe that wasn't such a bad thing.

He nodded slowly, the fog of doubt beginning to clear. "You're right," he said, his voice steadier now. "I can't compromise on this. I have to write the truth, even if it's not what Marlene wants to hear."

Nora's smile widened, a look of pride in her eyes. "I knew you'd make the right choice."

Jake looked out over the park, the quiet serenity of the night matching the calm that was slowly settling within him. "Thank you, Nora. For everything. You've helped me see things in a way I never would have on my own."

She squeezed his arm gently before letting go. "You've done the same for me, Jake. We've both learned a lot from each other."

They sat in companionable silence for a few moments, the weight of the day's events easing with each passing second. For the first time in weeks, Jake felt a sense of peace, a clarity that had been elusive for so long.

As he opened his laptop again, ready to finish his draft and send it off, Nora stood, giving him one last encouraging smile. "You've got this, Jake. Just be true to yourself. The rest will follow."

Jake watched her walk away, her figure blending into the shadows of the trees. He knew the decision he had made was the right one, even if it came with risks. He would submit the article as he had written it—honest, real, and true to the spirit of Heartsville.

And whatever happened next, he knew he could face it with integrity. For the first time, he was writing not just as a journalist, but as someone who cared—someone who had become part of the story.

Chapter 17
Building Bridges

In the wake of proposing a dual-location strategy for the clinic, Bethany and Nora recognized the importance of strengthening their alliances both within and outside the clinic. They set out to engage more deeply with the community and their staff, ensuring that everyone felt involved and invested in the clinic's future.

Bethany organized a series of meetings with local community leaders, including representatives from neighborhood associations, schools, and other local businesses. Her aim was to gather support for the clinic's expansion and to reassure the community that their interests remained a priority.

At the first of these meetings, held in the community center, Bethany presented the dual-location plan. "Our goal is to expand our services without losing the personal touch that has defined our clinic for over twenty years," she explained to the gathered audience. "By maintaining our current location and opening a second, more advanced facility, we believe we can serve our community even better."

A local business owner, Mr. Chen, was quick to express his support. "We've seen how much good your clinic does for the area," he said. "I think having more resources at your disposal will only increase the positive impact you have on our community."

Bethany was grateful for the endorsement, which seemed to ease some of the community's apprehensions. "Thank you, Mr. Chen. We're committed to being a partner in this community's wellbeing, not just a service provider."

Meanwhile, Nora focused on internal efforts, holding workshops with the clinic staff to discuss the logistical and operational changes that the dual-location strategy would entail. During one workshop, she addressed the staff's concerns about workload and responsibilities.

"I want to ensure that this expansion doesn't just mean more work for everyone," Nora stated clearly. "It's about working smarter, not harder. We will be hiring additional staff for the new location, and we'll provide training to make sure everyone feels confident in their roles."

George, always a voice of practicality, raised a concern. "It's important that we maintain our standards during this transition. How do we ensure that the quality of care doesn't drop as we grow?"

Nora nodded, acknowledging the validity of his point. "Absolutely, George. Quality control will be more important than ever. We'll implement regular reviews and feedback loops at both locations. And I'll be personally overseeing the integration to ensure our standards are met."

The proactive communication seemed to reassure the staff, and their feedback became increasingly positive as they discussed ways to optimize workflow and patient care across two locations.

As the week progressed, Bethany and Nora saw the fruits of their efforts to strengthen alliances. The community's response grew more supportive, buoyed by clear communication and visible commitments to local engagement. Similarly, the clinic staff expressed a renewed sense of purpose and teamwork, inspired by the leadership's transparency and inclusiveness.

One afternoon, after a particularly encouraging community meeting, Bethany and Nora met to discuss the feedback they had received.

"It feels like we're really building momentum," Bethany remarked, a note of relief in her voice. "The community and our team seem genuinely excited about what we can achieve with this expansion."

Nora smiled, pleased with their progress. "It's a testament to your hard work and vision, Bethany. And it's proof that when we listen and work together, we can overcome any challenge."

The meeting ended with both leaders feeling more confident than ever in their decision. They had not only managed to maintain their clinic's core values but had also laid the groundwork for future growth that would benefit both the clinic and the community.

As they left the meeting room, they knew that the challenges ahead would require continued diligence and cooperation, but the strengthened alliances within their team and with their community provided a strong foundation to build upon. The rest of the day passed in a flurry of activity, but the undercurrent of unity and shared vision was a constant reminder of the positive changes on the horizon.

Recognizing the need to broaden their message and garner wider support, Bethany decided to leverage the media to highlight the clinic's expansion plans and its continued commitment to the community. She arranged an interview with a local newspaper known for its community-focused reporting.

On the day of the interview, Bethany met with Janet Lee, a seasoned journalist who had covered the clinic's activities in the past. They sat down in the quiet back room of the clinic, away from the day's usual hustle.

"Thank you for taking the time to speak with me today, Bethany," Janet began, setting up her recorder. "I've heard about your plans to expand. Could you explain what this expansion entails and how you think it will impact the community?"

Bethany, poised and clear, responded, "Absolutely, Janet. We are planning to open a second location that will allow us to offer more specialized services that are currently not available locally. This includes advanced surgical procedures, specialized diagnostics, and comprehensive emergency care. However, we are committed to maintaining our existing clinic as a community-focused center, where we continue our wellness programs and routine care."

Janet nodded, jotting down notes. "So, you're essentially doubling your capabilities. What prompted this decision?"

"Our community's needs are growing, and we've reached a point where we need to expand to effectively meet those needs," Bethany explained. "But we're mindful of our roots. That's why we're keeping our original location open and integrated into our operation."

"That's an interesting approach," Janet remarked. "How are you planning to manage the potential challenges that come with running two locations?"

Bethany smiled, acknowledging the complexity of the task. "It's certainly going to be a challenge, but we're planning carefully. We'll be hiring additional staff and using technology to integrate operations across both locations. Our aim is to ensure that our standards of care and community involvement do not diminish but instead grow stronger."

Janet's next question touched on a potential concern. "There's often worry in the community when local businesses expand. How are you addressing concerns that the clinic might lose its personal touch?"

"We're very aware of those concerns," Bethany affirmed. "That's why we're involving our community every step of the way. We're holding town hall meetings, conducting surveys, and I'm personally available to discuss any concerns. Our commitment is to remain as accessible and community-focused as ever."

Janet seemed impressed. "It sounds like you've got a solid plan in place. How about the funding for this expansion? Are there investors involved, and what are their roles?"

"We are partnering with local investors who share our vision for community health. They are fully supportive of our dual mission to expand services while maintaining our community presence. It's important to us that any financial partnerships do not alter the clinic's values or our operational independence."

As the interview drew to a close, Janet stood, gathering her notes. "Thank you, Bethany. It's clear that you and your team are dedicated to both growth and your foundational principles. I think our readers will find this very reassuring."

Bethany stood as well, offering a handshake. "Thank you, Janet. We appreciate the opportunity to share our story and keep the community informed. We're excited about what the future holds and are eager to continue serving our community."

After Janet left, Bethany felt a sense of accomplishment. The interview had been an opportunity to articulate the clinic's goals and reassure the community that their interests were at the forefront of all planning and decision-making. As she returned to her office, she felt confident that the media outreach would play a crucial role in shaping public perception and support for the clinic's ambitious plans.

- - - - - - - - -

The tension that had been brewing over the clinic's expansion plans finally came to a head during a staff meeting that was initially intended to finalize the integration strategies for the two locations. As Bethany addressed the team, outlining the final steps and the expected roles everyone would play, it became evident that not all concerns had been fully assuaged.

During the meeting, George, a long-standing and highly respected technician, raised a significant concern that captured the attention of the entire team. "Bethany, I know we've talked a lot about this expansion and what it means for the community, but I'm still worried about how this will change our workload and the dynamics here. Are we really prepared to maintain our standards under this new pressure?"

Bethany appreciated George's forthrightness and recognized this as a crucial moment to affirm her leadership. "George, thank you for bringing this up. It's vital that we all feel confident in our ability to handle these changes. I want to assure you that we are not just expanding physically but also bolstering our support systems. We're bringing in additional resources, including more staff, to ensure that no one feels overwhelmed."

Lisa, one of the veterinarians who had initially supported the expansion, joined the discussion, expressing her endorsement of Bethany's approach. "I've seen the detailed plans, and while the changes are significant, the leadership has laid out a clear path to manage this transition effectively. I believe this can work if we all support each other through it."

However, Tom, another technician, still seemed unconvinced. "But what about the personal touch we're known for? Won't we risk losing that as we grow bigger and possibly more impersonal?"

Bethany acknowledged his concerns with a nod. "That's a valid fear, Tom. But part of our strategy involves specific training on maintaining client relationships and personal care standards. Growth doesn't have to mean becoming impersonal. In fact, it's an opportunity to spread our core values further."

The conversation shifted towards constructive dialogue, with team members expressing their thoughts and suggesting ways to preserve the clinic's ethos. Nora, who had been quietly observing the exchanges, finally spoke up, lending her support to Bethany.

"Nora here, and I've been through several phases of growth with this clinic. Each time, we've faced doubts and fears, much like now. But at the heart of our success has been our commitment to our core values and to each other. Bethany is leading us with that same commitment."

Her endorsement helped steer the mood towards a more hopeful outlook. Bethany seized this moment to further solidify her stance and reassure her team. "Thank you, Nora. I'm here not just as your leader but as someone who believes deeply in what we do. This expansion is about bringing what we do best to more pets and families while ensuring we all grow together, not apart."

As the meeting concluded, Bethany proposed setting up a follow-up session to address any additional concerns and to continue the dialogue. "Let's keep this conversation going. Your feedback is crucial as we navigate these changes."

The team left the meeting room with a lot to think about, but there was a general sense of cautious optimism that had not been present at the start. Bethany felt the weight of her responsibilities but also a renewed confidence in her ability to lead the clinic through this challenging yet promising phase.

The test of leadership had indeed been stringent, but by fostering open communication and addressing concerns head-on, Bethany had managed to keep her team aligned and focused on the collective mission. As she returned to her office, she felt more determined than ever to ensure the clinic's expansion would be a success, not just in terms of scale but, more importantly, in maintaining the trust and support of her team and community.

The challenges surrounding the clinic's expansion continued to unfold, culminating in a direct confrontation with Mr. Hartman, a local council member known for his skepticism about the proliferation of commercial developments in community-centric areas. Hartman had been vocal in his criticisms and now sought to directly challenge the clinic's expansion plans, citing concerns about commercialization overshadowing community welfare.

The confrontation occurred during a community forum held at the local town hall, a meeting intended to gather public opinion on the clinic's proposed expansion. The room was packed with residents, clinic staff, and local business owners, all of whom were eager to understand the implications of the clinic's new direction.

As Bethany prepared to present the benefits of the dual-location strategy, Hartman stood up, his voice carrying across the crowded room. "While I understand the clinic's intentions to expand, we must consider the broader impact on our community. Are we sacrificing our small-town feel and accessibility for the sake of growth?"

Bethany, standing at the podium, addressed his concerns directly. "Mr. Hartman, thank you for your concern, which I assure you we all share. Our plan for expansion is not just about growth but about enhancing our ability to serve our community more effectively without losing our personal touch."

Hartman, unconvinced, pressed on. "But how can you guarantee that this expansion won't lead to the clinic becoming more commercialized? How do we know that this won't just open the door for more businesses to come in and change the face of our town?"

Bethany responded calmly, aware that the community's eyes were on her. "Our commitment to this community is unwavering. The new facility will allow us to provide services we currently can't, due to space and technology limitations. As for commercialization, we are planning strict guidelines on how the clinic operates and grows, ensuring that our core values of community service and accessibility are upheld."

A local resident chimed in, offering support to Bethany. "I've been taking my pets to Heartsville Veterinary Clinic for years. I've always appreciated their personal approach and deep commitment to animal welfare. If they say they'll maintain their standards, I believe them."

The debate continued, with Hartman raising questions about traffic, environmental impacts, and potential disruptions. Bethany addressed each point, supported by data and testimonials from other community members who spoke about the positive impacts the clinic had on their lives.

As the meeting drew to a close, Bethany offered a final reassurance. "We invite all of you to visit our existing clinic, to talk to our staff, and see firsthand how we operate. We're committed to transparency and community dialogue throughout this process."

Hartman, while still skeptical, thanked Bethany for her responses. The crowd began to disperse, with many attendees expressing their support for Bethany's thoughtful and comprehensive handling of the situation.

Back at the clinic, Nora congratulated Bethany on her poise and effectiveness. "You handled that very well. It's not easy to face such direct challenges, but you did it with grace and professionalism."

Bethany felt a mixture of relief and determination. "Thank you, Nora. It's important that the community knows we are listening and taking their concerns seriously. This expansion will test us, but I believe it will ultimately allow us to serve better and grow stronger."

As the day ended, the confrontation with Hartman remained a significant moment for Bethany, marking her growth as a leader capable of navigating complex and sometimes hostile waters. She knew that the path ahead would require even more resilience and diplomacy, but she was ready to face whatever came her way, armed with a clear vision and a deep commitment to her community.

Chapter 18
The Article's Aftermath

In the wake of the community forum, Bethany recognized the necessity of broadening the clinic's communication strategy to better inform and engage with the public about their expansion plans. To this end, she decided to initiate a series of op-eds and blog posts, aiming to provide a deeper insight into the clinic's mission, its expansion, and how it intended to preserve its core values amidst growth.

Early one morning, before the clinic opened its doors to the day's appointments, Bethany sat in her office, surrounded by notes and drafts of what would soon be her first op-ed piece. The article was targeted at the local newspaper, which had a wide readership in Heartsville and was influential in shaping local opinion.

Bethany's focus was intense as she crafted her message. She started with an introduction about the clinic's history and its deep-rooted connection to the community. Then, she outlined the reasons behind the expansion, emphasizing how the new facilities would allow the clinic to provide advanced care that was currently out of reach for many local pet owners due to the limitations of their existing setup.

As she wrote, she made it a point to address the concerns raised by community members like Mr. Hartman, explaining in detail the measures they would take to ensure the clinic's ethos would not be diluted. This included commitments to community involvement, accessibility, and maintaining a high standard of personal care.

The sun was higher in the sky when Bethany finally leaned back in her chair, reviewing her draft. She felt a mixture of anxiety and hope—this article could significantly shape the public's perception of the clinic's future.

Later that day, Bethany met with Nora to discuss the draft. Nora read through the document carefully, occasionally nodding or making small annotations in the margins.

"This is very thorough, Bethany. It touches on all the key points and anticipates the concerns we've heard," Nora commented after finishing the read. "It's important that we're transparent about our intentions and the benefits this expansion offers not just to our clinic but to the entire community."

Bethany absorbed Nora's feedback, feeling reassured. "I want to make sure we communicate that we're not just growing for the sake of growing. Every decision we've made has been with the community's best interests in mind."

"That comes through clearly here," Nora affirmed. "Getting this published will help widen our reach and hopefully ease some of the tensions we've felt."

With Nora's approval, Bethany submitted the op-ed to the newspaper, and it was scheduled to run in the weekend edition. In the days leading up to the publication, Bethany also worked on additional blog posts for the clinic's website, aiming to create a series that would invite readers into a more regular dialogue about the changes and developments at the clinic.

When the op-ed was published that Saturday, it sparked a significant amount of feedback. Emails and social media comments began to pour in, many expressing a newfound understanding of the clinic's goals and plans. Others still voiced concerns, but the tone was more curious and less confrontational, opening the door for constructive discussions.

Bethany spent that weekend responding to comments and emails, engaging with the community in ways that further demonstrated the clinic's commitment to transparency and dialogue. Each interaction was a reminder of the power of communication and the importance of taking an active role in shaping the narrative surrounding important decisions.

As Monday approached, and the clinic prepared to open for another week, Bethany felt a cautious optimism. The op-ed had begun to shift perceptions, and her ongoing efforts to amplify the clinic's voice were laying the groundwork for more informed and balanced community interactions. She knew the path ahead would still hold challenges, but she was ready to meet them with the same openness and dedication that had guided her actions thus far.

- - - - - - - - -

The impact of Bethany's op-ed was more far-reaching than she had anticipated. The article not only resonated with the local community but also caught the attention of a regional news network, which requested an on-air interview to discuss the clinic's expansion and its implications for regional pet care.

Bethany prepared diligently for the interview, aware that this was an opportunity to further clarify and promote the clinic's mission on a larger stage. Sitting in the quiet of her office before heading to the television studio, she reviewed her main talking points with Nora, who provided feedback and moral support.

"You're doing the right thing by taking this proactive approach," Nora encouraged her. "It's important that people understand the 'why' behind our actions, not just the 'what.'"

At the studio, Bethany was greeted by the program host, Martin Fields, a well-respected journalist known for his thorough coverage of community issues. As the cameras rolled and the interview began, Martin's questions were direct but fair.

"Your recent op-ed about the Heartsville Veterinary Clinic's expansion has sparked a lot of conversations," Martin began. "Can you share with our viewers why you believe this expansion is necessary?"

Bethany nodded, feeling a surge of responsibility to convey her message clearly. "Thank you, Martin. Our clinic has been a part of the Heartsville community for over two decades, and during that time, we've seen an increasing need for specialized veterinary services that are currently not available locally. Our expansion allows us to provide these services, reducing the need for our clients to travel long distances for care."

Martin followed up, "There's been some concern about the clinic losing its community-focused touch with this expansion. How do you plan to maintain your community roots?"

"We're very aware of those concerns," Bethany replied. "That's why we're adopting a dual-location strategy. Our original clinic will continue to operate focusing on community wellness and education, while the new facility will handle more advanced medical care. We believe this approach allows us to enhance our services without losing the personal connection that defines us."

The interview touched on various aspects of the clinic's operations, from the types of new services that would be offered to the training and integration of new staff. Martin also asked about the feedback from the community, to which Bethany responded by emphasizing the ongoing dialogue with local residents and the clinic's commitment to addressing their concerns.

As the interview concluded, Martin thanked Bethany for her transparency and dedication to both animal care and community welfare. "It's clear that the Heartsville Veterinary Clinic is committed to advancing animal care while keeping the community's best interests at heart," he summarized, ending on a positive note.

Back at the clinic, the staff had gathered to watch the interview, and there was a collective sense of pride and accomplishment as they saw their mission being articulated so effectively on a regional platform. The positive exposure brought new inquiries and support from beyond their immediate locale, broadening their community impact.

Later, as Bethany debriefed with the team, she felt a renewed sense of commitment from everyone. "This interview was not just about me or the expansion," she addressed the group. "It was about all of us and what we stand for. Your hard work and dedication are what brought us to this point, and it's what will carry us forward."

The team's response was enthusiastic, with many expressing their appreciation for her leadership and the direction in which the clinic was heading. The sense of unity and purpose was palpable, reinforcing the clinic's role not only as a provider of veterinary services but as a pivotal community advocate.

As the day drew to a close, Bethany reflected on the widespread impact of their communication efforts. The power of the pen, coupled with the reach of the media, had amplified their voice in ways she had only hoped for, bringing their message of growth, community, and care to a much larger audience than ever before.

The increased visibility from Bethany's media outreach brought not only support but also a significant amount of backlash, particularly from a small but vocal group of local residents who were skeptical of the clinic's expansion and its implications for the community's character. This group, led by a community activist named Clara, organized a campaign to challenge the clinic's plans, armed with petitions and a series of pointed questions about the potential commercialization of community spaces.

The backlash came to a head during a public meeting organized by the city council to discuss the impact of local business expansions, including that of the Heartsville Veterinary Clinic. The meeting was well-attended, with Bethany and Nora present to represent the clinic and address concerns.

Clara stood and addressed the council with a firm tone, her eyes occasionally glancing towards Bethany and Nora. "We acknowledge the clinic's long-standing service to our community, but we must consider the broader impacts. How can we ensure that this expansion does not pave the way for more intensive commercial development that could alter the fabric of our town?"

Bethany took the floor to respond, maintaining a calm demeanor despite the tension in the room. "Thank you for your concerns, Clara. We are very mindful of the balance between growth and maintaining the community character. Our expansion plans have been carefully designed to enhance our services without disrupting the community feel that is so important to us all."

A council member then asked Bethany, "Can you elaborate on how you plan to manage the increase in traffic and the environmental impact of the new facility?"

"We've conducted a thorough traffic impact study and are working with planners to ensure that any increase in traffic is managed effectively," Bethany explained. "We are also investing in green building technologies to minimize our environmental footprint."

Despite Bethany's responses, murmurs of dissent flowed through the room, illustrating the divide in the community. Clara continued, "While we appreciate the clinic's efforts to mitigate impacts, there remains a concern about setting a precedent. Today it's a veterinary clinic, but what about tomorrow?"

Nora, sensing the need to reinforce their commitment, added her voice

to the discussion. "It's a valid concern, Clara. That's why part of our commitment is to remain actively involved in community planning processes, ensuring that our growth never comes at the cost of our town's character."

A resident from the audience, Mr. Jacobs, who had frequented the clinic with his pets, stood up to share his perspective. "I've known the folks at Heartsville Veterinary Clinic for many years. They've always put the community and their patients first. I believe their expansion is in our best interest—they've earned our trust."

The conversation shifted slightly as more residents began to voice support, sharing personal anecdotes of the clinic's positive impact on their lives and their pets. However, the room remained divided, with a clear line drawn between those embracing the change and those fearing the implications of growth.

Bethany addressed the assembly one more time, striving to articulate the clinic's vision. "Our intention isn't just to grow our clinic but to enhance the services we can provide to our community. This expansion will allow us to save more lives, offer more comprehensive care, and yes, it will bring change. But we pledge to manage that change with the utmost respect for the values and the environment of Heartsville."

As the meeting concluded, it was clear that while some skepticism remained, the dialogue had opened doors for ongoing communication and collaboration. Bethany and Nora stayed behind to answer individual questions, reinforcing their openness and commitment to transparency.

Later, back at the clinic, Bethany and Nora debriefed the meeting. "It's never easy facing public backlash," Bethany remarked, a hint of exhaustion in her voice. "But it's crucial that we keep the lines of communication open. We need to be where the hard conversations are happening."

Nora agreed, her expression thoughtful. "Yes, and every question, every concern, gives us a chance to reaffirm our commitment. We're not just building a bigger clinic; we're aiming to build a better community. And sometimes, that requires facing tough challenges head-on."

As they locked up the clinic for the night, the weight of their responsibilities lingered, but so did a sense of accomplishment. They had faced the community's concerns openly and had made progress, however incremental. Bethany felt a renewed sense of determination, knowing that each conversation, each meeting, was a step towards not just expanding a clinic, but nurturing a community.

In an effort to further address the community's concerns and shape the ongoing narrative about the clinic's expansion, Bethany agreed to a crucial interview with a prominent local radio station known for its influence in Heartsville. The interview, hosted by Sam Mitchell, a veteran radio personality who prided himself on tough but fair questioning, was scheduled to air during prime time, ensuring it would reach a broad audience.

As Bethany arrived at the radio station, she was acutely aware of the stakes. She greeted Sam with a confident smile, ready to articulate her points clearly.

"Welcome, Bethany," Sam began as they went on air, his voice smooth and professional. "There's been a lot of talk about your clinic's expansion plans. Why don't you start by telling us why this is the right move for Heartsville?"

Bethany took a deep breath before responding. "Thank you, Sam. At Heartsville Veterinary Clinic, we've always been committed to providing the best possible care to our patients and being a good neighbor in our community. The expansion allows us to offer more advanced treatments and surgeries that are currently not available locally, which means better care for pets and less travel for their owners."

Sam nodded, then followed up. "Some residents are concerned about the impact of the expansion on the local community's character. How do you address those concerns?"

"We understand that change can be unsettling," Bethany acknowledged. "That's why we're committed to maintaining our original clinic as a community-focused facility. The new location will simply allow us to enhance our services. We're also implementing environmental and traffic management plans to ensure that our presence remains a benefit, not a burden."

Sam's questions continued, probing into the specifics of those plans. "Can you give us more details on how you plan to manage the increased traffic that a new facility might bring?"

"Absolutely," Bethany replied. "We've worked with city planners to create a traffic flow that minimizes congestion. We're also exploring options like shuttle services from the old clinic to the new one to help those who might find the new location less accessible."

The interview then touched on the economic aspect. "What about the economic impact? How does the expansion benefit Heartsville economically?" Sam asked.

Bethany was ready with her response. "The new clinic will create job opportunities, not only within the clinic itself but also through partnerships with local businesses. We're investing in local construction firms for the building work and will continue to source locally whenever possible."

As the interview drew to a close, Sam gave Bethany a final opportunity to address the listeners directly. "Bethany, what would you say to those who are still on the fence about this expansion?"

Bethany leaned into the microphone, her voice earnest and sincere. "To those who are uncertain, I say this: we hear you. We're here to answer your questions and address your concerns. This expansion is about doing more good—providing better care for our pets and strengthening our community. We invite you to join us in this journey, to help shape what comes next. Your voice matters to us."

The interview concluded with Sam thanking Bethany for her time and transparency. "Thank you, Bethany, for being here today and for your candid responses. It's clear that Heartsville Veterinary Clinic is looking towards the future with the community's interests at heart."

As Bethany left the station, she felt a mixture of relief and accomplishment. The interview had provided a platform to clarify the clinic's intentions and reassure the community, an essential step in maintaining public trust and support.

Back at the clinic, the team listened to the interview, feeling proud and supported. Bethany's words resonated not just with the public but with her staff, reinforcing their collective mission and the positive impacts of their work, both present and future.

Chapter 19
The Community's Embrace

In the days following the publication of Bethany's op-ed and her subsequent radio interview, the clinic experienced a noticeable shift in public perception. The detailed explanations and transparent communication Bethany provided had begun to sway the tide of opinion, with many in the community expressing a new understanding and support for the clinic's expansion plans.

At the clinic, the mood was cautiously optimistic. Bethany noticed an increase in clients mentioning the article, often bringing it up during their visits to express their support or to ask more informed questions about what the expansion would entail. The staff, too, felt a renewed sense of purpose, seeing firsthand how their leader's efforts were harmonizing public opinion.

One morning, as Bethany reviewed the latest client feedback surveys, she was pleased to see positive comments about the clinic's commitment to transparency and community involvement. However, amidst the routine tasks and client interactions, an unexpected development unfolded that added a personal dimension to the ongoing narrative.

Dr. Michael Harrison, a veterinary specialist who had been collaborating with the clinic to help set up the new facility's advanced surgical center, stopped by Bethany's office. Michael had always been professional and supportive, but today, he seemed to have something more personal on his mind.

"Bethany, do you have a moment?" Michael asked, his tone a bit more hesitant than usual.

"Of course, Michael. What's on your mind?" Bethany responded, setting aside her paperwork.

"I've been meaning to talk to you about something a bit outside of our usual discussions," Michael started, clearly trying to choose his words carefully. "I've been really impressed with how you've handled the clinic's expansion and the public's response. It's clear you care deeply not just about the animals but about the community."

Bethany was taken aback by the personal nature of his comments but prompted him to continue.

"It's more than just professional admiration," Michael continued, his demeanor indicating the personal stakes. "I've developed feelings for you, Bethany. I find myself wanting to know more about you, not just as a clinic director but as the person who has handled all these challenges with such grace."

Bethany, surprised by his revelation, took a moment to process his words. Romance had been the furthest thing from her mind, especially amidst the clinic's expansion challenges.

"Michael, I'm flattered," she finally said, choosing her words with care. "I respect you a great deal as well, and I appreciate your support during this hectic time. But I think I need some time to think about this. There's a lot going on, and I want to be sure we consider all implications of such a change in our relationship."

Michael nodded, his expression understanding. "Of course, I wouldn't want to add any pressure. Just know that my support for you and the clinic remains unchanged."

The conversation ended with an agreement to continue their professional collaboration while Bethany considered her personal feelings. After Michael left, Bethany sat back in her chair, the weight of his words sinking in amidst the myriad responsibilities she was juggling.

This unexpected personal revelation added another layer to the already complex tapestry of her professional and personal life. As she returned to her work, Bethany found herself reflecting not just on the future of the clinic but also on the nature of her relationships and how they might evolve in this new chapter of her life. The day closed with Bethany feeling a mix of anticipation and uncertainty, aware that the decisions ahead were not just about the clinic but about her personal happiness as well.

- - - - - - - - -

The day of the city council vote on the clinic's expansion was marked by a palpable tension. Bethany arrived at the city hall early, equipped with folders of supportive documents, architectural plans, and the results of community feedback. The session was open to the public, and a sizable number of community members, including some of Bethany's staff, filled the seats, signaling the high stakes of the meeting.

Council chambers buzzed with whispered strategies and last-minute discussions as council members took their seats. The mayor opened the session, quickly outlining the agenda before giving the floor to Bethany for a final presentation before the vote.

Bethany stood, her notes organized before her, and addressed the council with a clear and steady voice. "Thank you, Mayor, and thank you to all the council members for allowing us this time. Our proposal for expansion is more than just a building project—it's about enhancing the quality of veterinary care available to our community and continuing our commitment to public education and animal welfare."

Councilwoman Rodriguez, a known advocate for local business development, was the first to respond. "Bethany, your clinic has certainly been an asset to our community. Can you clarify how you plan to manage the increased traffic this expansion might bring, especially concerns regarding congestion in the area?"

Bethany replied, "Absolutely, Councilwoman. We've worked with traffic analysts to create a plan that includes additional parking, optimized appointment scheduling to avoid peak traffic times, and we are also exploring a partnership with local transit services to encourage public transportation."

Councilman Hartman, who had expressed skepticism previously, interjected, "And what about the environmental concerns? Expanding a medical facility can have significant impacts, particularly waste management."

"We are fully committed to sustainable practices," Bethany explained. "This includes state-of-the-art waste management systems and building materials that are environmentally friendly. We're not just planning to meet current environmental regulations but to exceed them."

As the questions continued, each council member probing into different aspects of the plan, Bethany responded with informed and thoughtful answers, demonstrating the careful planning and community consideration that had gone into the proposal.

After the question-and-answer session, the council prepared to vote. The room grew silent, the tension mounting as each council member cast their vote. Bethany watched, her heart rate accelerating with each "yes" that echoed in the chamber.

Finally, the mayor announced the results. "With a majority in favor, the motion passes. Heartsville Veterinary Clinic is approved to proceed with its expansion."

A wave of relief washed over Bethany as applause broke out among her supporters in the audience. She exchanged a look with Nora, who was smiling broadly, pride evident in her eyes.

As the council session adjourned, several community members approached Bethany to offer their congratulations. "We really appreciate what you're doing for our pets and for Heartsville," one elderly gentleman told her, shaking her hand warmly.

Bethany responded with genuine gratitude, "Thank you. It's our community that makes all this worthwhile. We're excited to start this new chapter and keep serving you all."

The conversation around her buzzed with excitement and relief, but for Bethany, the approval was more than a professional victory; it was a validation of her leadership and vision for the clinic.

As she left city hall, Bethany felt a mixture of exhilaration and exhaustion. The council vote was a crucial hurdle, but it marked just the beginning of the next phase of her journey—both for the clinic and for herself personally, considering the new emotional dimensions Michael had introduced into her life. The challenges ahead were daunting, yet Bethany felt more equipped than ever to handle them, bolstered by the trust and support of her community.

- - - - - - - - -

Following the successful council vote, the clinic staff organized a small celebration back at the clinic. It was a moment for everyone to unwind and reflect on the hurdles they had overcome together. Bethany was there, mingling and thanking her team, but her thoughts were intermittently drifting to Dr. Michael Harrison's unexpected confession of feelings towards her.

As the celebration was winding down, Michael found Bethany standing alone, looking at some of the thank-you cards from clients displayed on the wall. He approached her cautiously, respecting the complexity of their situation.

"Bethany, if you have a moment, I wanted to check in with you," Michael began, his voice a mix of professional and personal concern. "I hope my earlier words haven't made things uncomfortable between us."

Bethany turned to face him, her expression thoughtful. "Michael, I appreciate you bringing it up. I've been so focused on the clinic that I haven't given myself much time to think about anything else, including what you said."

Michael nodded, understanding her position. "I get that completely. This expansion is a huge deal, and you've handled it incredibly well. I wouldn't want to add any more pressure."

Bethany smiled slightly, touched by his consideration. "Thank you for being so understanding. It's actually nice to know that you care, not just about the clinic but about how I'm handling things personally. It's been a lot."

There was a pause as both considered their next words carefully.

"I've always admired how dedicated you are, Bethany. And whatever happens between us personally, I want you to know that my commitment to the clinic and to our work remains unchanged," Michael said earnestly.

Bethany looked at him, genuinely reassured. "That means a lot, Michael. And honestly, I'd be lying if I said I hadn't thought about it. I've just been unsure about mixing personal feelings with our professional work."

Michael gave a small, understanding nod. "That makes sense. And whatever you decide, I'm here. We make a good team, no matter what."

Bethany appreciated his directness and sincerity. "Let's keep talking. I'm not saying no—I'm just saying not yet. There's a lot to figure out with the clinic, and I need to sort through my own feelings too."

"That sounds fair," Michael agreed. "I'm here when you're ready to talk more, Bethany. No pressure."

The conversation ended on a mutually respectful note, with both feeling a sense of relief that they could continue to work together amicably. Bethany felt a weight lift slightly—acknowledging the connection didn't mean she had to fully understand or act on it immediately.

As the evening came to a close and the last of the staff left the clinic, Bethany stayed behind, reflecting on the day's events. It had been a day of professional triumphs and personal revelations. The council's approval marked a new chapter for the clinic, and perhaps, in time, a new chapter for her personal life as well.

Bethany locked up the clinic, feeling a blend of satisfaction and anticipation. The road ahead was clear for the clinic's expansion, and her conversation with Michael had opened a door to potential new beginnings on a personal front. The complexities of her role seemed to intertwine more and more with her personal growth, each influencing the other in ways she was only beginning to understand.

- - - - - - - - -

As the clinic's expansion began to take tangible form with plans being set into motion and contractors starting on the new site, Bethany found herself at a crossroads of personal and professional transformation. Late one evening, after a long day of meetings with architects and planners, Bethany sat down with Nora to reflect on all the changes and what they meant for both of them.

Nora poured them each a cup of tea, her presence comforting as always. "It's been quite the journey, hasn't it? From all the community meetings to the council vote and now the actual building phase," she began, a note of nostalgia in her voice.

Bethany nodded, stirring her tea slowly. "It really has. And it's not just the clinic that's going through changes. I've been doing a lot of thinking about my personal life as well."

Nora looked at her with understanding. "Michael's confession?"

"Yes," Bethany admitted, her voice soft. "It was unexpected, and it's made me consider aspects of my life I've been neglecting. It's not just about the clinic for me anymore."

Nora sipped her tea, considering her words carefully. "It's important, Bethany, to remember that you're not just your job. You're a person who needs to find happiness in other areas too.

Michael is a good man, and he's been straightforward with you."

Bethany sighed, a mix of apprehension and anticipation in her tone. "I know. And the truth is, I think I might have feelings for him too. But I've always been so focused on the clinic. I'm not sure how to balance it all."

"That's the challenge, isn't it?" Nora said gently. "Finding that balance. But Bethany, if anyone can do it, it's you. You've managed this clinic through thick and thin, adapting to changes and facing challenges head-on. I think you'll find a way to manage this too."

"You really think so?" Bethany asked, looking for reassurance.

"I do," Nora affirmed. "Just remember to take things one step at a time. There's no rush to figure it all out at once."

Bethany smiled, feeling a bit lighter. "Thank you, Nora. It means a lot to have your support."

"As for the clinic," Nora continued, shifting the conversation back to professional matters, "we're on a good path. This expansion is going to allow us to help so many more animals and to continue making a difference in the community. It's a new beginning for us, in many ways."

"It is," Bethany agreed, her thoughts drifting to the future. "And I'm excited about that. Excited to see where we can take the clinic and what we can achieve."

Nora nodded, her eyes twinkling. "And I'm excited to see you grow, not just as a director but as a person, Bethany. You've got so much ahead of you."

As they finished their tea, the conversation drifted to other topics, but the themes of change and personal growth remained central. When Bethany finally left Nora's office, she felt a renewed sense of purpose and clarity, not only about the clinic's future but also about her own.

Walking to her car under the stars, Bethany felt the weight of her responsibilities intertwined with the possibilities of new beginnings. Her life, much like the clinic, was evolving, and she was ready to embrace whatever came next with an open heart and mind. As she drove home, the quiet streets of Heartsville seemed to echo her thoughts, reminding her that every end is just a new beginning.

Chapter 20
Decisions and Destinies

As the repercussions of Bethany's op-ed and subsequent media appearances began to manifest, the Heartsville Veterinary Clinic experienced an unprecedented surge in recognition, not only within the community but also regionally. The article had resonated deeply, striking a chord with pet owners and animal lovers alike, casting Bethany not just as a clinic director, but as a visionary in veterinary care and community engagement.

With this newfound attention came opportunities and challenges. The clinic saw a noticeable increase in client visits, with many new faces citing the article as their reason for choosing Heartsville Veterinary Clinic for their pets' care. Moreover, local schools and community centers began reaching out, inviting Bethany to speak about animal health and the role of veterinary services in public welfare.

One crisp autumn morning, as golden leaves drifted through the mild air, Bethany sat in her office, surrounded by notes and invitations from various community organizations. Each request was a testament to the clinic's growing influence and her own as a thought leader. Bethany took a moment to reflect on this shift, feeling a mixture of pride and responsibility.

It wasn't just the increase in appointments and public speaking requests that marked the article's impact. The local chamber of commerce awarded the clinic with a recognition award for Community Service Excellence, a first for a veterinary clinic in the region. The award was not only a recognition of the clinic's services but also its commitment to ethical expansion and community integration.

Bethany organized the award in her office next to a framed copy of the op-ed, a visual reminder of the journey the clinic had undertaken. The walls of her office, once sparse, now displayed thank-you letters from various community members and photos from recent events where the clinic staff had volunteered, helping with local animal shelters and health fairs.

As she prepared for another day, Bethany's schedule reflected the diversity of her new responsibilities. Beyond her administrative duties and client consultations, it included meetings with city planners to discuss the integration of the new clinic site and its impact on local traffic and community aesthetics.

Moreover, an unexpected but welcome invitation had come from a regional veterinary conference asking her to be a keynote speaker. The conference would gather professionals from across the state, providing a platform to share her insights on balancing business growth with community values—a topic now closely associated with her and the clinic.

Amid these preparations, Bethany maintained a meticulous focus on the clinic's daily operations. She ensured that new staff members were integrated smoothly and that the quality of care remained high despite the increase in client numbers. Her management meetings often ran late into the evening, discussing everything from patient care strategies to employee wellness programs.

The clinic's waiting room, once a quiet space, buzzed with the chatter of excited pet owners sharing stories and experiences. The community bulletin board in the corner, which Bethany had installed years ago, was now covered with notes of thanks, community announcements, and photos of pets that had been treated at the clinic.

As Bethany walked through the clinic, checking in on the day's operations and greeting clients and their pets, she felt a profound connection to her work and its impact. The expansion, once a source of anxiety and contention, was now taking shape as a beacon of community service and animal care excellence.

Reflecting on this transformation, Bethany felt reassured that the path they had chosen was the right one. The widespread recognition of the clinic was not just a personal achievement but a shared success, a testament to the dedication of her entire team and the support of the Heartsville community. As the day ended and Bethany closed her office door, she knew that the challenges ahead would be met with the same passion and integrity that had brought them this far, ready to turn new opportunities into lasting contributions for the community and the field of veterinary medicine.

- - - - - - - - -

While the initial wave of positive recognition had bolstered the clinic’s standing in the community, it also brought unforeseen challenges that began to surface. One such challenge arose during a routine staff meeting where operational issues were being discussed.

"Bethany, with the increased client volume, we're starting to see some strain on our appointment scheduling," Dr. Lisa, one of the veterinarians, expressed with a note of concern. "We're booked solid most days, and I'm worried we might be compromising on the quality of care we're able to provide each patient."

Bethany, attentive and nodding, acknowledged the issue. "Thank you for bringing that up, Lisa. It's important we address this head-on. Do you have any suggestions on how we might improve the situation?"

"I think we could benefit from streamlining our intake process and possibly extending our hours," Lisa suggested. "Maybe we could also consider hiring additional support staff to handle the administrative workload."

Bethany considered this thoughtfully. "Extending our hours could certainly provide some relief. I'll look into the logistics of that and the feasibility of hiring more staff. We need to ensure we're maintaining our standard of care without overburdening our team."

As the meeting continued, another challenge came from George, the senior technician. "There's also the issue of our equipment. With more complex cases coming in, especially from the new clients who've heard about our expansion, some of our diagnostic tools are proving inadequate."

Bethany was already aware of this growing problem. "You're right, George. It's time we upgraded our equipment. I'll prioritize that and see where we can allocate funds from our expansion budget."

The meeting moved on to discuss the integration of the new site, which was being prepared to handle more advanced medical procedures. Nora, who had been overseeing much of the logistical planning, added her perspective. "While we're all excited about the new facilities, there's a significant amount of training our staff will need to effectively use the new technology we're installing there."

Bethany nodded, her mind racing through potential solutions. "Let's set up a training schedule. Maybe we can bring in some specialists for a series of workshops. It's crucial everyone feels confident and competent with the new equipment."

As the meeting wrapped up, Bethany felt the weight of these new challenges. She stayed behind in the conference room, jotting down action items and preparing to tackle each issue systematically. She knew that addressing these challenges effectively was crucial not only for the clinic's operations but also for maintaining the trust and satisfaction of their clients.

Later that day, Bethany called a meeting with her management team to outline a detailed plan addressing the issues raised. "We need a multifaceted approach," she began, her tone determined but calm. "First, let's look into extending our operating hours as Dr. Lisa suggested, and identify recruitment agencies to find additional support staff."

She continued, outlining a plan for equipment upgrades and staff training that would help bridge the gap between current capabilities and the needs brought by increased demand. "For the equipment, let's prioritize diagnostics and emergency care tools. I want proposals on my desk by the end of the week."

The management team left the meeting with clear directives, and Bethany spent the rest of the day in back-to-back discussions with finance, HR, and operations to ensure that the new strategies were set in motion promptly.

As the clinic closed for the day, Bethany felt a mix of exhaustion and accomplishment. The challenges were daunting, but her proactive approach gave her hope that they were manageable. Reflecting on the day's meetings, she understood that with growth came complexity, but she was resolute in her commitment to navigate these waters without compromising the heart of their mission. The clinic had become more than a healthcare provider; it was a vital part of the community fabric, and she was determined to keep it thriving, responsive, and respected.

As the Heartsville Veterinary Clinic navigated the complexities introduced by its growing popularity and the imminent expansion, Bethany saw an opportunity to strengthen the bonds within her team and the community. Recognizing the increased pressures on her staff and the need for deeper community connections, she organized a series of team-building activities and community outreach events.

One crisp Saturday morning, the clinic was closed to the public to host a staff retreat at a local park. The day was carefully planned with activities that encouraged teamwork and communication, crucial for managing the clinic's growing demands. Bethany watched as her team participated in problem-solving games and trust-building exercises, pleased to see laughter and camaraderie weaving through the activities.

"Great work, everyone," Bethany called out as the team completed a particularly challenging activity. "Seeing you all work together like this reassures me that we can handle whatever comes our way."

In the afternoon, the clinic hosted a free pet health fair in the same park, inviting the community to bring their pets for check-ups and consultations. The event also served as a platform for Bethany to informally discuss the clinic's plans and gather feedback directly from pet owners.

As families arrived with their pets, clinic staff, fresh from their morning retreat, were energized and ready to engage. Bethany circulated among the visitors, answering questions and sharing insights into the clinic's future.

"This is what it's all about," Bethany remarked to Nora, who was overseeing a station on pet nutrition. "Connecting with the community, ensuring they know we're here for them and their pets."

Nora nodded in agreement, handing a dog owner some informational brochures. "It's these moments that remind us why we do what we do. It's not just about treating animals; it's about being a part of the lives of the people who love them."

The fair was a success, with numerous residents expressing their appreciation for the clinic's efforts and openness. Many were reassured about the expansion, now seeing it as a positive development that would bring more comprehensive services to the community.

As the day ended, Bethany felt a profound connection with her team and the community. The retreat and fair had not only served to alleviate some of the stress and uncertainty brought on by the clinic's growth but had also reinforced the foundational relationships that were essential to the clinic's success.

Driving home, Bethany reflected on the day's events. The laughter and shared purpose she'd witnessed among her staff were more than she could have hoped for, and the community's enthusiastic participation and feedback had bolstered her confidence in the clinic's direction.

The challenges of managing a rapidly growing clinic were manifold, but Bethany felt reassured that with a united team and a supportive community, they were more than capable of navigating the future. Today had been a reminder of the importance of maintaining and strengthening the bonds that held them together, ensuring that as they moved forward, they did so not just as a clinic, but as a vital and integrated part of the Heartsville community.

- - - - - - - - -

After a whirlwind of activity marked by heightened public interaction and internal team building, Bethany found herself in a rare moment of quiet late one evening at the clinic. The last of the staff had left, and the soft hum of the equipment in the background provided a soothing backdrop to her thoughts. She was joined by Michael, who had stayed late to finish up some patient charts.

Michael noticed Bethany's contemplative mood as he walked into her office. "You look like you're a million miles away," he said gently, taking a seat across from her.

Bethany smiled, grateful for the company. "Just reflecting on everything that's happened. It's been a lot to take in—the article, the expansion, the community feedback. It feels like we're turning a major corner."

Michael nodded, understanding the weight of her reflections. "It's a big step, but you've handled it incredibly well. The community really seems to rally behind your vision."

"It's more than just my vision now," Bethany responded, her eyes thoughtful. "It's about all of us—our team, our community. It's about making sure we continue to serve them as best we can, even as we grow."

The conversation turned to the personal side of things, a topic they had cautiously navigated since Michael's admission of his feelings. "And how are you holding up with everything else?" Michael asked, his tone careful but sincere.

Bethany took a deep breath, her gaze settling on a photo of the clinic staff at a recent community event. "Personally, it's been challenging. Balancing the professional with the personal isn't always easy. Your support means a lot to me, Michael, and I've been thinking about what you said."

Michael listened intently, respecting her process. "I hope you know there's no pressure from me. I care about you, Bethany, and I want what's best for you, whether that's us taking a step forward or just continuing to work together like this."

Bethany appreciated his understanding. "I do know that, and thank you. It's given me a lot to think about. I'm not sure what the future holds, but I'm open to finding out, step by step."

Their dialogue shifted back to the clinic's immediate needs, discussing the upcoming schedule and the integration of new technology at the facility. As they talked, Bethany felt a sense of partnership that extended beyond the professional, a connection rooted in shared goals and mutual respect.

As they concluded their conversation and stood to leave, Bethany felt a renewed sense of purpose. "Thanks for staying late to talk, Michael. It's these moments of reflection that really help put things into perspective."

Michael smiled, his affection for her evident even in his professionalism. "Anytime, Bethany. We're in this together, after all."

Walking out of the clinic together, the night air was cool and refreshing, a stark contrast to the day's earlier heat. The quiet streets of Heartsville seemed to mirror the calm that had settled between them, a calm that came from understanding and shared experiences.

As they parted ways, with Michael heading to his car and Bethany taking a moment to gaze at the starry sky, the reflective pause offered both a respite and a reminder of the journey ahead. The clinic was evolving, and so were they, individually and together. With each challenge and achievement, they were not just building a better clinic but also a deeper connection to each other and to the community they served.

Chapter 21
A Shared Vision

The Heartsville Veterinary Clinic was abuzz with activity, not just from its daily operations but from the preparations for the upcoming Canine Gala, an annual event that had grown in prominence alongside the clinic. This year, the gala was particularly significant as it was the first major public event since the announcement of the clinic's expansion. Bethany was determined to make it a night to remember, celebrating the clinic's growth and the community's support.

A few days before the event, Bethany and Nora were busy finalizing the arrangements. They sat together in Bethany's office, surrounded by decorations, seating charts, and lists of attendees.

"Do you think we have enough volunteers for the check-in table?" Bethany asked, looking over the list of staff and volunteers.

"I believe so," Nora replied, scanning the document. "Let's double-check with Lisa. She coordinated the last training session, so she'll know if we're covered."

Bethany nodded and picked up her phone to call Dr. Lisa. "Hi Lisa, just wanted to make sure we're set with volunteers for the gala night. Do we have enough hands on deck?"

Lisa's voice came through, cheerful and confident. "Yes, we're all set, Bethany. Everyone's really excited, and we've got backups just in case. Also, the gift bags are prepared, and the catering confirmation came through this morning."

"That's great to hear, Lisa. Thanks for staying on top of this," Bethany replied, relief evident in her tone.

As they continued to discuss logistics, Michael walked in with a stack of brochures and posters for the event. "Just got these from the printer," he announced, placing them on Bethany's desk. "They turned out really well."

Bethany picked up a brochure, examining it with a critical eye. "These look fantastic, Michael. They'll make a great impression at the entrance."

"Glad you think so," Michael responded, watching her reaction closely. "I included a section on how the funds raised will be used towards the new facility's community programs. It should help our guests understand exactly where their donations are going."

"That's perfect. It's important that our supporters see how their contributions make a difference," Bethany said, appreciating his attention to detail.

The conversation then shifted to the evening's program. Nora was looking over the schedule. "Bethany, have you decided if you're going to speak before or after the dinner service? I think opening the night with a few words might set a wonderful tone."

Bethany considered this for a moment. "I think you're right, Nora. Kicking off with our vision for the future could really energize the crowd."

Michael chimed in, "And maybe we can screen that short video we made about the clinic's history right after your speech? It's a good segue into the fundraising part of the evening."

"Excellent idea, Michael. It'll remind everyone of how far we've come and why we're moving forward," Bethany agreed, pleased with how the team was pulling together.

As they wrapped up their meeting, the trio looked over the venue layout one last time. "Everything seems in order, but let's do a final walk-through of the venue tomorrow," Bethany suggested. "We need to ensure everything is as perfect as it can be."

"Agreed," Nora and Michael said in unison, their expressions a mix of anticipation and determination.

As the day of preparation drew to a close, Bethany felt a mix of nerves and excitement. The gala was more than just a fundraiser; it was a showcase of the clinic's evolution and a celebration of the community that had supported them throughout the years. She knew that the success of this event could further solidify the clinic's place in the hearts of the community members and their pets.

Leaving the office that evening, Bethany looked back at the clinic, its windows aglow with the late evening sun. She felt a deep connection to this place and the people it served.

Tomorrow's gala was not just an event; it was a milestone, and she was ready to make it a memorable one.

- - - - - - - - -

The evening of the Canine Gala arrived, bringing with it a flurry of excitement and a buzz of activity. The venue, a beautifully decorated hall with elegant table settings and soft lighting, was abuzz as guests began to arrive, greeted by the welcoming committee of staff and volunteers from the Heartsville Veterinary Clinic.

Bethany, dressed in an elegant gown, stood near the entrance, greeting each guest with a warm smile and heartfelt thanks for their support. Nora and Michael were also there, assisting with the greetings and ensuring that the guests felt welcomed.

"Everything looks wonderful, Bethany," Nora commented as they had a moment to themselves. "You've really outdone yourself this year."

Bethany glanced around, taking in the scene. "It's a team effort, Nora. I couldn't have done it without everyone's help. This night is a testament to what we can accomplish together."

As the guests settled into their seats, Bethany took the stage to open the event. The room quieted down as she began to speak, her voice clear and resonant. "Good evening, everyone. Thank you for joining us at our annual Canine Gala. Tonight is not just a celebration of what we've achieved but also a look forward to the exciting developments at our clinic."

She continued, detailing the plans for the new facility and how it would enhance their services. "With your support, we can make these plans a reality and continue to provide the highest quality of care to our beloved pets."

After her speech, the video Michael had mentioned earlier was played, showcasing the clinic's history and the community's involvement in its success. The video was met with applause, and many guests seemed visibly moved by the clinic's story.

The dinner service began shortly after, with tables buzzing with conversations about the video and Bethany's speech. Michael, sitting next to Bethany, leaned over to speak with her. "You did a great job up there, Bethany. You really captured the essence of what we're all about."

"Thank you, Michael," Bethany replied, offering him a grateful smile. "It's easy to speak passionately about something you deeply care about."

As dinner wound down, the fundraising portion of the evening began. Nora took the stage this time, her presence commanding and sincere. "Now comes an important part of our evening," she announced. "Your generosity tonight will help us bring our vision to life. Every donation, no matter the size, will contribute directly to the health and wellness of countless animals."

The fundraising was a tremendous success, with guests enthusiastically raising their bid paddles for auction items and pledging donations. Bethany watched, overwhelmed by the support and love the community showed.

After the formal events concluded, the floor opened for dancing and mingling. Bethany found herself surrounded by colleagues, friends, and supporters, each expressing their admiration for the clinic's work and their excitement about its future.

As the evening drew to a close, Bethany shared a quiet moment with Nora and Michael. "Tonight was incredible," she said, her eyes reflecting the soft lights of the hall. "I can't thank you both enough for everything."

"It was a beautiful night, Bethany," Nora replied. "And it's just the beginning of what's to come."

Michael nodded in agreement. "We're building something great here, Bethany. And it's an honor to be a part of it."

The gala was indeed a night of celebration, but also a profound affirmation of the community's faith in the Heartsville Veterinary Clinic. As the guests departed and the team began to clean up, Bethany felt a deep sense of accomplishment and optimism. The night had not only celebrated past achievements but had also paved the way for a future filled with promise and continued dedication to the care of animals and the community that loved them.

- - - - - - - - -

As the Canine Gala wound down and the last of the guests trickled out, Bethany found herself lingering near the back of the hall, helping the staff with some final tasks. The night had been a resounding success, and the energy of the event still hummed through the air. It was during these quiet moments of winding down that Michael approached her, a serious look on his face that suggested he had more on his mind than just the gala's success.

"Bethany, can we talk for a moment?" Michael asked, his voice low, ensuring they had a semblance of privacy amid the cleanup crew.

"Of course, Michael. What's on your mind?" Bethany responded, sensing the importance of the conversation he intended to have.

"I've been doing a lot of thinking," Michael started, pausing to choose his words carefully. "About us, about this evening, and everything leading up to it. Seeing how beautifully everything came together tonight, and knowing your vision drove us here... it's just reinforced how I feel about you."

Bethany felt a flutter of anticipation, mixed with a myriad of other emotions. She remained silent, giving him space to continue.

"I know we agreed to keep things professional, and I've really tried to respect that boundary," Michael continued. "But I can't help feeling there's something special between us. I don't want to put any pressure on you, but I also don't want to regret not telling you how much you mean to me, not just as a colleague, but as the incredible woman you are."

Bethany took a deep breath, her heart racing a bit as she processed his words. "Michael, I... I'm grateful to hear you say that. I've been feeling a lot of the same things, but I've been worried about how it might affect our work, our friendship."

"I understand that," Michael said, nodding. "I would never want to jeopardize what we have professionally, or the great work we're doing at the clinic. If you feel there's a chance for us, I'm willing to do whatever it takes to make sure it doesn't interfere with our jobs."

Bethany looked around the nearly empty hall, considering the weight of his words against the backdrop of their shared achievements. "I admire you so much, Michael. Your support has meant the world to me, especially through all the challenges we've faced. I think... I think I'd like to explore what's between us, slowly and carefully."

Michael's expression brightened, a mixture of relief and happiness crossing his features. "I'd like that very much. And I agree, we should take things slow, see where they lead without any pressure."

They agreed to have more detailed discussions about how they could pursue a relationship without disrupting their professional environment. As they spoke, it was clear that both valued their work and the clinic too much to let anything jeopardize it.

As they finished their conversation, they agreed to meet for coffee the following weekend, a small step toward understanding what this new personal dimension might look like for them. They walked out of the gala together, a subtle shift in their dynamic that felt both thrilling and right.

Bethany drove home that night with a lot on her mind. The success of the gala, the clinic's bright future, and now, the possibility of a new relationship with Michael. It was a lot to take in, but for the first time in a long while, she felt a profound sense of completeness. The road ahead would certainly require careful navigation, but she felt ready to face it, armed with clarity about her professional vision and a newfound openness to the personal happiness that might accompany it.

The day after the gala, as the clinic resumed its usual pace, Bethany found a moment to share her conversation with Michael with Nora. She knew Nora not only as a mentor but as a confidant, and her advice had always guided Bethany through many of the clinic's and her personal milestones.

Finding Nora in her office, Bethany knocked gently on the open door. "Nora, do you have a moment?"

Nora looked up from her paperwork, her expression softening as she saw Bethany's slightly nervous demeanor. "Of course, Bethany. Come in. What's on your mind?"

Bethany took a seat across from Nora, taking a moment to gather her thoughts. "It's about Michael. He and I had a conversation last night after the gala. It was... personal."

Nora nodded, an understanding look crossing her face. "I had a feeling something might be developing there. What did he say?"

"He told me how he felt about me—more than just as a colleague," Bethany explained. "And honestly, Nora, I think I might feel the same. But I'm worried about what this could mean for the clinic, for our working environment."

Nora listened attentively, then spoke with a calm reassurance. "Bethany, you're both adults and professionals. It's natural to develop feelings in such close working conditions, especially when you both share such a strong commitment to what you do."

"But what if it affects our work? Or the team dynamics?" Bethany asked, her concern evident.

"Here's how I see it," Nora began, her voice steady and encouraging. "You both have the clinic's best interests at heart. As long as you maintain that professionalism, set clear boundaries, and communicate openly, I don't see why personal relationships should interfere with work."

Bethany considered Nora's words, finding comfort in her pragmatic approach. "Do you think the staff will see it that way?"

"I believe they will respect your privacy and integrity," Nora responded. "You've both earned that respect. And if you ever feel the situation is affecting work, address it promptly."

Bethany felt a weight lift, knowing Nora supported her. "Thank you, Nora. I really needed to hear that. Michael and I agreed to take things slowly, see where they lead without any pressure."

"That sounds like a wise approach," Nora said with a smile. "And Bethany, you deserve happiness too. Don't forget that. It's important to find joy not just in your work but in your life as a whole."

Bethany smiled, feeling reassured. "I'll keep that in mind. And I'll make sure to keep everything transparent, for the clinic's sake and for ours."

Nora gave a nod of approval. "That's all I ask. And Bethany, I'm here for you, whatever you need."

As Bethany left Nora's office, she felt more confident in her ability to navigate this new aspect of her life. The support from Nora was invaluable, and it reinforced the strong foundation of trust and respect they shared. Bethany was ready to face whatever challenges might come, knowing she had the support of her mentor and friend.

This conversation not only settled some of her immediate anxieties but also reminded Bethany of the importance of balance in life—balancing professional responsibilities with personal happiness. As she went back to her office, she felt a renewed sense of clarity and purpose, ready to continue her work and explore the possibilities of a new relationship with Michael, with honesty and integrity at the forefront.

Chapter 22
The Strength of Heartsville

Jake sat at his desk in the Heartsville Inn, his heart pounding in his chest as he hovered over the "send" button. The article was done, the final version polished and ready to go. It was the most honest piece he had ever written, one that reflected not only the reality of Heartsville's struggles but also the strength and unity of its people. He had poured everything into this article, and now it was time to face the consequences.

With a deep breath, Jake clicked "send," watching as the email containing his article shot off to Marlene's inbox. There was no turning back now. He leaned back in his chair, closing his eyes for a moment as he tried to calm the storm of emotions swirling inside him. He had done what he believed was right, but the uncertainty of how it would be received weighed heavily on him.

The hours that followed were agonizing. Jake tried to distract himself by walking through town, visiting the familiar places and faces that had come to mean so much to him. But the tension followed him like a shadow, a constant reminder that his career was hanging in the balance. Would Marlene see the value in his perspective, or would she dismiss it as too soft, too optimistic?

His phone buzzed in his pocket, snapping him out of his thoughts. He pulled it out to see Marlene's name flashing on the screen. The moment of truth had arrived. Jake answered, bracing himself.

"Jake," Marlene's voice came through, sharp and brisk as always. "I got your article."

Jake swallowed hard, forcing himself to stay calm. "And?"

There was a long pause, one that stretched out into what felt like an eternity. When Marlene finally spoke, her tone was cool, measured. "It's not what I expected."

Jake's heart sank, but he kept his voice steady. "I know. But it's the truth."

"I get that," Marlene said, her voice softer now, but still laced with a hint of frustration. "But you and I both know that truth isn't always what sells. I was looking for something with more bite, something that would grab people by the throat. This... this is different."

Jake took a deep breath, choosing his words carefully. "It's different because the story is different. Heartsville isn't a town on the brink of collapse—it's a town fighting to survive, to thrive. I couldn't write something sensational when that's not what I saw."

Marlene sighed, and Jake could almost picture her rubbing her temples, trying to make sense of it all. "I get where you're coming from, Jake. And it's well-written, I'll give you that. But I'm just not sure it's what we need right now."

Jake felt a pang of disappointment but held firm. "I understand, Marlene. But I'm not going to compromise on this. If that means the article doesn't run, then so be it."

There was another pause, this one shorter, and then Marlene spoke again, her tone resigned but with a hint of respect. "Alright, Jake. We'll run it. But don't expect it to be front-page material. It's going to be a hard sell."

Jake let out a breath he hadn't realized he was holding. "Thanks, Marlene. I appreciate it."

"Don't thank me yet," she replied with a hint of her usual sharpness. "Let's see how it does."

They exchanged a few more words before ending the call. As Jake put his phone away, he felt a mixture of relief and lingering uncertainty. The article would run, but it wasn't the victory he had hoped for. Still, he had stayed true to his principles, and that counted for something.

As the day wore on, Jake tried to push thoughts of the article from his mind, but it was impossible. The tension in his professional life was palpable, and he couldn't shake the feeling that his decision might have lasting consequences. He walked the familiar streets of Heartsville, seeking solace in the places that had become so dear to him.

It wasn't long before word began to spread. The article was live, and the people of Heartsville were reading it. Jake felt a growing sense of anxiety as he wondered how they would react. Had he captured their story in a way that did them justice? Or had he missed the mark?

He didn't have to wait long for an answer. As he passed the general store, he was spotted by Mr. Harris, who waved him over with a broad smile. "Jake! I just read your article. It's... well, it's exactly what we needed. Thank you."

Jake felt a rush of relief, mixed with a humble pride. "I'm glad you think so. I just wanted to tell the truth, as I saw it."

Mr. Harris clapped him on the back. "You did more than that. You told our story. And for that, we're grateful."

As Jake continued through town, he was met with similar reactions. Mrs. Thompson, Kyle, Nora—all of them expressed their gratitude, their appreciation for the way he had portrayed Heartsville. The warmth and acceptance from the community filled him with a sense of belonging he hadn't expected.

But with that warmth came a deeper realization. Jake had crossed a line—he wasn't just a journalist in Heartsville; he was now a part of it. His article had solidified his place in the community, but it had also created a tension with his professional life that wouldn't easily be resolved.

That evening, as the sun dipped below the horizon, painting the sky in hues of pink and gold, Jake found himself back at the inn, reflecting on the day's events. He had made his choice, and while it had brought him closer to the people of Heartsville, it had also set him on a path that might lead him away from the career he had known.

But as he looked out over the town, the lights twinkling in the growing darkness, Jake felt a sense of peace. He had done what was right, both for himself and for the people he had come to care about. Whatever the future held, he knew he could face it with integrity, knowing he had stayed true to his principles.

And in that moment, Jake accepted the changes in his life—the shifting priorities, the new connections, and the uncertain future. Heartsville had changed him, and he was ready to embrace whatever came next.

- - - - - - - - -

The morning after Jake's article was published, Heartsville was buzzing with a quiet, palpable energy. The sun had just begun to rise, casting a soft golden light over the town, but already the streets were filled with people starting their day. There was something different in the air, a sense of anticipation mingled with curiosity, as word spread about the article that had been published online the night before.

Jake stepped out of the Heartsville Inn, his mind still reeling from the events of the previous day. The conversation with Marlene, the decision to stick to his principles, the sleepless night wondering how his article would be received—it all felt like a blur. But now, as he walked through the town, he couldn't help but feel a knot of anxiety in his stomach. How would the people of Heartsville react? Would they feel he had done them justice, or would they see it as an outsider's misguided attempt to capture their story?

His thoughts were interrupted as he turned the corner onto Main Street and nearly collided with Mrs. Thompson, who was just leaving the bakery with a fresh loaf of bread tucked under her arm.

"Jake!" she exclaimed, her eyes lighting up as she recognized him. "There you are, dear. I was just talking about you with Mrs. Harris. We read your article this morning—well, she read it to me because, you know, I'm not too good with these newfangled computers."

Jake's heart skipped a beat, unsure of what was coming next. "And? What did you think?"

Mrs. Thompson smiled, her expression warm and sincere. "It was wonderful, Jake. You captured our town so beautifully. You told our story, not just the parts that people might want to sensationalize, but the heart of it. And for that, we're all so grateful."

A wave of relief washed over Jake, and he found himself smiling back. "Thank you, Mrs. Thompson. That means a lot to me. I was worried I might have missed the mark."

"Not at all, dear," she said, reaching out to pat his arm. "In fact, I'd say you hit the nail right on the head. Heartsville isn't just about our struggles—it's about how we come together, how we support each other. And you showed that."

As she continued on her way, Jake felt a lightness in his chest that hadn't been there before. Mrs. Thompson's words echoed in his mind, reassuring him that he had made the right choice. But there was more to come.

As he made his way down Main Street, more familiar faces greeted him—some with handshakes, others with pats on the back. Mr. Harris waved him over from his woodworking shop, his face beaming with pride.

"Jake, my boy," Mr. Harris called out, his voice filled with enthusiasm. "You did it! You really did it. That article... it was like you reached into the soul of this town and put it into words. I've never been prouder to call Heartsville my home."

Jake couldn't help but laugh, feeling a mixture of pride and humility. "Thank you, Mr. Harris. I just wanted to tell the truth, to show what I've come to see in all of you."

"And you did," Mr. Harris said, nodding firmly. "We've had our share of reporters come through here, looking to dig up dirt or make us look like some struggling backwater. But you... you told it like it is. You're one of us now, Jake."

Those words, simple as they were, struck a deep chord within Jake. "One of us." It was something he had never expected to hear, something he hadn't even realized he wanted. But now that it was offered, it filled a place in his heart he hadn't known was empty.

As the day went on, Jake continued to encounter more townsfolk, each one offering their thanks and congratulations. Even the teenagers who had been wary of him at first approached him with newfound respect. Kyle, who had been instrumental during the search for Sparky, clapped Jake on the shoulder as they crossed paths near the park.

"Great job on the article, Jake," Kyle said with a grin. "It's about time someone showed the world what Heartsville is really like. And hey, thanks for not making us look like a bunch of helpless small-town kids."

Jake chuckled, ruffling Kyle's hair. "You and your friends are far from helpless, Kyle. You're the future of this town, and that's something worth showing off."

As the day wore on, Jake found himself back at the Heartsville Inn, the events of the morning replaying in his mind. He had never imagined that the town would embrace him so fully, especially after the initial skepticism he had faced when he first arrived. But now, as he reflected on the journey he had taken with these people, he realized that Heartsville had become more than just a story to him—it had become a home, a place where he truly belonged.

That evening, as the sun set over the town and the sky turned a brilliant shade of orange and pink, Jake sat on the porch of the inn, his heart full. The acceptance he felt from the community was a stark contrast to the distance he had kept when he first arrived. He had come to Heartsville as an outsider, but now, he was leaving as one of their own.

The door behind him creaked open, and Nora stepped out, a gentle smile on her face as she joined him on the porch. "Mind if I sit with you?"

"Not at all," Jake replied, his voice soft with contentment.

They sat in comfortable silence for a moment, watching the sky darken as the stars began to peek through. Finally, Nora broke the silence, her tone reflective. "You've come a long way since you first got here, Jake."

Jake nodded, his gaze fixed on the horizon. "Yeah, I have. I didn't realize how much I needed this place... until I found it."

Nora smiled, her eyes shining with affection. "And we needed you, too. You showed us that our story was worth telling, that we have something special here. Thank you for that."

Jake turned to her, the depth of their connection clear in his eyes. "I think Heartsville showed me more than I could ever put into words. I'm just glad I could do it justice."

Nora reached out, taking his hand in hers, and they sat together in the fading light, a sense of peace and belonging settling over them both. For the first time in a long time, Jake felt truly at home—not just in Heartsville, but in his own skin, knowing that he had made the right choices, both as a journalist and as a man.

The story of Heartsville was his story now, too, and it was one he would carry with him wherever he went. But for now, he was content to stay, to be part of the community that had welcomed him with open arms, and to continue writing the next chapter of his life—right here, in the place that had come to mean everything to him.

The evening air was cool, with a gentle breeze rustling the leaves of the trees that lined Heartsville's quiet streets. Jake and Nora walked side by side, their footsteps slow and unhurried as they made their way through the town that had become so much more than just a place on a map. The day had been filled with emotion, from the town's response to Jake's article to the quiet acceptance that had settled over him as he finally understood where he belonged.

They reached the park, its open space bathed in the soft glow of the streetlights, casting long shadows across the grass. Jake gestured to a nearby bench, and they sat down together, the silence between them comfortable and familiar. For a moment, they simply sat there, taking in the stillness of the night and the closeness of each other's presence.

Nora was the first to speak, her voice gentle but filled with a hint of uncertainty. "So... what now, Jake? You've told our story, and you've found a place here. But what happens next?"

Jake looked at her, the depth of his feelings for her clear in his eyes. "I don't know, Nora. When I first came here, I thought I'd write my article and move on to the next story. But now... I'm not sure I want to leave."

Nora smiled softly, but there was a question in her gaze. "And what about your career? You've always been so focused on being the kind of journalist who goes where the big stories are. Can you really see yourself staying in a small town like Heartsville?"

Jake sighed, running a hand through his hair. "It's strange, but I've never felt more like a real journalist than I do now. Writing that article, being part of this community... it made me realize that there's more to the truth than just chasing headlines. There's a truth in the everyday lives of people, in the way they come together, in the way they care for each other. That's the kind of story I want to tell."

Nora's eyes softened as she listened, her heart swelling with emotion. "You really mean that, don't you?"

Jake nodded, his voice firm. "I do. I've been all over, seen a lot of things, but nothing has ever felt as real or as important as what I've found here. Heartsville isn't just a story to me anymore—it's home. And you... you're a big part of why I feel that way."

Nora's breath hitched slightly, her eyes searching his. "Jake, I've been feeling the same way. Ever since you arrived, I've felt this connection with you, like we were meant to meet. But I was always afraid that when your article was done, you'd leave, and I'd lose whatever this is between us."

Jake reached out, taking her hand in his, his thumb gently stroking her skin. "I'm not going anywhere, Nora. Not if you want me to stay. You've changed my life in ways I didn't even realize I needed. And I think... I think we could build something here, together."

Nora's heart raced as she heard his words, the sincerity and vulnerability in his voice touching her deeply. "You really mean that, Jake? You're willing to stay, to build a life here with me?"

Jake leaned in closer, his gaze never leaving hers. "I've never been more certain of anything. I've spent so much time running, chasing after the next big thing, but here... with you... it feels like I've finally found what I've been looking for."

Nora's eyes filled with tears, not of sadness, but of overwhelming happiness. She had been so guarded, so careful not to let herself hope for too much, but now, sitting here with Jake, she knew that this was real. "I want that too, Jake. I want us to be together, here in Heartsville. We can build a life together, make this town our home."

Jake smiled, the weight of his earlier doubts lifting from his shoulders. "Then let's do it, Nora. Let's make this our future."

Nora leaned in, closing the small distance between them, and pressed her lips to his in a tender, lingering kiss. It was a kiss filled with promise, with the unspoken understanding that they were both choosing this path together. When they finally pulled apart, both were smiling, their hearts full.

"I love you, Jake," Nora whispered, her voice trembling with emotion.

"I love you too, Nora," Jake replied, his voice steady and sure. "More than I ever thought possible."

They sat there for a while longer, their hands intertwined, the future stretching out before them like a blank page waiting to be filled with the story they would write together. For Jake, the decision to stay in Heartsville was more than just a choice—it was the beginning of a new chapter in his life, one that he would share with the woman who had become his anchor, his inspiration, and his love.

As the night deepened and the stars twinkled above them, Jake and Nora knew that whatever challenges lay ahead, they would face them together. And for the first time in a long time, both felt a deep sense of peace and belonging. Their journey had brought them to this moment, and now, they were ready to embrace the future, hand in hand, heart to heart.

- - - - - - - - -

Jake sat on the front porch of Nora's house, the morning sun casting a warm glow over the quiet street. The aroma of freshly brewed coffee filled the air, and the birds chirped a cheerful melody from the nearby trees. It was a peaceful scene, one that Jake had come to cherish more than he ever thought possible.

Nora stepped outside, two steaming mugs in hand, and handed one to Jake as she joined him on the porch swing. "Here you go, Mr. I'm-Not-Leaving-Heartsville," she teased, a playful smile on her lips.

Jake chuckled, taking a sip of the coffee. "Thanks, Ms. I-Knew-You-Wouldn't-Leave."

Nora leaned against him, her head resting on his shoulder. "So, you've really decided then? You're staying?"

Jake nodded, his voice firm. "Yeah, I am. It wasn't an easy decision, but it's the right one. I've spent so much of my life chasing after stories, moving from place to place, never really settling down. But here... this feels different. It feels like home."

Nora looked up at him, her eyes sparkling with affection. "You know, when you first came here, I didn't think you'd stay more than a few days. You were so... detached, like you were just passing through on your way to something bigger."

"I was," Jake admitted, his tone thoughtful. "But somewhere along the way, this place got under my skin. The people, the community... you. I realized that the story I was looking for wasn't out there somewhere—it was right here."

Nora smiled, reaching up to gently touch his cheek. "I'm glad you found it. And I'm glad you're staying."

Jake placed his hand over hers, his expression serious. "There's something else, too. I've been thinking about what comes next, about my writing. I don't want to stop, but I want to do it differently. I want to focus on stories that matter, stories that show the strength of communities, the goodness in people. Heartsville has shown me that there's so much more to the world than just the headlines, and I want to be the one to tell those stories."

Nora's smile widened, her heart swelling with pride. "I think that's a wonderful idea, Jake. You have a gift for seeing the truth in people, for capturing what makes a place special. You could do so much good with that kind of focus."

"That's what I'm hoping," Jake said, his voice filled with determination. "And I want to start here, in Heartsville. There's so much more to tell, so many stories that deserve to be heard. And I want to do it with you, Nora. I want us to work together, to build something here that we can both be proud of."

Nora's eyes softened, and she leaned in, pressing a gentle kiss to his lips. "I'd love that, Jake. There's nothing I'd rather do than build a life with you, right here, in the place that brought us together."

Jake smiled against her lips, the warmth of her words settling deep within him. "You have no idea how happy that makes me."

Nora pulled back slightly, her gaze playful. "So, what's our first project, Mr. I-Want-To-Write-Positive-Stories?"

Jake laughed, shaking his head in mock exasperation. "You're never going to let me live that down, are you?"

"Not a chance," Nora teased, her laughter joining his. "But seriously, what's next?"

Jake's expression grew thoughtful as he considered her question. "I was thinking... the community center could use some help. It's been the heart of this town for years, but it's starting to show its age. What if we organized a fundraiser, got the whole town involved? We could write about the history of the center, the people it's helped over the years, and why it's so important to keep it going."

Nora's eyes lit up with excitement. "That's a great idea! The center has been a lifeline for so many people, especially during tough times. And I'm sure everyone would love to be part of something like that."

Jake nodded, already feeling the spark of creativity igniting within him. "We could do a series of stories, interviews with people who've been impacted by the center, maybe even some of the older residents who helped build it. And we could use the articles to drum up support, get people excited about preserving it for future generations."

Nora squeezed his hand, her heart full. "I love it. This is exactly what Heartsville needs right now—something positive to rally around, something that brings us all together."

Jake turned to her, his expression tender. "And it's exactly what I need too. I've found my purpose here, Nora. And I've found you. I can't imagine anything better."

Nora's smile was radiant as she leaned in for another kiss, this one lingering and filled with the promise of their future together. "I feel the same way, Jake. This is just the beginning, for both of us."

As they sat there on the porch, the sun climbing higher in the sky, Jake felt a deep sense of contentment settle over him. He had found his place, his purpose, and the person he wanted to share it all with. The road ahead might be filled with challenges, but he knew that with Nora by his side, there was nothing they couldn't face together.

Looking out over the town that had come to mean so much to him, Jake felt a sense of peace he hadn't known in years. He was home, in every sense of the word. And as he and Nora began to plan their first project together, he knew that this was just the start of a new chapter—one filled with love, purpose, and the promise of all the stories still waiting to be told.

Chapter 23
Roots and Wings

With the expansion of the Heartsville Veterinary Clinic well underway and the new challenges it brought, Bethany realized the importance of not just internal but also extensive community support. To further engage the community and ensure ongoing support, Bethany and her team organized a series of community outreach programs designed to educate, involve, and ultimately rally the community around the clinic's initiatives.

One crisp Saturday morning, Bethany met with her outreach team to plan a community health fair that would serve both as an educational event and a showcase for the clinic's expansion progress. The meeting took place in the clinic's newly designated community room, a space designed to host such events.

"Okay, team, let's make sure we have everything covered. Michael, how are the preparations going for the veterinary health talks?" Bethany asked, looking over the agenda.

Michael responded with a confident nod. "All set. We have three talks lined up—one on preventive pet care, another on the importance of vaccinations, and the last on common pet emergencies. I've also arranged for some interactive demonstrations that should keep the audience engaged."

"That sounds fantastic," Bethany replied with a smile. "Nora, what about the logistics? Do we have enough volunteers for the day?"

Nora, who had been coordinating the volunteer efforts, looked up from her notes. "Yes, we're good on that front. We have volunteers assigned to all the major areas, including registration, information booths, and activity stations. Plus, we'll have staff on hand to answer any specific questions about our services and the expansion."

Bethany's attention then turned to the promotional aspects of the event. "And the promotional materials? Are we all set with the flyers, posters, and social media announcements?"

"Yes, Bethany. We've distributed flyers in the community, posted details on our social media pages, and even got a mention in the local newspaper's events section," replied Jessie, the clinic's communications coordinator.

"Great work, everyone. This health fair is a fantastic opportunity to strengthen our bond with the community and show them how the expansion will benefit not just our clients but their pets as well," Bethany expressed, her tone reflecting the importance of the event.

As the meeting concluded, the team felt energized and ready to make the health fair a success. Over the next couple of weeks, they worked diligently to ensure every detail was perfect. Bethany personally visited several community centers to promote the event, talking to local leaders and pet owners about the benefits of attending.

The day of the health fair arrived, and the clinic grounds transformed into a bustling hub of activity. Tents and booths lined the area, each manned by cheerful volunteers ready to engage with visitors. Bethany, overseeing the event, felt a deep sense of pride as she watched families and their pets come through, participating in activities, listening intently to the health talks, and leaving with better knowledge and appreciation of pet care.

Throughout the day, Bethany spoke with many attendees, answering questions and sharing her vision for the clinic's future. The response was overwhelmingly positive, with many expressing their support for the expansion and appreciation for the clinic's proactive approach to community involvement.

As the event wound down, Bethany and her team gathered to debrief and discuss the day's outcomes. The feedback was positive, and the sense of community spirit was palpable.

"Today was a testament to what we can achieve when we come together," Bethany reflected aloud to the group. "Thank you all for your hard work and dedication. It's days like today that remind us why we do what we do."

The team shared a moment of quiet pride, knowing they had not only pulled off a successful event but had also taken a significant step towards rallying the community around the clinic's future. As they packed up, Bethany felt reassured that the clinic was on the right path, one that honored its commitment to both animal care and community partnership.

In the wake of the successful health fair, Bethany and her team decided to capitalize on the positive momentum by hosting a community gathering at the clinic. The purpose of this event was not only to foster further engagement with the local population but also to provide an update on the clinic's expansion progress and gather feedback directly from the community.

The gathering was scheduled for a late afternoon, allowing people to come after work or school. The clinic's parking lot was transformed into a welcoming space with chairs set up in a semi-circle and a small podium at the front. Refreshments were available at a side table, and informational posters about the clinic's services and expansion plans lined the perimeter.

As the community members began to arrive, Bethany greeted each one with a warm smile, expressing her gratitude for their presence. Once everyone was seated, she took her place at the podium, her posture relaxed yet confident.

“Good evening, everyone, and thank you for joining us today,” Bethany began, her voice carrying clearly across the gathering. “We're here to talk about our clinic's future, but more importantly, about how we can continue to serve you and your pets better.”

She continued, detailing the phases of the expansion that were already underway and what they meant for the community. Bethany highlighted the new facilities that were being constructed, including an advanced diagnostic center and a community education room.

"As we grow, we want to ensure that our clinic remains a resource for all of you," she explained. "That's why we're including a community education room in our plans, where we can host events, workshops, and more, all aimed at improving pet care awareness."

The floor was then opened for questions. Community members took turns asking about everything from the expected completion dates for each phase of the expansion, to the types of workshops the clinic might offer in the future.

One local resident, Mrs. Henderson, asked, "Will the new facilities affect our current access to emergency services during construction?"

"That's an excellent question," Bethany responded. "I can assure you that access to emergency services will not be hindered during our expansion. We have taken extensive measures to ensure that our services remain uninterrupted."

Another resident, a young man named Carlos, inquired about volunteer opportunities. "With the new education center, will there be chances for us to get involved, maybe help out with community programs?"

"Absolutely, Carlos," Bethany replied, her eyes lighting up with enthusiasm. "Volunteer involvement will be crucial. We're planning to launch a 'Pet Health Ambassador' program that will train volunteers to help educate our community on basic pet health and safety."

As the discussion continued, it was clear that the community was not only supportive of the clinic's plans but also eager to be involved in the process. The feedback was overwhelmingly positive, with many expressing their appreciation for the clinic's efforts to keep the public informed and engaged.

The gathering concluded with a casual mix and mingle, where people stayed to chat with Bethany and her team, discuss ideas, and share their stories and experiences at the clinic.

Bethany moved among the groups, listening and engaging, her heart full from the community's enthusiasm and support. The gathering had not only served as an informative session but had also strengthened the bonds between the clinic and the Heartsville community.

As the sun set and the gathering came to a close, Bethany helped her team clean up, feeling grateful and motivated by the community's response. She knew that the path ahead would be demanding, but with the community's backing, she was confident that the clinic's expansion would be a success, enhancing their ability to serve and care for the pets of Heartsville.

- - - - - - - - -

In the days following the community gathering, Bethany decided to further deepen the clinic's ties to the community by collecting testimonials from clients who had experienced significant and positive interactions with the clinic. These stories were intended to be featured in an upcoming newsletter and on social media, highlighting the personal impacts of the clinic's work and fostering a stronger emotional connection with the community.

Bethany and her team set up a small, comfortable area in the clinic where clients could share their stories on camera. The setup was simple, with soft lighting and a backdrop of the clinic’s logo, creating a warm and inviting atmosphere.

One of the first clients to participate was Mrs. Thompson, a long-time client whose Golden Retriever, Max, had recently undergone a complicated surgery at the clinic.

As the camera started rolling, Bethany began the interview. "Mrs. Thompson, thank you for joining us today. Could you share with us a bit about your experience with Max’s surgery?"

Mrs. Thompson nodded, her expression softening as she began to speak. "Oh, Bethany, I can’t thank your team enough. Max is not just a pet; he’s a part of our family. When we found out he needed surgery, we were devastated. But from the moment we walked into the clinic, we felt supported. Your team was not just professional; they were genuinely caring."

"That’s wonderful to hear," Bethany replied, genuinely moved by her words. "How is Max doing now?"

"He's doing fantastic, thanks to you all. He's back to his old self, running around and playing fetch like nothing ever happened. We couldn't have asked for a better outcome," Mrs. Thompson said, a smile spreading across her face.

Another testimonial came from a younger client, Carlos, who had previously expressed interest in volunteering. "Carlos, you've had a few interactions with our clinic. What's been your impression?" Bethany asked as the camera focused on him.

Carlos leaned forward, his enthusiasm evident. "It's been amazing, honestly. Not only did you take great care of my cat when she was sick, but the educational sessions you hold have been eye-opening. It shows how much you care about not just treating animals, but also educating us on how to better care for them."

"Thank you, Carlos. We believe education is just as important as the medical care we provide," Bethany responded, pleased with his feedback.

As more clients shared their stories, the theme was consistent: the clinic not only provided exceptional medical care but also fostered a caring and supportive environment for both the pets and their owners.

Once the testimonials were collected, Bethany and her team edited the footage, choosing the most impactful statements to feature in their outreach materials. Each testimonial was a powerful reminder of the clinic's vital role in the community and reinforced the importance of the ongoing expansion to improve and extend their services.

When the newsletter was published, featuring the heartfelt testimonials alongside updates about the clinic's expansion, the response from the community was overwhelmingly positive. Social media posts with the video testimonials received hundreds of likes, shares, and comments, further solidifying the community's support and involvement.

Bethany watched as the testimonials spread across the community, reinforcing the bonds between the clinic and the residents of Heartsville. It was clear that these personal stories resonated deeply, making a compelling case for the continued support of the clinic's mission.

Reflecting on the success of this initiative, Bethany felt a renewed sense of purpose. The testimonials were more than just marketing tools; they were genuine expressions of trust and appreciation from the community, a powerful testament to the clinic's impact. As she planned the next steps for the clinic's growth, she knew that maintaining this deep community connection would be key to their ongoing success and mutual growth.

With the community increasingly rallied behind the Heartsville Veterinary Clinic thanks to the heartfelt testimonials and ongoing engagement activities, Bethany felt a profound sense of accomplishment. Yet, she knew that the real work was just beginning. The full realization of the clinic's expansion, which now seemed more attainable than ever, required sustained effort and a united front from her entire team.

In the weeks that followed, Bethany organized a series of strategic planning sessions with her staff, designed to integrate all the feedback they had received from the community and to refine the clinic's short- and long-term goals. These meetings were crucial for ensuring that every team member was not only aware of the clinic's direction but also actively involved in shaping its future.

One morning, as the team gathered in the newly set up conference room, Bethany stood at the head of the table, her presence commanding yet inclusive. "Thank you all for being here today," she began, her voice steady and clear. "This clinic isn't just a place of work; it's a community asset, and each of you plays a vital role in its success. Today, we need to align our goals with the expectations and needs of the community we serve."

The team listened intently as Bethany outlined the key areas of focus: enhancing patient care, expanding educational programs, improving client communication, and optimizing internal operations. Each point was backed by data gathered from client feedback and community interactions.

"We have a unique opportunity to set a new standard in veterinary care," Bethany continued, encouraging her team to brainstorm innovative approaches to client care and community involvement.

As the meeting progressed, ideas flowed freely among the team members. Suggestions ranged from introducing mobile vet services to enhance accessibility, to hosting monthly pet health workshops for the community, and even starting a partnership program with local schools to educate children on pet care from a young age.

Bethany facilitated the discussion with a skilled hand, ensuring that every suggestion was considered and that every team member had the opportunity to contribute. "It's essential that we not only listen to our community but also anticipate their needs. This proactive approach will keep us ahead and ensure our continued relevance and impact."

The planning session concluded with concrete action items assigned and deadlines set. Bethany's leadership had effectively channeled the team's enthusiasm into a structured plan that would guide the clinic into the future.

In the days that followed, the clinic began to implement some of the new initiatives discussed. The community's response was overwhelmingly positive, with increased engagement and appreciation shown across various platforms.

As Bethany reviewed the progress with Nora, she reflected on the journey they had undertaken. "Nora, seeing the team and the community come together like this, supporting our vision—it's more than I could have hoped for."

Nora nodded, her expression one of pride and satisfaction. "Bethany, you've done an incredible job leading this charge. It's your vision and commitment that have brought us to this point. The clinic is a true reflection of its community, and that's something incredibly special."

Bethany felt a surge of gratitude for Nora and for every team member who had stepped up to the challenge. The clinic was not just expanding its facilities but also its impact and its role within the heart of Heartsville.

As the sun set on another busy day at the clinic, Bethany felt assured that the united front they presented would lead them through any challenges that lay ahead. The clinic had truly become a beacon of community health, innovation, and compassion, a legacy that Bethany was proud to be part of shaping.

Chapter 24
The Future Begins Here

As the Heartsville Veterinary Clinic approached the final stages of its expansion, a new hurdle emerged that threatened to disrupt the progress they had made. A small group of community members, led by a local business owner who was concerned about the potential traffic and noise the expanded clinic might bring, began to rally opposition. With a crucial city council meeting approaching, where the final permits for the expansion were to be decided, Bethany and her team prepared to defend their project.

The morning before the meeting, Bethany gathered her key staff members in the conference room to strategize. Michael, Nora, and the clinic's lawyer, Sandra, were present, each bringing their expertise to the table.

"Thank you all for coming in early today," Bethany began, her tone serious but calm. "As you know, we've hit an unexpected snag with a group of community members who are opposed to our expansion. Today, we need to finalize our approach for tomorrow's council meeting."

Sandra, the lawyer, adjusted her glasses and looked at the notes in front of her. "Based on the objections that have been raised, our strongest arguments are going to be centered on the comprehensive planning we've done to mitigate traffic and noise, and the overall benefit our expanded services will provide to the community."

Michael chimed in, "We should also emphasize the community outreach we've done throughout this process. We've held multiple open houses and information sessions to explain our plans and listen to concerns."

Nora nodded in agreement. "Exactly, Michael. We've not only listened but actively incorporated community feedback into our plans. For example, the green space we included to provide not just aesthetics but also a buffer zone to reduce noise."

Bethany took notes as they spoke. "Good points, both of you. Sandra, can we also talk about the economic benefits? Hiring more staff, using local contractors for the building work, and the increase in services should all contribute positively to the local economy."

"Yes, absolutely," Sandra responded. "Highlighting the economic impact will help counterbalance some of the opposition's arguments about the clinic's expansion harming the community. It's not just about animal care; it's about community and economic development as well."

"Let's also prepare for some of the tougher questions," Bethany suggested. "We should anticipate them bringing up issues like waste management and the potential for increased traffic during construction. Sandra, could you outline our responses?"

Sandra nodded and detailed the clinic's plans for managing construction waste, ensuring minimal environmental impact, and managing traffic flow with the help of a professional traffic consultant.

As the meeting drew to a close, Bethany looked around at her team, feeling a surge of gratitude for their dedication and support. “Everyone, I know this has added a layer of stress, but I can’t tell you how much I appreciate your hard work. We’re not just building a clinic; we’re ensuring that our community has the best possible animal care facilities. Let’s keep our focus on that mission.”

The team nodded, feeling rallied by Bethany’s words. They dispersed to finalize their individual contributions for the presentation.

That evening, Bethany stayed late to review every slide of the presentation, every statistic, and every piece of testimonial evidence they planned to present. She rehearsed her speech, refining her delivery, determined to convey not just the facts but also the passion and vision behind the clinic’s efforts.

As she finally turned off the lights in her office, Bethany felt prepared and resolute. The next day’s council meeting wasn’t just a bureaucratic hurdle; it was a chance to affirm the clinic’s place in the community and to secure its future. She left the building, the weight of the upcoming battle firm on her shoulders, but with a resolve that was steeled by the knowledge that what they were fighting for was worth every effort.

- - - - - - - - -

The day of the council meeting dawned clear and bright, a stark contrast to the tension that simmered within Bethany as she and her team made their way to the city hall. The large room was already bustling with activity as various community members, council staff, and media had gathered. The stakes were high, and the atmosphere charged with anticipation.

Bethany, Michael, Nora, and Sandra found their seats, arranging their notes and presentations meticulously. The opposition group, recognizable by their coordinated attire and stern expressions, sat across the aisle, occasionally casting wary glances toward Bethany's team.

The meeting was called to order by the council chair, a middle-aged woman with a reputation for fairness. "We are here today to discuss the proposed expansion of the Heartsville Veterinary Clinic," she began, setting the tone with her firm, clear voice. "We will hear from both supporters and opponents of the project. Each side will have thirty minutes to present their case, followed by a question and answer session."

Bethany was the first to speak for her team. She approached the podium with a calm demeanor, though her hands betrayed a slight tremor. "Thank you, council members, for allowing us the opportunity to discuss our project," she started, her voice gaining strength as she proceeded. "Our expansion plan is not just about growing our clinic but about enhancing the services we provide to our community and their beloved pets."

She detailed the meticulous planning that had gone into the project, emphasizing the benefits, including the economic boost from job creation and the improved animal care facilities that would serve the community's needs. She concluded with heartfelt words about the clinic's commitment to the community's well-being.

Next, the opposition leader, a local business owner named Mr. Hargrove, took the podium. His argument focused on the potential disruptions: increased traffic, noise, and the change in the neighborhood's character. "While we understand the clinic's intentions, we must consider the broader impacts on our community's daily life," he stated firmly.

The tension in the room spiked as council members began their questioning, which revealed the depth of the council's concerns about both the logistical and environmental impacts of the clinic's expansion.

Sandra, armed with legal and environmental assessments, addressed the concerns about regulations and standards. "We have adhered to all local environmental laws, and in many cases, exceeded them. We are committed to sustainable practices that will ensure minimal impact on our community," she explained, providing detailed data and projections.

Michael discussed the traffic management plans, including collaborations with local authorities to mitigate any potential issues. "We are proactively addressing traffic concerns by implementing a staggered appointment system to avoid peak traffic times," he elaborated.

As the debate continued, Nora provided testimonials and data from other communities where similar expansions had positively impacted both the local economy and the quality of life.

After both sides had presented and the council's rigorous questioning session had ended, the room was left in a heavy silence, everyone awaiting the decision. The council chair called for a recess before the final vote, allowing everyone a moment to reflect on the arguments presented.

During the recess, Bethany and her team huddled together, reviewing their performance and discussing the potential outcomes. "Whatever happens, I know we've done everything we can," Bethany said to her team, her expression one of resolve but also fatigue.

When the council reconvened, the tension was palpable. The chairwoman took a moment before announcing, "After careful consideration and review of all presented materials and arguments, we will now proceed to vote."

The vote was tense, each council member casting their vote in turn. The room held its breath, waiting for each yes or no that echoed in the chamber.

As the final vote was cast, a mixture of relief and triumph washed over Bethany. The council had approved the expansion, albeit with some conditions regarding ongoing community engagement and traffic monitoring.

The victory was hard-won, and as the crowd began to disperse, Bethany felt both the weight of the upcoming challenges and the joy of the opportunity to move forward. She thanked her team, knowing that the real work was just beginning. As they left the city hall, the sunset painted the sky with colors of fire and gold, reflecting perhaps the fiery trials they had undergone and the golden opportunities that lay ahead.

The approval of the Heartsville Veterinary Clinic's expansion by the city council did not mark the end of resistance. The local business owner, Mr. Hargrove, who had led the opposition at the council meeting, was not ready to concede defeat. In the days following the decision, he mobilized a more structured opposition, planning to appeal the council's decision by gathering a significant petition from the community and seeking legal avenues to challenge the approval.

Mr. Hargrove's efforts began to materialize in a series of meetings he held at his business, where he invited other local business owners and residents who shared his concerns. Their strategy was to emphasize not just the potential traffic and noise but also the procedural aspects they claimed had been overlooked in the council's decision-making process.

Meanwhile, Bethany, aware of the brewing counter-moves, maintained a vigilant stance. She increased her engagement with the community, attending local gatherings, visiting neighborhood associations, and keeping an open line of communication through the clinic's newsletters and social media channels. Her aim was to keep the community informed and involved, reinforcing the benefits of the expansion.

One afternoon, as Bethany reviewed the latest updates from her community liaison, she received a call from Sandra, the clinic's lawyer, informing her of the official appeal filed by Mr. Hargrove.

"Bethany, Mr. Hargrove has filed an appeal against the council's decision. He's managed to gather a considerable amount of support," Sandra reported. "He's citing procedural errors and insufficient assessment of environmental impacts."

Bethany listened intently, her brow furrowed. "What's our next step, Sandra? How do we address this?"

"We need to prepare a detailed response," Sandra explained. "We'll reinforce the transparency of our processes and the thoroughness of our environmental assessments. I'll also monitor the appeal's progress closely and keep you updated. It might be beneficial to arrange a meeting with the council members to reassure them of our compliance and readiness to address any further concerns."

"Let's do that," Bethany agreed. "And maybe we should also organize a community forum. It could be a platform where people can ask questions directly and where we can address any misinformation or concerns they might have."

As Bethany implemented these plans, the community's reaction was mixed. Many continued to support the clinic, expressing their trust in Bethany's leadership and the clinic's longstanding positive impact on the community. However, there was a noticeable portion swayed by Mr. Hargrove's arguments, fueled by fears of change and disruption.

Over the next few weeks, Bethany and her team worked tirelessly. They organized the community forum, which was well-attended and allowed for direct dialogue between the clinic's representatives and community members. Bethany addressed the gathering, her words measured and reassuring.

"We are here not just to expand but to improve and give back to the community that has supported us for so long," she stated. "We understand the concerns some of you have, and we are committed to addressing them transparently and thoroughly."

Despite the opposition's efforts, the proactive approach taken by Bethany began to sway public opinion back in favor of the clinic. Her continuous presence in community activities and the transparent sharing of information about the expansion's benefits gradually rebuilt the trust that had been shaken by the opposition's counter-moves.

As Bethany navigated these challenges, she was reminded of the complexities of leading a community-centered business. Each decision she made, each interaction with the community, and each setback faced was a learning experience—an opportunity to reaffirm her commitment to her work and the community she served.

Though the road was tough and the outcome of the appeal still uncertain, Bethany remained steadfast, supported by her team and the many community members who appreciated the clinic's dedication. The opposition had mounted a significant counter, but Bethany's resolve and her deep commitment to community engagement ensured that the clinic remained a united front, ready to continue its mission regardless of the challenges ahead.

- - - - - - - - -

The tension that had enveloped Heartsville Veterinary Clinic and its community reached a climax as the date for the hearing on Mr. Hargrove's appeal approached. Bethany and her team, along with their legal counsel, Sandra, spent countless hours preparing their defense, ensuring every possible detail was accounted for. They gathered extensive documentation, from environmental impact studies to traffic analysis reports, and prepared testimonials from other community members who supported the clinic's expansion.

On the day of the hearing, the city hall was packed, a tangible buzz filling the air as both supporters and opponents of the clinic's expansion awaited the council's final decision. Bethany felt a mix of apprehension and determination as she sat with her team, her gaze occasionally meeting those of Mr. Hargrove and his supporters across the room.

When the hearing began, the council chair reiterated the purpose of the session and reminded everyone present to maintain decorum, regardless of the outcome. Mr. Hargrove presented his case first, reiterating his concerns about the clinic's expansion, emphasizing the potential negative impacts on the neighborhood's character and quality of life.

When it was Bethany's turn to speak, she stood confidently, though her voice betrayed a hint of the enormous pressure she felt. "Honorable council members, we have not only complied with all local regulations but have gone beyond them to ensure that our expansion will benefit not just our clinic but our community as a whole," Bethany stated. "We've engaged with the community extensively, and we've listened to their concerns. We are committed to being good neighbors, and our plans reflect that commitment."

Sandra then took over, methodically addressing each of Mr. Hargrove's points, showcasing evidence and citing specific data that refuted his claims. "The allegations of procedural errors are unfounded. Here are the environmental assessments, traffic studies, and community outreach records that show our commitment to transparency and community engagement."

The council members listened intently, occasionally asking pointed questions that reflected their deep engagement with the issue. After both sides had presented, the room was left in a tense silence as the council retired to deliberate.

The wait felt interminable. Bethany, Michael, Nora, and the rest of the team sat together, exchanging quiet words of support and reassurance. Finally, the council members returned, their expressions unreadable.

The council chair cleared her throat before announcing the decision. "After careful consideration of all the evidence and arguments presented, we find that the Heartsville Veterinary Clinic has met all requirements and has made considerable efforts to address community concerns. Therefore, the appeal is denied, and the clinic's expansion plan is upheld."

Relief washed over Bethany and her team, their tension dissolving into quiet tears of joy and hugs of relief. Mr. Hargrove, looking defeated, quietly left the room with his supporters.

As the crowd dispersed, Bethany thanked the council members and then turned to her team. "We did it," she said, her voice thick with emotion. "Thank you, everyone, for your hard work, your faith in this project, and your dedication to our clinic and our community. This isn't just a win for us; it's a win for all of Heartsville."

Back at the clinic, the team celebrated their victory, but Bethany knew that the real work was just beginning. The approval meant that they could move forward with the expansion, but it also meant they had to fulfill their promises to the community—to integrate seamlessly and beneficially into the lives of the people and pets they served.

As the celebrations ended and Bethany prepared to close up for the day, she took a moment to stand in the quiet of her office, reflecting on the journey. The battle was over, but the mission to serve and the commitment to excel for the sake of their community continued. With her team by her side, Bethany felt ready to face the future, no matter what it held.

Chapter 25
Home at Last

The final approval for the expansion of the Heartsville Veterinary Clinic brought a palpable sense of relief and triumph to Bethany and her dedicated team. To mark this significant milestone, Bethany organized a celebratory event not just for the clinic staff but for the entire community, reflecting her deep gratitude for their support and patience throughout the process.

The event was planned to be held in the local community center, which was decorated with balloons in soft blues and greens, streamers, and tables laden with refreshments and appetizers. The atmosphere was festive, with light music playing in the background, setting a joyful tone for the evening.

As the community members began to arrive, Bethany, dressed in a light, flowing dress that mirrored her buoyant mood, greeted each guest with a warm smile and words of thanks. Michael, Nora, and other key staff members were also on hand, mingling and expressing their gratitude to the attendees.

"Thank you so much for coming," Bethany said to a group of local business owners, including some who had initially been skeptical about the expansion. "This celebration is as much yours as it is ours. Without your feedback, support, and sometimes even your criticisms, we wouldn't be where we are today."

One of the business owners, a middle-aged woman named Marjorie, who had been particularly vocal at council meetings, nodded appreciatively. "Bethany, seeing how you've handled this whole process has really changed my mind. You've shown that you truly care about this community and its needs."

"That means a lot to hear, Marjorie," Bethany replied, genuinely touched. "It's been a learning curve for all of us, and I'm just glad we could find a way to move forward together."

As the evening progressed, Michael took a moment to address the gathering. "Everyone, if I could have your attention," he called out, his voice carrying over the murmur of conversations. The room quieted down as all eyes turned toward him. "I just want to echo Bethany's words and add my own thanks. This clinic isn't just a place of work for us; it's a passion, and seeing everyone here tonight, supporting us, it's incredibly affirming."

Nora joined in, her voice emotional yet strong, "This clinic has been my life's work, and as I prepare to step back a bit, I can't think of a better note to start that transition on. Thank you, Bethany, for leading us here, and thank you to all of you, our community, for trusting us with your care."

The crowd applauded, and as the clapping died down, Bethany invited everyone to enjoy the food and drink. "Please, everyone, help yourselves. Tonight is about celebration and community. Let's enjoy it to the fullest."

Throughout the evening, laughter and lively discussions filled the room. Community members shared their stories of the clinic, discussing how it had helped their pets and families over the years. The clinic's staff, in turn, listened and shared their own stories, strengthening the bonds between the clinic and the community.

As the event wound down, Bethany stood by the exit, thanking guests as they left. The expressions of contentment and the words of encouragement she received were a profound reminder of the positive impact the clinic had on the community.

Driving home later that night, Bethany felt a profound sense of fulfillment. The challenges of the past months had tested her resolve, but the outcome was as rewarding as she had hoped. With the expansion set to proceed and the community firmly behind them, the future of the Heartsville Veterinary Clinic looked bright and promising. Bethany knew that the real work was just beginning, but she also knew that they were well-prepared to meet the challenges and opportunities that lay ahead.

The celebratory event had left everyone in high spirits, and as it wound down, Bethany, Michael, and Nora found themselves sitting together, lingering over the last of their drinks, relishing the calm after the festive storm. It was a perfect moment for deeper reflection and expressions of gratitude among them.

Nora leaned back in her chair, her eyes twinkling with a mix of nostalgia and contentment. "You know, when I first started at the clinic, I never imagined it would become what it has today. Bethany, watching you take the reins and drive this expansion has been one of the highlights of my career."

Bethany smiled warmly at Nora. "I couldn't have done any of this without you, Nora. You've been more than a mentor; you've been the heart of this clinic. Your dedication has inspired me every single day."

Michael nodded in agreement, his expression sincere. "And it's not just about the expansion. It's about how you've both built a place that genuinely reflects its community. This clinic isn't just a building; it's a part of people's lives. You've both done something extraordinary here."

Bethany looked between Nora and Michael, her heart full. "I feel incredibly lucky to have had both of your support through all of this. Michael, your innovative ideas and energy have brought so much to our services. And Nora, your wisdom has guided us through countless challenges."

Nora reached across the table, placing her hand over Bethany's. "And we'll continue to face whatever comes, together. That's what makes this place special. It's not just the care we provide; it's the relationships we build."

Michael raised his glass, a light clink echoing softly. "To relationships, then. May they always be the foundation of everything we do here."

Bethany raised her glass to join his. "To relationships, and to new beginnings. With the expansion, there will be challenges, but there will also be opportunities to make even more meaningful connections within our community."

The trio sat in a comfortable silence for a moment, each lost in their thoughts, reflecting on the journey they had undergone and the future that lay ahead. It was Bethany who broke the silence, her voice thoughtful.

"Thinking about everything that's happened, it makes me realize just how important it is to stay connected to the why of what we do. It's not just about treating sick pets; it's about enhancing the lives of the people who care for them."

Nora nodded, her voice soft but firm. "Exactly, Bethany. And it's about showing up, not just as professionals but as neighbors, friends, and fellow animal lovers. That's what builds trust and that's what keeps people coming back."

Michael leaned forward, his eyes bright with resolve. "Let's make sure that as we grow, we don't lose sight of that. Let's keep the community—and our relationships—at the heart of everything we plan for the expansion."

"Agreed," Bethany said, her resolve strengthening. "Let's make that our pledge: to grow, to innovate, but never at the expense of our core values."

As they stood to leave, there was a mutual feeling of accomplishment and anticipation. They were not just a team; they were a family, bound by a shared mission and mutual respect.

Walking out of the community center together, they each felt renewed and ready to face the future. The challenges of tomorrow seemed less daunting, knowing they would face them together, with the community firmly by their side. The night ended not with goodbyes but with promises of continued commitment and shared dreams for the future of Heartsville Veterinary Clinic.

- - - - - - - - -

The weeks following the clinic's celebratory event were busy but fulfilling. Amid the ongoing work and community engagements, a personal relationship blossomed further between Bethany and Michael. They had managed to navigate their developing feelings alongside their professional roles, maintaining their commitment to both the clinic and each other.

One cool evening, as the sun set with a promise of early autumn, Michael planned a special surprise for Bethany. He had invited her for a walk in Heartsville Park, under the guise of discussing some new ideas for community programs.

As they strolled along the park's winding paths, surrounded by the gentle rustle of leaves and the last golden rays of daylight, Michael seemed unusually reflective.

"Bethany, these past months have been incredible," Michael began, his tone earnest. "Not just professionally but personally as well."

Bethany smiled, sensing the shift in his mood. "I feel the same, Michael. It's been a journey, hasn't it?"

"It really has," Michael agreed, pausing as they reached a beautifully illuminated gazebo, which he had arranged to be decorated with soft fairy lights and a few discreetly placed bouquets of flowers. The scene was set just as the sun dipped below the horizon, casting a warm glow over the park.

"This isn't just about work, Bethany," Michael continued, his voice slightly nervous now. "These months working closely with you, sharing successes and challenges, have made me realize how much you mean to me. More than I could have imagined."

Bethany, taken by the beauty of the moment and the sincerity in Michael's voice, felt her heart beat a little faster. "Michael, I—"

He took a deep breath, then reached into his jacket pocket and knelt on one knee, holding out a small, elegantly designed ring box. "Bethany, I love you. I love every moment we spend together, and I can't imagine my life without you. Will you marry me?"

The question hung in the air, mingled with the soft whisper of the evening breeze. Bethany's hands flew to her mouth, tears of joy welling in her eyes. After a moment of overwhelmed silence, she nodded vigorously, managing to say, "Yes, Michael, yes!"

Michael stood and slipped the ring onto her finger, his own eyes bright with emotion. They embraced, the park around them fading into a blur as they shared a long, tender kiss.

"Michael, this is more than I ever hoped for," Bethany whispered as they parted, her gaze fixed on the ring, which glittered in the twilight. "I was so focused on the clinic, on our community... I didn't realize how much I needed someone to share it all with."

"And now we get to share everything, together," Michael replied, his voice thick with emotion. "I promise to be there, for you and with you, no matter what comes our way."

As they walked back through the park, hand in hand, the world seemed to pause just for them. The evening was quiet, save for the soft sounds of nature and the distant laughter of families enjoying the park. The challenges of their work, while significant, felt surmountable with the strength of their partnership.

The proposal not only marked a new chapter in their personal lives but also symbolized a deeper commitment to their shared goals and visions, both for the Heartsville Veterinary Clinic and for the community they cherished.

When they finally left the park, the stars were out, and the air was cool and crisp, whispering promises of the future. They drove home, not just as partners in work but as fiancés, ready to face whatever the future held, together.

- - - - - - - - -

The successful resolution of the clinic's expansion issues and Bethany's engagement to Michael marked a period of joyful anticipation and planning for the future. The clinic was not just expanding its physical boundaries but also its role within the community, with Bethany and Michael at the helm, now united in both personal and professional capacities.

One bright morning, after a staff meeting where the latest expansion updates were shared, Bethany and Michael took a walk around the new facilities, reviewing the progress and discussing the upcoming official opening.

"It's really coming together, isn't it?" Michael said, gesturing towards the new wing, which was bustling with workers adding the final touches.

"It is," Bethany replied, her eyes taking in every detail. "I can't believe we're almost ready to open this section. It feels like just yesterday we were drawing up the plans."

"As we prepare for the opening, we should also think about our long-term goals," Michael suggested. "Not just in terms of the clinic's operations but our community programs and how we integrate them into our overall mission."

Bethany nodded thoughtfully. "Absolutely. I want us to continue being a resource for pet owners, not just for healthcare but for education and support. We should expand our outreach programs—maybe even start a scholarship fund for veterinary students from the community."

"That's a great idea," Michael agreed. "Engaging with future veterinarians early on could really help shape the kind of care and community involvement we envision for the clinic."

Their conversation was filled with ideas and plans, weaving together their visions for both their professional and personal futures.

Later that day, Bethany sat down with Nora to discuss her transition into a less demanding role, ensuring that her mentor and friend remained an integral part of the clinic's future.

"Nora, your guidance has been one of the pillars of this clinic," Bethany said earnestly. "As we move forward, I hope you know your role here will always be vital, no matter how you choose to shape it."

Nora smiled, her eyes reflecting a mix of pride and affection. "Thank you, Bethany. I've seen you grow into a remarkable leader. I'm looking forward to stepping back a little, knowing the clinic is in capable hands. And I'm excited to see where you and Michael take it."

As they discussed specifics, Nora expressed her desire to focus on mentoring and educational outreach, areas where she felt she could make the most impact without the day-to-day stresses of clinic management.

With everything falling into place, Bethany felt a profound sense of contentment. The challenges of the past had forged a stronger clinic and a united team, ready to face the future with optimism and resolve.

In the weeks that followed, as the clinic prepared for the grand opening of the new wing, Bethany and Michael also planned their wedding, intertwining their personal joy with their professional achievements. The community responded with enthusiasm, eager to celebrate both the new beginnings at the clinic and the union of two of its most beloved members.

As the narrative of their lives and work continued to unfold, Bethany often reflected on the journey. Each step, each decision, and each challenge had brought them here—to a place of growth, commitment, and shared dreams. Looking forward, she saw a path filled with possibilities, guided by a vision of care and community that had always been at the heart of their mission.

The expansion completed, the clinic stood not just as a testament to their hard work but as a beacon of hope and health in the community—a place where care extended beyond medicine, touching the lives of all who entered its doors. And as Bethany and Michael looked to the future, they did so with the knowledge that together, they could face anything, supported by the community they loved and the team they trusted.

Conclusion

As the weeks turned into months, Jake settled into his new life in Heartsville, the town that had transformed from a temporary stop into a permanent home. The fundraiser for the community center was a resounding success, thanks in no small part to the series of heartfelt articles Jake wrote, each one highlighting the town's rich history and the people who had shaped it. The stories resonated far beyond the town's borders, drawing attention to the unique spirit of Heartsville and even inspiring donations from former residents who had moved away but still felt a deep connection to the place they once called home.

Jake's writing continued to evolve, reflecting the deep connection he felt to the town and its people. His articles were no longer just reports on events; they were chronicles of a community that had taught him the true meaning of resilience, kindness, and belonging. Each piece he wrote was infused with the love and respect he had come to feel for Heartsville, and in turn, the town embraced him fully, seeing him not as an outsider, but as one of their own.

Nora and Jake's relationship blossomed alongside their professional partnership. They became an inseparable team, not just in their personal lives, but in their efforts to uplift the town. Together, they spearheaded new projects, from organizing town events to launching initiatives that brought new life to Heartsville's local economy. Their love for each other and for the community grew stronger with each passing day, their bond deepened by the shared purpose of making a difference in the place they now both called home.

As seasons changed and the town thrived, Jake found himself reflecting on the journey that had brought him here. He had started out as a journalist searching for a story, but what he found in Heartsville was so much more. He had discovered a community that showed him the value of connection, a place where he could lay down roots and build a life filled with meaning. And in Nora, he had found a partner who understood him in a way no one else ever had—a woman whose strength and compassion had inspired him to become the best version of himself.

One crisp autumn evening, as the sun set over Heartsville, painting the sky in hues of orange and pink, Jake and Nora stood together on the porch of their home, watching the town settle into the peaceful rhythm of nightfall. The warmth of the moment, the quiet contentment that enveloped them, was a reminder of all they had built together and all they had yet to experience.

"This is it, isn't it?" Jake said softly, his arm wrapped around Nora's shoulders. "This is the life we were meant to have."

Nora smiled, leaning into him. "Yes, it is. And I wouldn't trade it for anything."

As they stood there, side by side, watching the stars begin to twinkle in the evening sky, Jake knew that he had found everything he had ever been searching for—not in the bustling cities or in the pursuit of the next big story, but here, in the quiet, steadfast heart of Heartsville. It was a place of simplicity, of deep roots and enduring ties, a place where love and community could flourish.

And with Nora by his side, Jake was ready to face whatever the future held, knowing that they would continue to write their story together, page by page, day by day, in the town that had become their forever home.

www.ingramcontent.com/pod-product-compliance
Ingram Content Group UK Ltd.
Pitfield, Milton Keynes, MK11 3LW, UK
UKHW041457190125
4177UKWH00036B/262